DEATH OF THE

DRUGGIST

Rick Morrow

Mike and Elizabeth,

Thanks so much for supporting
the Pharmacy Opportunity Fund.
Enjoy the read!

Rick Morrow

8/11/20

For Sherry
In loving memory

1

"WHAT THE HELL HAPPENED TO MY LIGHT?" GREG ASKED.

He was answered by the crunching of thin glass shards as his feet hit the single wooden step. Greg shivered in the early April downpour as he pushed open a travel-sized umbrella, locking his fingers around the stays to prevent the wind from inverting it. The fresh ozone aroma reminded him of mid-summer as he danced down the alley, dodging rain-filled fissures and potholes. In spite of his evasive efforts, Greg felt his socks turning wet and cold. A flash of lightening revealed his pale blue car in the midst of the gray sheets of rain.

"Hey Ebert! Is that y'all playin' hopscotch?"

Greg's initial reaction was to question why an announcer from an oldies station was hanging out in the alley. The booming voice was distinctive but Greg couldn't identify it as belonging to anyone he knew.

"I'm Greg Ebert. What do you want?"

"Head back toward your damn drug store. You'll find out soon enough. And, in answer to your first question it was me what took care of your light," the man said. His voice demanded obedience.

When Greg turned, he had a rain-filtered image of someone standing under the awning of the insurance agency next to his store. As Greg got closer, he made out an enormous man with yellow hands, one of which was holding a pipe. The pipe turned out to be a silencer attached to the barrel of a gun.

"Your wife is Lynda. You live on Foster Street. You're going to do everything I tell you to, the way I tell you to. Understand?"

"Understand," Greg said. He hoped the rain concealed the sound of his gulp.

"Well? Let us in, dammit," the man commanded.

Greg first tried what must have been the store's front door key. Once he found the correct key, he tried to put it in upside down. On his third shaky attempt, Greg managed to unlock the dead bolt. Then he stuck that same key into the lock in the center of the knob.

"Wait Jerknuts," the man said. "I better not hear a friggen' alarm when that door opens."

"It has a thirty second delay. I've got to put in a code that lets me turn it off for ten minutes. The system only lets me use it once a night though."

The man gouged the gun into Greg's back and said, "Ten minutes ought to be enough. Go in

first and take care of the alarm. I'll be right behind
you."

Greg tossed the dripping, open umbrella into
a corner and started pushing buttons on the security
system console. Once the alarm was inactivated
Greg looked up and the man motioned with his gun
toward the pharmacy's prescription counter. Even
in the dim after-hours lighting, Greg could see that
the man had a broad, acne-scarred face. His long,
dirty red hair was pulled back into a tight ponytail.
He was dressed in faded denim, like many of the
people who worked at nearby horse farms. Under
other circumstances it would have been comical to
see this gigantic man wearing disposable blue
booties over his work boots as well as an extra-large
pair of yellow rubber gloves like the ones Greg's
mom wore when she scrubbed pans.

Greg thought about the newspaper account
of a recent pharmacy robbery that had occurred
twenty miles to the northeast. The pharmacist had
described the robber as a big calm man who wore a
Donald Duck mask. Even though she claimed to
have cooperated, the robber had hit her hard enough
to misalign her jaw and loosen a tooth. She had
passed out from the pain.

"Alright, Jerknuts. Here's what you're going
to do. You're going to give me all of your Dilaudid,
Demerol, Oxy and fentanyl if you've got it and all
your cash. But I don't want no change or checks.
Get on it."

A lightning flash that was barely separated
from its corresponding booming thunderclap

punctuated the 'get on it'. The lights flickered but stayed on.

The man was tall enough to see over the prescription counter into the alcove where Greg kept controlled drugs. Being visible didn't matter since Greg harbored no illusion of anything heroic even with access to the ancient pistol he kept loaded in the safe. He had been held up twice before. Neither time had there been any reference made to his family. Nor did he have the impending inevitability of bodily injury. The other two crooks seemed less sober … less methodical.

Greg opened the safe and removed the day's cash receipts, two packets of fifty singles, and the drugs the man had requested. He reached onto an adjacent shelf and added several bottles of pseudoephedrine into a plastic bag with an Ebert Drugs label. Greg hoped the man would appreciate how much he was trying to cooperate.

"I've got what you asked for. Plus there's another sixty in bills in the front register. I threw in some Sudafed in case you wanted them," Greg said, managing to avoid having his voice shift into a higher octave.

"Did I say I wanted Sudafed, Jerknuts? Pay attention. I leave cookin' meth to the hillbilly crankers.

Stop. Don't take it out.

You're really pissin' me off.

Before you bring everything around to me Jerknuts, real careful like, pick up that gun. Grab it by the barrel and slide it into the bag."

Greg did as he was told and slowly stood up. He tensed his shoulders and pulled his arms tightly into his sides in a failed attempt to stop shaking. He walked back around to the front of the counter, wondering if there was any way he could prepare himself to be pistol-whipped.

Am I going to end up toothless, knocked out, maybe have a concussion? How soon before somebody finds me?

"Here," Greg said. He suppressed a swallow.

Get on with it. Please, get this over with.

"Your kid's name is Zach ... right?" the man asked.

He pulled the gun out of the bag, checked to see if it was loaded. He half-laid, half-dropped it onto the floor before saying, "I wouldn't fire that old thing lest I cleaned it myself."

"Come on. I've done what you asked. I didn't set off the alarm. I gave you everything. Please. Leave my family alone."

"I'll leave 'em alone like you should've left the fuckin' cave alone."

"The cave? How come you know so much about me?

Hey! Where's your mask?

This isn't a robbery, is it?" Greg spewed out the questions as quickly as his thoughts came together.

The man answered by raising his gun and cocking it. He pointed it at Greg's face. But he didn't shoot.

Does he want to torture me? Why is he waiting? What's he trying to decide?

As if Greg asked the questions out loud, the man said, "I'm waiting on the storm."

Greg saw a flash of lightning. He never heard the thunder.

2

THE KING-SIZED BED THAT VIC FYE ONCE SHARED WITH HIS EX-WIFE TRACY gave the bedroom the crowded feel of a bargain-priced cabin on a five-day Caribbean cruise. The townhome's other bedroom was larger by eight square feet. It served as Vic's office and it provided a corner for a large dog crate. The townhome complex workout facility, attached garages, and proximity to the freeway only partially compensated for the unit's claustrophobia-inducing layout.

Vic had been asleep for almost six hours thanks to a Benadryl washed down by a third Fat Tire. He'd found Ambien to be an equally effective sleep aid until he had the dream about fighting velociraptors and other Jurassic Park predators with a pair of light sabers. When he emerged from the nightmare, he was standing in the kitchen with a rolling pin and a spatula in either hand.

A cut from Aerosmith awakened him, this time from dreamless sleep, demanding that he walk the way Steven Tyler wanted. Tracy had chastised Vic any number of times, saying that his ringtone was inconsistent with the professional image he ought to be projecting. But Aerosmith had been keys with her. She told me she wasn't sure why she said that. Anyhow, that's when Sheriff Billings pulled up, followed right away by an ambulance and a fire truck. Lynda doesn't remember much that happened after that. Everything was chaos.

As soon as he could, the sheriff brought her back here. Back to their house. He called the doctor and then me. I've been here ... as I said, I'm with Lynda now ... ever since. Billings said that the safe was wide open and that it looked like money and drugs were taken. He called a crime unit in from Lexington."

Julie's voice dropped to a hoarse whisper. "The sheriff told me Greg was shot and that an old gun was on the floor beside him.

Billings seemed rattled. It was like he needed to talk. Like he needed to come to grips with how any of this could happen in 'his Burgoyne'. He called it an execution. He said that it looked like part of Greg's head was gone. 'Shot off' he said.

Are you still there?

Vic?"

"Yeah. This is hard to take in. Sorry, Julie. I know you've been dealing with it all night.

God! I can't imagine what Lynda must be going through. This doesn't seem possible. I'm just glad she wasn't the one who found him.

Zach. What about Zach?"

"The doctor has Lynda sedated. She's asleep here on the couch but she's tossing around a lot. Zach. He's in Nashville at a Model U.N. conference. He doesn't know about his dad yet. That's the other reason I called. I, or we I guess, need your help.

Could you come down and be here when Zach gets back? Lynda wants you here when she has to tell him."

Vic said. "When's he supposed to get there?"

"Not until late this afternoon, she thinks. Oh, and I left a message for Reverend Rex at the church office. I'm not sure whether he'll get it and I didn't want to bother Lynda for his cell number."

"You're in Burgoyne, remember. He'll know."

"You're right, Vic. I'll see you later today then?"

"Sure. And I'm sorry. I'm sorry for everything Julie"

"Me too."

This is wrong any way I think about it. I spent half of my DEA career under cover, living out deceptions with crazed druggies and their suppliers, the most paranoid and volatile kind of criminals. Greg was a pharmacist. He referred to himself as the last of the small town druggists. And it's Greg, not me, who gets shot by some scumbag. I deluded myself into believing I was protecting society. I couldn't even protect Greg.

I hope I'll be able to console and smooth things for Lynda and Zach. I'd like to do even more. But even if I was still an agent, the DEA would never let me anywhere near this case. As a private citizen, my hands will be tied even more. Lynda will need my help with the store and with Zach. How's a sensitive kid like Zach ever going to be able to handle this?

I'm not sure how I'll deal with it. I convinced Greg to delay the fishing trip by a week. Greg shouldn't have been working last night. I wouldn't have wanted any other pharmacist to be shot. But damn! Not Greg.

3

VIC PADDED ON BARE FEET INTO THE KITCHEN. The all black appliances and accouterments his decorator promised would make things "warm and cozy", that morning, made the room feel dreary and cramped. He brewed a cup of Italian roast in his Keurig coffee maker with no real expectation that caffeine would improve anything. He tried a bite of Raisin Bran Total but it didn't clear the back of his throat. He spit it into the disposal side of the double sink that was also black. He tried a sip of the dark coffee and was grateful when it didn't make him retch. He swallowed a bigger drink but the warm bitterness provided no comfort. When he glanced toward the only four square feet of usable wall space in his no-frills kitchen, his eyes were drawn to the matted and framed Topps Baseball Card autographed by Joe Morgan. Greg had given him Joe Morgan's 1965 Rookie card last year on his birthday. Vic thought back to a sultry June evening when he was ten or eleven. His dad had taken him to a Cincinnati Reds game.

It was Father-Son Night at Riverfront Stadium. Dad and I were sitting beside Greg and his father in the right field upper deck. Our dads, who didn't know each other, exchanged a few words about how hot it was and how they hated staring into the sun during the early innings. Dad was teaching me how to keep score. Between pitches, Greg was reading a book. It was a Reds-Dodgers game and he was reading a book!

In the bottom of the sixth inning, I out scrambled Greg and a dozen or so other kids to snag a Joe Morgan home run ball. After we got back to our seats Greg's dad handed him his book. I recognized the title. <u>Stormie the Dog Stealer</u>. It was one of several young adult books about a fictional detective named Hawkins. Harper Lee immortalized other books in the series. Greg and I, like Scout in <u>To Kill A Mockingbird</u>, were avid readers of the Hawkins stories. As we talked, Greg bragged that the author was his great grandfather ... a fact confirmed by his dad.

As we headed to our cars, Greg loaned me <u>Stormie</u>. I gave him the ball. The Dodgers had won 3 to 2. Morgan's homer seemed futile to the fans that night. Greg and I came to believe differently.

4

VIC TURNED HIS EYES AWAY FROM THE BASEBALL CARD when he heard the Louisville Courier-Journal slap against his driveway. He grabbed a pack of Post-It notes and started a list of what he needed to get done.

As if on cue, Sheldon loped into the room, his paws softly tapping across the faux hardwood flooring. He slurped several gulps of raspberry-flavored water from his bowl and nuzzled Vic's arm to signal his desire to go outside. Sheldon, a greyhound with a successful but abbreviated racing career, had a cutesy pedigree name, his professional name. Tracy and Vic, the new owners, summarily renamed him. They had rescued him and he soon became their surrogate child. Based on his lanky body, his obsessive dietary and exercise habits, and his persistent pacing when anyone sat in "his spot" ... which happened to be the entire length of their loveseat ... he became Sheldon ... a tribute to the "Big Bang Theory" lead character.

In the divorce decree, Tracy and Vic were granted joint custody of Sheldon. Identical loveseats became fixtures in both of their townhomes. Also spelled out, they have a standing appointment the last day of every month at a mutually agreed upon kennel. This gives Sheldon a day of transition, allegedly to lessen his anxiety when passed between his joint owners. In reality, it reduced Tracy's and Vic's jealous disappointment when the fickle Sheldon refused to pick a favorite owner and became frantically excited at the sight of either of them. By decree, April was one of Vic's months. Sheldon would need to go to the kennel early.

Vic dreaded sharing the news of Greg's death with Tracy, knowing it would upset her almost as much as it had him. Anytime Tracy and Greg had been together, the routine was for one maybe both of them laughing and saying, "See. Vic does love you best." Tracy and Greg had delighted in ganging up on Vic, making fun of his exercise regimens, his compulsive car maintenance routines, and even his life long fear of water.

And now Vic had lost them both.

As exes, Tracy and he maintained a civil, their counselor referred to it as "adult", relationship. It helped that there were no children to complicate negotiations and that they had managed to avoid brutalizing each other during their divorce proceedings. While they each held onto some hurt feelings, when situations warranted, they didn't have to fake behaving like friends. People after seeing them interact said things like, "Are you two getting back together?" or "I thought you two are supposed to be divorced."

Tracy and her physician boyfriend were spending the weekend at Boothbay Harbor … a

Maine hideaway that she and Vic had first visited ten years earlier.

Is there anything from our marriage Rothstein hasn't usurped?

Vic was well informed as to American divorce and adultery statistics. His certainty of Tracy's and his love had led him to believe that those staggering numbers didn't apply to them or to their marriage. She'd asked him numerous times to leave the DEA. She had told him how his extended undercover assignments scared her, especially after Vic let his hair grow. She half believed that the nasty scar on the back of his hand, a remnant of a knife wound, was self-inflicted. She hated that it, like the grotesque tattoo covering his left upper arm, was a part of his disguise.

When Vic finished his last undercover case and promptly gave up his commission, Tracy informed him that she was relieved but that his "gesture", as she called it, was too late to save the marriage. She had already decided to move out. Only later did he learn that Rothstein had long since become an ordained part of her life ... or of what she envisioned her new life was going to be.

The DEA higher-ups, from whom he had asked to take a leave of absence, had chided him for "walking away", inferring that he must be reacting to being passed over for a promotion or some other such slight. That was before informing him that unless he was pregnant or enrolling in law school, his options were to withdraw his request or to resign. It didn't seem to matter that he had exemplary performance reviews. Meritorious service didn't translate into permission to take time off to deal with a "personal issue".

He ended up resigning in the hope that he could salvage his life with Tracy. At the time he didn't consider his decision to be a sacrifice although he knew full well how much he would miss living with the constant undercurrent of anxiety, broken up by occasional episodes of outright terror. Like many in the DEA, he'd allowed the adrenalin surges of the job to become an addiction. He wondered if he'd ever adjust to his lackluster life as a divorced pharmacist living in a cramped townhome.

VIC IMAGINED TRACY ALREADY WOULD BE POWER WALKING in the dim light of the earlier East Coast dawn. Her defiant stride along with her sub-four mile per hour pace engendered awe in most other morning walkers and helped insure that she'd find the solitude she sought.

"Hello Victor," she answered his call after a pronounced pause while she caught her breath. Vic's mother and Tracy were the only two people who called him Victor.

Setting aside their usual banter, he said, "Tracy. Sorry to call you so early. Can you talk?"

"Yeah. I've been down to the dock area. I'm going into cool down mode and I'm heading back to the B & B … to the inn."

Vic knew the inn. He knew its water view. He knew Cerise, its hostess and Cerise's blueberry coffee cake and her passionate and persistent endorsement of the Boothbay Botanical Center. He could visualize the inn's late nineteenth century furnishings ... the dark, oversized wood furniture, the needlepoint artwork, and the feather mattresses that Tracy and he had nicknamed pioneer waterbeds. He could well imagine how Tracy and David had been exploiting their soft but constantly in motion bed while acrobatically trying to minimize the hardwood floor creaks and moans. His imagination was making this call even worse than he'd anticipated.

"Victor. Victor. You're not talking."

"I'm here. There's no easy way to tell you this. Greg … uh, Greg … he was killed last night."

"Killed? You do mean our Greg, right? What happened?"

"He was shot. They're calling it a robbery. It sounds like it was cold blooded. Maybe somebody who was high. Anyhow, I'll be driving down to Burgoyne in a little while."

"By yourself? You sure you're okay to drive?"

"No, I'll be fine. Just so you know, the visitation and funeral will be Monday."

"No other details?"

Vic said, "All I know for sure is that it was a robbery. Greg was shot, maybe with his old gun that the robber, the killer I guess, left at the scene. I can't see Greg pointing the thing at anybody and I definitely can't see him shooting it."

"Damn, Victor. Greg and Lynda are practically our only friends who didn't take sides. Greg, as close as he was to you, still always told me he loved me when we talked.

David and I will be getting back to Louisville Sunday night. I can drive down in time to be there the next day. Do you know how Lynda and Zach are holding up?"

"Lynda had to be sedated," he answered. "Zach's out of town. I'm going to try to be there when Lynda tells him."

"You're a good uncle. He'll need you to be there."

"Godfather, not uncle," he corrected, although he knew that putting aside the lack of DNA corroboration, "uncle" was more accurate since Zach called them Uncle Vic and Aunt Tracy.

Sensing they were heading into their awkward pattern of correcting each other's minor miscues, she interjected, "Okay. Tell Lynda and Zach how sorry I am and that I'll see them soon."

"I'll be dropping Sheldon at the kennel later this morning. Will you be able to finish out April for me?"

"Sure, as long as I still get him all of May."

"Gee! I hope this isn't one of those I'll have my attorney contact your attorney things."

He knew it was a lame joke but fortunately Tracy forced a laugh and said, "I'm going on vacation in July for two weeks and you'll get Sheldon then if he'll have you."

"Yeah, right. That'll work."

"Okay. See you Monday," she said. Vic heard a tremble in her voice.

5

VIC SENT A QUICK TEXT MESSAGE TO HIS BUSINESS PARTNER HEIDI. Their company, Pharmacists-PRN, supplied pharmacists to stores on a temporary basis. Pharmacists interpret 'prn' on prescriptions to mean 'as needed'. Vic wanted to make sure Heidi knew he'd be in Burgoyne and that he was uncertain how soon he'd be able to return to Louisville. This was more than a courtesy message because the two of them were often emergency fill-ins for their seventeen associates when scheduling became complicated.

Once Vic handled this and some other departure details, he dropped off an unusually rambunctious and reluctant Sheldon at the kennel. Whereas he was maliciously scornful of people who anthropomorphize their pets, he couldn't keep himself from attributing Sheldon's naughty behavior to his "knowing" he was being boarded before Vic's month was supposed to be completed.

He vacuumed the car and took his second shower of the day. He packed his usual road trip clothing, Apple electronic necessities, and workout gear. He added a suit, a dress shirt and tie, his personal gen4 Glock 17 and his pocket-sized backup gun. His license to carry was lifetime. He stowed all of it in the back seat and miniscule trunk of his four month-old British Racing Green Mini Cooper convertible He'd purchased the Mini the afternoon he learned that Tracy had his replacement picked out before she'd filed for divorce.

Instead of the engine's soothing rumble, Vic heard a series of clicks. The Mini had started less than thirty minutes before.

Damn! If I'm in Burgoyne for only a few days a rental might work.   But it's likely to be longer than that if I'm filling in at the pharmacy. I've got to take the Ford.

Vic transferred everything he'd packed into the massive trunk of the '57 Ford Fairlane Town Sedan that his father and he had restored. The Ford was identical to his dad's first car. It was two-tone black and white, with automatic transmission, a 312 Thunderbird engine with a 4-barrel Holley carburetor, and a penchant for frequent universal joint replacements. As favorites of police departments in the late '50s, they were driven hard. That model became the automotive equivalent of an endangered species. Except when his parents came to visit, the Ford was Vic's to maintain and drive. He often drove it to Burgoyne since the classic car license plates gave no hint that he had any connection to Louisville. University of Kentucky basketball fanatics, and there were lots of those in Burgoyne, didn't take kindly to anyone who might support the rival Louisville Cardinals.

VIC EASED HIS WAY PAST THE DISABLED MINI. He reminded himself that he'd be driving without power steering, power brakes, air conditioning, satellite radio, and cup holders. On the other hand, maintaining cruising speed would be easy for this forerunner of the muscle cars of the '60s and '70s. It could go 0-60 in under 10 seconds and he'd had it up to 108 mph.

Vic headed toward 265. From there he merged onto I-64. He'd made this drive many times and already knew where he would stop for lunch before making his way to Greg and Lynda's house in Burgoyne.

VIC DROVE UP THE RAMP at the first Frankfort exit and veered north onto U.S. 127 toward the more picturesque sections of Kentucky's capital city. He immediately caught a glimpse of the shiny gold dome atop the elegant capital building that dominates the landscape and the cultural fabric of this tiny city. Just as there are towns that are extensions of academic enterprises, there are quintessential capital cities. Frankfort is one such place.

He drove past his restaurant destination on the left. The curb-clipping U-turn let him pull directly into the Frankfort Frisch's Big Boy. He backed into his favorite parking spot that was situated so that the restaurant dumpster was adjacent to the driver's side. Tracy relished telling their friends "Victor's hobby is avoiding door-dings". Vic agreed only because hobby sounded less pathological than obsession.

Once inside and seated, the server forced a smile and activated her corporate play button. "Have you dined with us before?"

"Sure. Quite a few times," Vic said.

"Welcome back. May I bring you something to drink other than water?" She asked before stepping aside to make room for a waiter.

Her server colleague set down a tray filled with oversized sandwiches, dripping in cheese and mayonnaise based sauces at an adjacent booth. He dealt out the sandwiches like so many poker hands to a family of five. The kids at the table, without prompting, abandoned their crayons and games to mimic the food frenzy of their nutritionally negligent parents.

In less than a minute, his waitress placed a large Diet Coke on a napkin. "Are you ready to order?"

"I'll have a fish sandwich."

"Would you like fries with that?"

"No thanks. Just the sandwich."

Vic hadn't eaten at a Frisch's for several months. He avoided going there because it was Tracy's and his go to restaurant when neither of them had planned anything for dinner or, more often, when they simply wanted to go to Frisch's. His boycott reminded him of losing Tracy. It accomplished nothing other than depriving him of his favorite comfort food. His server wasn't the only one glad he'd come back.

Vic knew well in advance that there'd be no deviation from his standard order since, in his opinion, Frisch's serves the best fish sandwich in the U.S. In-N-Out restaurants are touted as having the best burgers. Prior to their corporate-wide change in frying oil, many believed that McDonald's had the best fries. But Frisch's Big Boy, at the restaurants Vic had been to, had the best fish sandwiches.

Although he'd bypassed breakfast, Vic still had little appetite. Once the order arrived, he could only force down about a third of the sandwich. He conveyed to his waitress that he hadn't saved room for Frisch's signature strawberry pie.

While neither the fish nor the Diet Coke was as appealing as he'd anticipated, he didn't blame Frisch's. He paid the check, affirmed with the cashier that "everything was wonderful", and headed toward the parking lot.

VIC'S VINTAGE CAR HAD ACQUIRED A HUMAN HOOD ORNAMENT. A bulky man with a shaggy mop of dyed-blonde hair sat on the front of his Ford. Vic judged him to be in his early twenties and, based on his attire, pegged him as a kitchen worker or a busboy. The man had positioned his feet so that he could brace himself against the bumper to keep from sliding off the hood with its many coats of wax. He sat rubbing his straggly, and incongruously dark-brown goatee. He didn't seem the type to be lost in contemplation. Instead he appeared to be milking away crumbs or perhaps kitchen grease. A cigarette dangled from his mouth. His nametag indicated he was Gus. Gus was in quotes.

Several ways of dealing with the interloper crossed Vic's mind. He decided to be polite but direct. "Fella, would you mind slowly getting off my car? I don't want the rivets on your jeans to scratch my paint."

"How 'bout y'all let me finish my cigarette first?" Gus asked with a smirk.

He pointedly flicked ashes down the right fender. Vic had been trying hard to keep his anger in check since early that morning. As he was thinking about his next option, it came to him that this insolent asshole represented a segment of society whose behavior was based on personal entitlement. *I can rob your drug store. I can shoot a man and deprive his family and friends of their loved one. I can have sex on a feather bed with the only person you ever loved. I can even sit on your painstakingly restored car.*

Vic locked eyes with the guy, slowly approached him from his left side, and said, "Yeah. Maybe if you've got one of those to spare."

"I just might, " Gus said, expressing with a smug smile *I got the best of this dude and I'm going to sit on his car for as long as I like.*"

The man reached toward a shirt pocket for his cigarettes. Vic moved quickly. He pushed the guy's feet off the bumper with his left hand, grabbed Gus's beard with his right, and pulled down and forward on the filthy goatee as hard as he could. An audible thud coincided with Gus's yelp of pain. His amply padded backside probably prevented him from cracking his tailbone. He staggered to his feet with clenched fists, thought better of it, and tentatively caressed first his chin and then his butt. He no longer made eye contact.

Vic roughly turned the man around and shoved him toward the employee back entrance and said, "Your break's over. Try not to let anybody see you crying."

"I ain't crying."

"I can take care of that if you don't get back inside."

The man slowly moved toward the door, gingerly massaging the base of his spine and turning every few steps to scowl at Vic. As he pulled open the door, he pivoted again and said, "Hope you and your car get what you deserve."

Vic waved, revved the engine loudly enough that everyone in the kitchen could appreciate the baritone reverberations of the Ford's fiberglass mufflers, and drove away. He made out Gus's one finger salute in his rearview mirror.

6

BEFORE VIC LEFT FRANKFORT, HE STOPPED TO TOP OFF HIS GAS TANK. The gauge showed three quarters but the Ford demanded high-octane gasoline without ethanol, a blend not always easy to find in a smaller town. He used a rag to wipe up any trace of gas that might have dribbled onto the rear bumper. Then ... the second reason he'd stopped ... he inspected the front of the car. It looked like the Ford's hood survived scratch-free. Before leaving, he pulled the car into direct sunlight and repeated the inspection. Satisfied that there was no damage, he merged back onto Interstate 64. He stayed in the right lane before exiting and continuing south onto a two-lane state highway. The highway number was not part of the working vocabulary of Burgoyne natives who only knew the road as the Frankfort Pike.

Vic's contentment at cruising through Bluegrass Country sidetracked him from thinking about Greg. The terrain was hilly enough to confirm that the Ford's shocks and struts were in good condition. Since the highway closely followed the contours of the countryside there were few straight stretches of road.

The houses, stables, and other out buildings he passed were well maintained and most yards and fields had a sprinkling of light green from newly leafed out red buds, magnolias, and fruit trees. In spite of this part of the state being short on moisture, the grass was a darker shade of green. A few horses were visible in the pastures enclosed by the requisite white fences. Vic cranked down the driver's side window and opened the wing so he could appreciate the aromas of the Kentucky spring. The air felt soft on his bare arm.

Calling this part of the state "Bluegrass Country" had fallen into some degree of disfavor. The Bluegrass style of music has many loyal fans but is considered to have a bit too much twang for many of the aficionados of today's mainstream country-western sound. To fortify their image, several counties in the Frankfort and Lexington general environs identify themselves as being part of the Bourbon Trail ... Kentucky's answer to Napa Valley. The idea is to convince tourists to drive from distillery to distillery, taking tours, enjoying tastings of specially aged whiskeys, and perhaps purchasing a bottle or two of distinctly labeled, and priced, bourbon. Bed and breakfasts had started to spring up, in some cases spruce up, and adjacent towns are revitalizing their downtown areas to cater to tourists. Greg recently told Vic that there was a push for such a renaissance in Burgoyne.

VIC THOUGHT IT IRONIC THAT IT WAS JULIE WHO CALLED TO ASK FOR HELP. Vic had been a less than reluctant victim of her manipulation once before.

Julie and Vic started at the University of Cincinnati the same year. She was a business major who had been a high school classmate of Greg. Vic was attracted to her before their freshman year, dating back to summers when he stayed in Burgoyne visiting Greg.

Julie had turned away when Vic approached her at a U.C. watering hole. Two days later she'd called and told him that she needed his "expertise." She convinced him that she was having trouble with calculus and understood from Greg, who naturally had become his freshman roommate, that Vic might be able to tutor her. Greg later denied having had such a conversation. Julie quickly caught on to what Vic was explaining and was able to easily apply it to her other homework problems. Vic learned some months later that her math SAT was 30 points higher than his.

At one point during the tutoring, she'd closed her calculus book and asked Vic whether he might help her with another concern. They sat thigh to thigh, her hand lightly moving on his wrist. The outcome was inevitable. Who was Vic to leave her dateless for her sorority formal?

He'd bought all of her drinks the night of the dance before she left with a pledge sister who "was sick". Vic had hoped it was her friend who was ditching her date but he wasn't self-assured enough to try to find out. Later, Julie turned him down for his own fraternity dance, saying that too many of her sorority sisters were already going … an argument he had no ability to refute since it lacked any basis in logic.

As Vic started getting close to Burgoyne, he saw the round barn that was a landmark for a county road that led to Riverton. Riverton was a collection of twenty or so summer cottages on a one-lane gravel road that bordered the eastern bank of the Kentucky River. The oldest of those cottages belonged to the Eberts and, at one time, Greg's great grandfather. Greg and he had spent a lot of time on the riverbank when he visited, often pretending to be characters in the Hawkins' books. But that was all in the past. Greg was dead and his belief that those books weren't purely fictional would die with him. Vic didn't take the turn toward Riverton. He needed to get to Burgoyne.

7

AN ALL FRAME EXTERIOR, A NOTEWORTHY ABSENCE
OF PILLARS and a prominent front porch
distinguished Greg and Lynda's goldfinch-yellow
home from the other houses on the cul-de-sac. The
Eberts' house was a half-century newer than those
of its neighbors. The trees and shrubs were
considerably smaller than those gracing the lawns
of other neighborhood homes. But with Lynda's
flair for plantings and her use of interesting-shaped
slabs of native limestone, the Ebert home held an
honorary title. Some of their friends declared it to
be the best-landscaped house NOT featured on the
Burgoyne Home Walking Tour. It did not look like
old South nor, more to the point, did it convey the
image of old Burgoyne money.

After an extensive remodeling a few years
back, Greg and Lynda had hosted a neighborhood
open house. All the neighbors had come, admired
the changes, ate the hors d'oeuvres, and drank the
wine. No return invitations had been forthcoming
from the guests.

VIC PULLED UP AND PARKED ON THE STREET. He
wondered whether the classic Ford with its fifties
vintage exhaust system would be in keeping with

the snobbish neighborhood ambiance. Fortunately, there was an offsetting Jaguar, Julie's no doubt, already parked on one side of the double driveway.

Two women, dressed like they were attending a country club luncheon, stood talking in the yard next door. As he got out of his car, they looked toward him and stopped speaking. He nodded and gave them a quick wave. They returned the nod, maintaining close-lipped smiles, as if to acknowledge that Vic was about to do something they were dreading. Their obligatory expressions of condolence to Lynda would come later, probably in the form of casseroles. Vic's impending visit couldn't wait. Nor would he be able to symbolically separate himself from Lynda and her sorrow with outstretched offerings in Tupperware containers.

Julie opened the front door. She was dressed like a model in one of Tracy's Chico's catalogs, stylish in tan capris and a black and green abstract print blouse. Her tan complemented not only her outfit but also her subtly highlighted, shoulder-length hair. They hugged each other briefly before she took his hand. Still not speaking, she led him through the family room, all leather and mahogany, and the kitchen, all quartz and metallic, onto the patio that surrounded the family's teal-colored pool.

"Lynda, Vic is here, " Julie said, even though Lynda had already turned and was starting to get up. Lynda wore an all microfiber outfit similar to what Julie was wearing except she also had on a matching jacket, designed to perpetually hang open. She was as dark as Julie. The two of them and several friends of Lynda took annual late winter cruises to bolster their tans. Her auburn hair was mussed and her nose was red. She held a wadded up tissue in her left hand.

Lynda and Vic held each other until they wordlessly acknowledged that neither of them was experiencing the mutual comfort they sought. As they separated, Vic kissed Lynda lightly on the cheek and muttered, "Lynda, I'm so sorry."

"I know," she said, her voice breaking. "I know it's your loss, too. Greg didn't get to say goodbye to either of us ... or to Zach."

Struggling not to cry, Vic managed to say, "I'm down here as long as you need me. Tell me what I can do to help with things ... with anything."

Without waiting for her to reply, he went on to say, "As starters, I'm going to make sure that someone from Pharmacists-PRN, probably me, will be here to help with the store."

"Yeah. Julie already promised that you'd see to that."

Julie and Vic exchanged meaningful half smiles.

As a tear involuntarily rolled down her cheek, Lynda went on, "Most important right now, I guess, is I'd like you here when I tell Zach."

Then, looking at Julie, Lynda said, "You've been here all night and all morning. I can't imagine what I would have done without you. But now, please go home and get some rest. Vic and I can manage."

Julie didn't argue. She must have sensed that her being there would only make the conversation with Zach more awkward with one more well-meaning witness to his discomfort as he struggled to come up with how he was supposed to react. Or Julie may have been tired. In any case, she smiled at Lynda, walked back into the house, and said, "I'll call you later. I love you."

"I love you too," Lynda whispered after swallowing twice.

They sat down and shared a smile when Lynda and Vic heard the Jaguar respond to Julie power shifting into second and the subsequent deep-throated roar of acceleration. He let his hand rest on hers and squeezed it reassuringly each time she suddenly twitched.

Finally she sighed deeply and said, "The last thing I said before he left for the store was 'Don't forget your umbrella.' I didn't tell him I loved him."

He gently squeezed her hand again. As if she could read his mind, Lynda said, "You know he loved you too."

"We should have told each other."

"You didn't have to."

"I talked to him a couple of days ago. He told me he'd gotten around to cancelling our reservations at Otsego Lake in Cooperstown. That was the last step in his scheme to move our fishing weekend down here. He reminded me again how sure he was he'd found Hawkins' cave and insisted, it didn't matter what I said or how afraid I was of water. The two of us were going to explore it together, maybe take Zach."

"So there'd be three of you boys," Lynda said. "What's the old saying? 'Men are boys who learned how to behave in public.'"

It hadn't been quite a year since Lynda and Vic sat together with Greg and Tracy in these same poolside chairs, watching the Derby through the four-door wide opening between the patio and the kitchen area. Obligatory groupings of roses intermingled with early blooming peonies from the Ebert backyard filled both of the glass-topped tables. They had surrendered further to tradition by sipping mint juleps that afternoon. Lynda had made a small pitcher, enough for four and only four, since as traitorous as it was considered to be so close to Churchill Downs, none of them cared much for the way mint adulterated the taste of a good sipping bourbon. They were snobbishly loyal to their Woodford County distillate and refused to drink the more affordable Jim Beam. Greg used to say, "If you want something to mix with fruit or Coke, don't waste money on Woodford Reserve".

Lynda broke the silence. "I appreciate your agreeing to take care of things at the pharmacy for a while but I can't help but worry. Greg could have made almost more money working for someone else but like the cottage and his preoccupation with those old books, the store was another nostalgic tradition he couldn't let go.

We own the cottage but we still owe big-time on this place. And Greg borrowed more to remodel the store. I'm sorry. I know you don't need to think about this."

"No, Lynda. I understand. I'll do any …," Vic started to say before they heard the front door open and click shut.

They looked at each other, shared a deep sigh, and let go of each other's hand. Vic hoped his showing up was enough. He hadn't given much thought as to how to tell Zach. He rationalized that this wasn't something that rehearsal or forethought could make go any smoother.

"Hey Mom! Hey Dad! Hey Uncle Vic!"

Zach had recognized the Ford and assumed that they'd all be sitting in the back yard, knowing they migrated there any time that it was 60° or warmer. Zach stepped out onto the patio. He was a slimmer, taller version of his father with his dad's unruly hair. He had inherited his mom's olive skin tone and her intensely dark brown eyes. He wore a tee shirt from a past mock U.N. trip, long, baggy shorts, and high topped Converse basketball shoes with no socks. He kissed Lynda, and shook Vic's hand. Then he glanced around.

"Is Dad home?"

"No, Zach. Something happened at the store. There was a robbery. Greg, your dad that is, was shot."

"Is Dad okay?" Zach asked with the cautiously certain optimism of any sixteen-year old.

"Honey, Dad didn't make it. I'm sorry, Zach. I'm so sorry."

"What? What are you saying? This isn't real. It can't be."

Zach covered his eyes with widespread palms. He slowly moved his hands down until they covered only his nose and mouth, as if to suppress a sneeze. His eyes were visibly redder. He dropped his hands to his sides and inhaled deeply and exhaled sharply through his mouth as if he could blow away what he'd heard.

Vic moved toward Zach, but made no effort to touch him, respecting his need to decide when to move and what to say and how to act. Zach went to Lynda and the two embraced tightly, her head on his chest.

Zach suddenly pulled away and ran into the guest bathroom in the hall. Through the closed door they could hear him retching and then throwing up. The toilet flushed. A few minutes later it flushed again and Zach came out.

"I need water," he said on his way to the kitchen.

"It's okay, Honey," Lynda reassured him when he stepped back outside.

"Mom, why didn't you call or text me?" Zach asked in a hushed but accusing voice.

"I don't know. Maybe I thought I could protect you a little longer. I guess I could pretend it hadn't happened as long as you didn't know."

Zach moved away from them both, needing to express anger toward someone or something. He glared in the general direction of Vic not making eye contact. With muted but obvious hostility, he turned to Lynda.

"Who did it?" he asked. His bitterness was unmistakable.

Zach continued, elaborating on his own question, and posing exactly what Lynda and Vic had separately been wondering. "There was that other robbery. Nobody was killed in that. Why was Dad murdered? He'd have co-operated? He's been robbed before. He always told me to do whatever they say. Give them what they want. Don't look them in the eye. Be polite. Treat them like a customer ... like somebody you're trying to help."

He turned to Vic with his original question, "Who did this?"

"We don't know, Zach," he answered. "The sheriff has called in the Lexington Crime Unit and they will have notified the DEA. There were some controlled substances taken."

"Oh yeah, you're not doing that DEA stuff any more, are you?"

Zach went on, "This is total bullshit. Dad was a pacifist. He was too smart to let this happen. He wouldn't put up any resistance.

Everyone likes him. I used to resent being known as 'Greg's boy' and some people even went ahead and called me Greg. Dad and I talked all that through though."

The doorbell rang. Before anyone could answer, the door opened and closed. Accompanied by a whiff of musky flowers, a slender blonde teenage girl in a pink neon tee shirt and skin-tight jeans joined everyone in the rear of the house. The blue eyes that might have dominated her face were made less noticeable by her triple ear, one nose, and two lip piercings. She seemingly needed no assurance that she was welcome and it was clear she knew where she was going. Her confidence waned only slightly when she saw Zach. The two young people shared a hug that lasted a bit longer than the ones teenagers sometimes substitute for the exchange of "hellos".

"Thanks for coming, Steph. This is Zach's Uncle Vic," Lynda said by way of justifying how and why Vic belonged there. He was happy to be assigned uncle status. He'd try to assume that role as much as he could for the next few days.

"Hi." Stephanie said, glancing obligingly in Vic's general direction. She concentrated instead on hugging Lynda.

"Mom. I've got to get out of here. I'm taking the car."

"I'll go with you," Stephanie said.

Zach looked down, frowned, and shook his head no.

Stephanie took Zach's hand, looked into his eyes and said, "No. I'm going with you."

Zach and Stephanie drove away in Greg's car a deputy had left parked on the street. Lynda said, "I'm glad Steph insisted on going with him. I know he'll be alright."

Vic again asked Lynda what he could do but she shooed him toward the door. He told her which motel he'd be checking into and let her know that he was available anytime before the visitation and funeral.

A TALL MAN WITH A FRIENDLY SMILE, SHAVED HEAD, and a broad but crooked nose that set off his otherwise handsome face walked up the driveway toward Vic. If he hadn't been expecting to see him, Vic might not have recognized Rex Thurman in a golf shirt. Vic extended his hand and then before their hands could meet they briefly hugged.

Rex said, "Hi Narco."

"Hi Rev," Vic countered.

Rex was known as Reverend Rex by the members of what had become the largest congregation in the greater Lexington area attracting members from other struggling churches in Burgoyne and from the western suburbs of Lexington. Many of the congregants of this mega-church were formerly categorized as "non-churched."

"Rev" was a relative newcomer to the fishing group that had first gotten together the summer after all the others graduated from college. Vic was christened "Narco". The other members of their fishing group, Pat and Will, had jobs too boring for them to be given nicknames. Pat was a hospital administrator and Will was an actuary. And Greg. Greg referred to himself as "the druggist", but that didn't translate into a nickname

"I don't envy you, Rev. You better have your 'this is why God lets bad things happen to good people' explanations ready for Lynda."

"I'm relying on spiritual guidance. I've been praying and reminding myself that I have the conviction of my own answers ever since I first heard about Greg."

"I'm sure you'll do fine Rev. I'll see you, if not tomorrow, the day after."

"Take care, Narco".

There was only one car in the driveway. The black Altima, based on its prominent cross decal in the back window, belonged to Rex. Stephanie didn't impress me as someone willing to take long walks. Vic surmised then that she must live in one of the seven other houses in this, one of Burgoyne's wealthiest neighborhoods. He had to assume that Stephanie's family must be reasonably well off.

8

LYNDA AND ZACH STOOD BY THE CLOSED CASKET
with Greg's mother and brother, Lucile and Roscoe.
The family kept things together, displaying the
proper balance of personal sorrow and gratitude for
sincere but at times awkward words of condolence.

A PowerPoint of digitalized pictures
featuring Greg that repeated itself every
seven minutes was shown on a screen to the right of
the casket. Like almost everyone else that afternoon,
Vic searched for pictures of himself in the nostalgic
and often humorous photo display. There was a shot
of Greg and Vic as boys with Greg's dad laughing
and pointing to a fish that was barely bigger than
the night crawler that enticed the pathetic thing to
its early death. Another picture showed a beaming
young Lynda with Greg and Vic in their caps and
gowns at their University of Cincinnati graduation
ceremony. Another was a shot of Lynda, Tracy,
Greg, and Vic mugging on Kentucky Derby Day.
The four wore sunglasses and fancy hats and had
binoculars strung around their necks. They were
pointing at bourbon balls and a Derby pie, both
prominently labeled for their Kentucky-naïve
Facebook friends. He replayed in his mind their

"Sure, Ali, I'll do that," Vic said, lying yet again, "And, by the way, she goes by Lynda, not Lynn."

Ali had been waging an on-going campaign to outbid Greg for the contracts with two assisted-living facilities that Ebert Drugs served. Ali's idea of consulting was to provide cursory oversight and to devise creative yet technically legal ways of billing third party providers for questionable services. To Ali, the patients and their health care needs were incidental to her financial aspirations.

Ralph Billings, the sheriff, walked up, saving Vic from any more of Ali's sales pitches. Ralph had been the sheriff of Burgoyne for ten years. He moved more slowly than Vic remembered, and appeared slightly stooped as if the burdens of law enforcement were beginning to wear him down. His prematurely white hair and his deeply lined face contributed to his looking considerably older than Vic, even though he was only two years his senior. Those two years made the biggest difference when as kids Ralph and Julie's older brother Timmy tormented Greg and Vic at every opportunity.

Ralph was seemingly sheriff for life. The last two elections he ran unopposed with loyal supporters from both political camps. Ralph's slogan, as if he needed one, was "Sheriff Billings keeps Burgoyne safe." Up until two days before, there had been no murders in Burgoyne in most people's memory. Reckless driving and public intoxication constituted the town's idea of serious criminal activity.

"One of your DEA associates was supposed to see me again today. I let her into the store but she'll have to wait to debrief me until tomorrow with the funeral and all," Ralph said without so much as a "hello".

"Who's the agent in charge?" Vic asked.

"Patrice Wilkins."

"She's very good. She's thorough and she's smart. She'll want to move fast. Which she should and which you should. It'd be nice to put a stop to these crimes and to find out who killed Greg. She's not here simply to determine what drugs are missing and definitely not to get in your way. People who are willing to murder in order to get drugs don't think like the rest of us. They'll continue to rob and kill people until someone catches up to them.

And, Ralph … don't try to work around her. She believes in being a good team member and will expect you to do the same. Trust me, I wouldn't cross her. How'd she take being told to wait?"

"Oh, I just explained how close Greg and I were."

"Close? Since when? You broke his arm giving him a body slam onto a pile of rocks."

"Come on, Vic. We were kids. That's all in the past. Greg let it go; you should too. He's been helping me out every year doing drug talks at the middle school," Ralph said.

"I suspect Greg thought he was helping the kids, not you."

"Whoa. I must have hit a nerve somewhere. Am I going to be dealing with you too? Are you going to be part of the investigative team?"

"No. I resigned from the DEA. I'm here for Zach and Lynda."

"Oh yeah. I heard that. Well, I'll talk to you later," Ralph said, awkwardly edging away.

9

"MR. FYE, I'M EDWIN RYDER. I think you met my daughter Stephanie the other day. I'm chairman of the Burgoyne Downtown Revitalization Project.

I'm sorry for your loss," Ryder added, before releasing Vic's hand. "Are you Greg's or Lynda's brother?"

"Neither. I'm Zach's godfather. He's always called me Uncle Vic."

Edwin Ryder learned Vic's identity from his daughter and saw it as a means to forging a connection. Ryder might have been a genuinely caring man. But even if that was true, he still set off Vic's 'slick-o-meter'. He impressed Vic as someone who solicited funds for a college or who spent a lot of time evangelizing for a church. Ryder was more boyish-looking than handsome. His conversation was punctuated by awkward grimaces ... his way of trying to suppress his perpetual and anything but solemn grin at the visitation.

"Tell me about the revitalization project," Vic said, playing dumb.

"A group of the local business leaders have hired me to help coordinate their plans for making Burgoyne into a tourist destination. I came here from Galena, Illinois. Galena is a good model for what we're trying to do in Burgoyne. They're so much like us ... an easy drive from several big cities and with rural countryside, ripe for development in the immediate vicinity. We've got old architecture, fall foliage, interesting history, and of course the horse farms. Oh, and our distillery is designated as a stop on the Bourbon Trail. Sorry, if I sound like a chamber of commerce brochure."

"That's okay," Vic assured him, "Ever since I was a kid, I've spent a lot of time here in Burgoyne. You don't have to sell me.

What's supposed to happen downtown, Edwin?"

"Some of the businesses should stay the same but we need more antique shops, art galleries, artsy-craftsy places, restaurants, upscale clothing places ... you know, enough so people can spend three or four hours wandering around and shopping. If Burgoyne turns into a Galena, people will be coming here by the busload."

"So what business leaders are backing this?" Vic asked.

"Well, Johnny Laine's consortium hired me. He and that crowd are the most involved. Other businesses are falling in line. I'd been talking to Greg about maybe moving his drug store out to the mall but keeping his Hallmark franchise and opening a soda fountain downtown. He was thinking about it."

DURING THE SHORT BREAK BEFORE THE FUNERAL, Will and Pat joined Lynda, Julie, and Vic. "How are God's gifts to wildlife conservation?" Vic asked.

"You guys do understand that 'catch and release' means that you first have to catch the fish."

Pat was quick to reply, "We're good but disappointed. We tried to practice casting last night at the Lawrence High School football stadium. A hundred yards didn't give us enough room. We kept getting our lines tangled in the goalpost at the opposite end of the field."

"Lawrence doesn't play football. Maybe it was their tetherball pole with its ten foot diameter play area," Vic countered

Lynda forced a smile and then said, "While we're on the subject of fishing, I think that's the topic, I should tell you that Zach and I have talked this over. We agree that you are more than welcome to spend next weekend at the cottage. The last thing Greg would want would be for you to cancel 'fishfest' or whatever you call it."

"That was last year. This year its 'Catfishpalooza'," offered Will.

"Anyhow, Vic will be in town to set things up and I've already asked Hal, our other pharmacist, to work next weekend. It's decided. Anglers you will be."

Nobody argued. Each of them gave Lynda an extra hug.

"Where's my hug?" Julie asked.

They obliged, not reluctantly, since she looked stunning even in all black. Her outfit set off her highlighted-hair that she was wearing up with dangling silver earrings. Julie had encountered few straight males who could resist doing anything she asked of them, especially if it involved physical contact.

"These hugs obligate you to do some heavy duty fish cleaning for us next weekend," Pat said.

"Guys, I think Krogers' fish comes packaged both fin and bone-free. Maybe I'll bring you some buns for sandwiches," Julie retorted, clearly having some insight into the group's lack of fishing prowess.

Vic noticed his ex-wife coming into the church. He excused himself and walked across the outer sanctuary to intercept her.

"Victor. How are you coping?" Tracy asked after they had exchanged perfunctory cheek kisses.

"I'm doing okay. On the surface, Lynda and Zach seem to be doing fine. I'm a little worried about both of them once they get through today. "

"At least you'll be here to help them. And they've always lived here in Burgoyne, so its not like they'll be alone.

Speaking of alone, I didn't see any point in picking up Sheldon and having him stay by himself all day. I'll get him tonight."

"By himself". I guess that means Tracy and David aren't living together.

TRACY NOTED THAT THE SANCTUARY WAS FILLING. She turned back to Vic and said, "I'd like to sit with you if that's alright ... if it doesn't make you too uncomfortable."

"Of course not. With Johnny and Julie, we surrogates will practically outnumber the real family. Speaking of ... uh, there he is now."

Johnny Laine continued to expertly work the room, shaking hands with late arrivals he encountered. Most returned his smile. He joined Julie in time for an usher to seat them beside Tracy and Vic in the pew immediately behind the family.

The flower-draped coffin was brought to the front of the sanctuary, followed by Lynda on Zach's arm, and, finally, Reverend Rex. As he did for most of his services, he wore a dark suit, not the more traditional ornate white robe. Uncharacteristically, Rex fumbled with his notes and turned several pages before finding the scripture reading. Rev had never presided over a funeral for a close friend. Greg had been the chairman of the church's Minister Call Committee, had helped Rex find and finance his house, and had hired Claudia, Rex's wife, as his pharmacy technician. But it was their regular Friday morning meetings over coffee that cemented their friendship.

It was clear that Rex prayed and spoke from the heart. Like most of Greg's many friends Rex struggled to disguise his feelings. At one point he addressed the family. "I speak on behalf of the entire congregation when I promise that you do not mourn alone. Your loss and your grief are our loss and our grief."

After his homily, he looked to the organist and in his best pastoral voice announced the final hymn. Greg was to be cremated and so there were no instructions as to how to proceed to a burial site. Instead, Rex announced a light lunch in the church basement and closed the service by leading the congregation in prayer.

Vic and Tracy stayed long enough to say goodbye to several people. Tracy cornered him before they left and explained how she needed to rush back to Louisville. She exaggerated her urgency. In truth, she was afraid she might start crying. Rex's eulogy was moving, of course, and she was deeply troubled by how devastating Greg's death was for Lynda and Zach and, yes, for Vic. She felt a loss as well but her sense of loss extended further. She saw, not for the first time, that by divorcing Vic she was drifting away from his friends and other enjoyable parts of his life they had shared.

THAT EVENING VIC HEADED FOR THE RESTAURANT. He was so lost in thought that he failed to appreciate the admiring stares and waves his Ford inevitably attracted. Without thinking, he pulled into one of the six parking spaces at an otherwise empty small neighborhood park. The park was ten blocks from where Greg grew up and for the first summer Vic visited it represented the furthest distance that the two of them were allowed to go to by themselves ... at least so far as Dale and Lucille Ebert knew. Vic leaned back, tightly gripping the unpadded steering wheel. He resisted the urge to pull or push for fear that in his rage he would snap it off. His shoulders shook with anger. He tried to delude himself into thinking that he was upset because of Lynda and Zach. Self-pity didn't fit Vic's preferred image of himself but it hadn't been far below the surface for the past several months.

From the time they were kids Greg and Vic always had each other's back. They thought of themselves as being like Butch and Sundance but they never could agree as to which of them was Sundance. It went beyond pretending. If Greg had needed him, Vic would have tied a pistol to his hand before they stumbled out of the cantina together, firing futilely at half of the Bolivian army. Greg was no longer able to ask but Vic answered him anyway. *I'm here now, Greg. I'm here to take care of Lynda and Zach. If I can I'll get the soldatos, ... no, I guess not the soldiers ...I'll get the bandito.*

10

VIC CONTINUED ON TO THE RESTAURANT, grateful to be thought of as part of the family. He knew it wasn't the case but he couldn't help feeling like he could be doing something else. He needed to settle into a routine at the pharmacy as quickly as possible. Only then could he concentrate on helping Lynda with her precarious financial situation, seeing after her and Zach, and finding a way for them and him to move on.

The last to arrive, Vic snaked his way through the maze of tables into the back room. Unintentionally, he announced his entrance by noisily scooting several chairs with glide-free wooden legs across the well-worn tile floor of Vinnie's Restaurant. In case the Dean Martin background music, the red, green, and white menu, and the unmistakable garlic-oregano aroma weren't enough to convince patrons that the fare was Italian, the plastic place mats on the tightly spaced tables featured maps with line drawings of a gondola, the Coliseum, the Leaning Tower, and other icons representing the cities and regions of Italy. Since Sunday was the restaurant's biggest day, Vinnie's was closed to the public on Mondays. They opened for a few hours that evening to serve the Ebert party.

Mrs. Palermo was their server. The chef, Vinnie Palermo, prepared a single entre ... the house specialty ... a spicy sausage lasagna. Regular patrons of Vinnie's would most likely have chosen to order the lasagna. There were over-sized bowls of salad, baskets of garlicky Italian bread, and carafes of the house Chianti already sitting on the large square table the Palermos had puzzled together from four smaller ones.

Greg's younger brother, Roscoe, was the only person who appeared as if he didn't want to be there. His frozen scowl and his incessant fidgeting reminded Vic just how irritating his behavior could be. Roscoe was a smaller version of his older brother except he had longer yet still unruly hair. He sported a small stud in his left ear lobe. And he had several partially visible tattoos. After leaving the funeral, he had changed to a lightweight sports jacket over a black tee shirt and faded jeans. Roscoe was too short and pudgy to pull off whatever GQ look he was trying to project.

Roscoe lived with his and Greg's mother, Lucille, in Newport. Ostensibly, he supported himself by working in a framing shop. He supplemented his wages by selling original landscapes and an occasional ceramic piece. Roscoe's standard of living stayed above a subsistence level through the grace of Lucille. She seemed to enjoy having Roscoe around so long as his needs didn't exceed her notion of generosity. Greg's dad Dale had amassed a comfortable nest egg, using profits from the pharmacy business to invest in real estate. When Dale died from a lymphoma, Lucille liquidated the Burgoyne properties. She reinvested in real estate in Newport, her girlhood home. Roscoe, in return for his room and board, helped to maintain those properties. Lucille believed she maintained financial parity between the brothers. In fact, Greg had used the proceeds from a survivorship insurance policy to complete the purchase of his father's half of the pharmacy partnership.

Lucille over the years had become good friends with Lynda's parents, Tom and Karen, to the extent that they had traveled together on several vacations. They chatted quietly with one another, content to tune out most of the conversations around them. They interrupted their discussion to listen, though, when Lynda began her explanation as to why Zach hadn't joined everyone else at the restaurant.

"Steph's family, the Ryders, asked Zach to eat with them tonight. Zach and Stephanie have been friends since the Ryders moved here eighteen months ago. Steph seems to be able to console him right now better than I can. Zach, I think, would like for he and Steph to become more than friends but Stephanie is much more sociable. Zach probably isn't adventurous enough for her. Anyhow, that's why Zach isn't here."

"Has Zach decided on a college yet?" Karen asked her daughter.

"Zach needs to figure out what he wants to do first. His science grades and test scores are good enough to get into a pharmacy school. But, working at the store and listening to his father ... I don't think there will be a third generation of Ebert pharmacists. He's talked about enrolling in business but he's not excited about that either."

"Lynda, how many seventeen year olds do you know that think beyond their latest text message or Snap Chat exchange?" chimed in Lucille, eliciting a surprised look from Roscoe who didn't believe his mother was versant in technology more sophisticated than her garage door opener.

"Yeah, I know Lucille. He's a good kid. I wish he'd have more friends is all."

"Doesn't he hang around with the other track team guys and the Model U.N. people?" offered Julie.

"He doesn't do anything with them after the meets or practice. The U.N. thing involves kids from all over the state, sometimes both Kentucky and Tennessee. He does like to run and he spends a lot of time texting and tweeting. These electronic friends must be people I don't know about. He's fine I guess."

Johnny sensed a break in the conversation and tried to segue into community politics ... a topic he knew would make him the center of attention. "Well, at least we can be sure that most of our kids aren't into drugs ... hard drugs anyway. Sheriff Billings has done a good job, he and the high school counselors. Ralph puts the fear of God into anyone who is supplying out of the high school and so far has only busted kids who don't live in the township. Some parents think he ought to be tougher but those aren't the parents of the local kids he's caught."

"So basically there's not much drug use in Woodford County?" Vic asked, not bothering to disguise his sarcastic intent.

"Oh, I guess there's still a lot of underage drinking and I hear there's quite a few kids smoking pot. I understand very few kids smoke but vaping, e-cigarettes I guess, seems to be picking up. But from what Ralph says, he and his deputies almost never find any crack or meth, or at least no kids with it."

"DEA priorities have changed with increased legalization of marijuana for recreational use, not in Kentucky, but in several states. There's an emphasis on prevention. The targeted issues for agents are distribution to minors, drugged driving, and revenue going to support other criminal activity, especially trafficking of other illegal substances. But I've got to admit, this county didn't demand a lot of our attention," Vic said, hoping his account would take some pressure off Johnny and maybe bring closure to the touchy topic. Zach's grandparents had gotten quiet and seemed uncomfortable hearing about any threat to their grandson's youthful innocence.

Lynda obliged by saying, "I need to figure out what to do about the pharmacy. I'm not sure how our store is going to fit in with the revitalization. Plus there's added competition from the new Wal-Mart over in Lawrence. We're doing okay with our nursing home business and our regular in-town customers but the younger families in Burgoyne don't seem to mind driving into Lexington or over to Lawrence.

Hal is fine with working a few more than his thirty hours a week for the immediate future but he's talking about him and his wife spending their winters in Florida. It would be ideal if I could get somebody to buy into the store, although I'm not sure why they'd do that given how tough it is for independent businesses."

"Lynda. You know, and I've said this before, I'll make sure that you get taken care of," Johnny said with what was probably a mirror-practiced look of empathy. "You don't need to be worrying about this. Greg and I had talked about us setting him up somewhere else or whatever we need to do to make this work. I promise I'll take care of you."

"Don't forget, Vic has agreed to help you with the store," said Julie, putting her spin on things. "Maybe he could stay in Burgoyne for a few weeks. He wouldn't have to convince somebody else to try and keep up the practice while putting up with a DEA investigation at the same time. He'll be your pharmacist and maybe could stay long enough to help you figure out what you want to do."

"Yeah, Vic, lucky you. You get to be in Burgoyne," broke in Roscoe.

Roscoe was openly critical of his boyhood home. He made fewer and fewer trips back to Burgoyne, and those were mostly to paint landscapes along the river in the spring and in the fall. He had lost track of acquaintances he used to shoot with at the local gun club. Simply put, Roscoe preferred not to acknowledge his Kentucky small town roots …as if Newport was most peoples' idea of a sophisticated metropolis.

"Now Roscoe, I'm thinking about rewording my trust so that you'll be required to live in Burgoyne," said Lucile, trying to offset Roscoe's snide manner with her own brand of irony. But immediately Lucille realized this was not a time for allusions to inheritances or wills. She blushed and tried not to make eye contact with anyone, busying herself with the croutons in her salad.

There was some polite laughing. Mrs. Palermo saved the day by refilling everyone's wine and efficiently serving the steaming-hot aromatic dinners. The portions were large. But as the conversations became lighter everyone's appetites improved. When people readied themselves to leave, no one requested a take-out container.

11

VIC EXPECTED AN UNINTERRUPTED NIGHT'S SLEEP. This hope was bolstered by the clerk's assurance that there'd be no road noise in rooms on the rear side of the motel. But every time Vic fell asleep either the cycling heater, the ice machine across the hall, or a flushing toilet from the room next door jolted him back to consciousness. Vic understood the benefits of a deluxe showerhead and he appreciated the convenience of the complimentary breakfast, but questioned whether they offset his noisy, fretful experience.

Vic completed his TRX cable work out without damaging the bathroom doorframe. He'd had to expense three frames already this year. He read for a while before lacing up his running shoes. He made it a practice to run when it was light enough to see hazards not merely feel them underfoot. It was a practice not a rule. It wouldn't begin to get light for half an hour, but Vic couldn't wait any longer.

He clanked down the steel stairs at the end of the hall, pushed open the windowless metal exit door and stepped into the chilly predawn. Momentarily confused by the darkness and by his exiting through a side door, he paused to figure out which way would lead him toward downtown. A four or five mile run would be enough for him to maintain his desired endurance level and to ramp up his metabolism. He used upcoming races as his motivation to run on a regular basis. He had signed up the mandatory year in advance for a half marathon that was several weeks away. He hoped his commitments in Burgoyne wouldn't derail his plan. Not a big deal, but he genuinely hated the thought of missing out on another trip to Indianapolis. He had run in the Indy Mini-Marathon, seven of the previous eight years.

Vic followed conventional safety rules and ran on the left shoulder of the two-lane road, facing Frankfort commuter traffic. It would be more than a mile before he'd reach the streetlight-illuminated sections of Burgoyne and the first trace of sidewalk. He wore a reflective vest and his running shoes had luminescent stripes. He ran slower than race pace so he could react to loose gravel, recessed and raised areas, and the biggest pieces of litter. His running became somewhat tenuous the two times he was temporarily blinded by the headlights of approaching cars on his side of the road. The driver of one vehicle gave him a wide berth, pulling into the oncoming lane. The other driver didn't waver from the accustomed distance from the white line.

He heard a truck accelerating behind him and turned in time to see that it had no lights and that it was swerving onto his side of the road. Vic slowed to maneuver into the weeds on the other side of the road's shoulder. He heard the crunch of the truck's tires on gravel. Something hard smacked into his right leg. The something turned out to be an orange that bounced off his thigh and back onto the road. It was still dark and Vic was too surprised to get a meaningful description of the accelerating truck. With no illumination front or back, catching a license number was out of the question.

He sped up out of anger, not because he had any chance of overtaking the truck. It was only the second vehicle to have passed him heading toward town. When Vic rounded a curve, he saw a couple of pick-ups being fueled at a 7-Eleven and four others parked by the entrance. As with most convenience stores, commuting hours were busy times. He crossed the street, continuing to run until he got to the door. The only reason he could come up with for stopping was to use the rest room. He latched the door, waited fifteen seconds or so, flushed the toilet, turned the water on and off, hit the air dryer button and exited. There were six male customers. Three of them were in line at the register to check out and the other three were filling 20 ounce coffee cups and selecting pastries and breakfast sandwiches. All six looked at him. He wondered whether it was his running clothes, that he was a stranger in town, or that he merited their interest as the only guy in the store who wasn't clinically overweight.

Vic realized how futile it would be, not to mention how childish it would sound, to ask something to the effect of, "Which one of you guys threw an orange at me?" Instead, he waited his turn in line before asking, "Do you sell oranges?"

"I've got o.j. Sir, but no oranges," the clerk said.

"No. I'm looking for an orange."

Vic turned, only to find that none of the patrons, those now standing around a tall table and those behind him in line, avoided eye contact. None of them showed the slightest indication that they knew what he was talking about. The further fact that no one appeared to be left-handed told him that none of those six guys had harassed him.

VIC ENTERED THE DOWNTOWN AREA. He left the sidewalk and ran down the middle of the street between Greg's store and the county court house. The three-story, gray monstrosity was no more attractive in semi-darkness than during the day. A fragment of fluttering crime scene tape tied to the door handle of the pharmacy reminded him what he would soon be facing. To the general public and to the Kentucky Board of Pharmacy Examiners, Vic would be the licensed pharmacist-in-charge, the person allowing the prescription-filling portion of the enterprise to legally remain operational. To a nucleus of people, his presence in Burgoyne meant that Lynda believed Ebert Drugs could survive as a business enterprise. Vic would operate under the premise that Lynda wanted more than survival for Ebert Drugs. His priorities would be to maintain, if not increase the customer base and to increase revenue … business 101.

This had to begin immediately. The store was only closed for a few business hours the day before. But when customers, for any reason at all, patronize another store, a few will stay away permanently. Patient-pharmacy monogamy can be fleeting. Some people, those most motivated by price or convenience, will be especially prone to take their business to other stores. Plus it was likely that there were some who remained loyal customers of Ebert Drugs because of their long friendship with Greg. In essence, Vic, as the new kid on the block, had his work cut out for him.

Vic turned around at the cross street. Except for the mild, throbbing pain in his right thigh, he felt rejuvenated. A distinct orange glow was starting to appear in the east. He picked up the pace, to get back in time to take advantage of the multi-flow, water-saving shower nozzle and to fortify himself with a cup or two of motel coffee and a make-your-own waffle. He had earned himself an extra 240 calories. He picked up his pace. He could now see where he was going and where he was stepping.

12

CLAUDIA THURMAN WAS HIS PHARMACY TECH. She was better known in Burgoyne simply as Reverend Rex's wife. She and Vic had spoken briefly at Greg's funeral but other than meeting her after church services a few times Vic couldn't claim to know her. His only other insight came from late night, beer-fueled talks on fishing trips. Both Greg and Rex portrayed Claudia as energetic and no-nonsense.

She was the ideal minister's wife for Rex's dynamic, rapidly growing congregation. She attended every service, which meant listening to the same sermon three times a weekend. After each service she stood by his side to greet parishioners. She knew their names as well or better than Rex. Having grown up a PK, a preacher's kid, she unabashedly critiqued his sermons … at least their first iterations.

She had short blonde hair and a fair complexion that contrasted sharply with her dark-rimmed glasses. She had attractive features and would have been described by Vic's less than politically correct father as "big-boned". Claudia was dressed in a pale green lab jacket over black slacks and comfortable work shoes.

She authoritatively showed Vic the store layout and explained "her system" for inventory control. Vic had little doubt that his designation as "pharmacist in charge" was nominal until he earned Claudia's full confidence. Claudia's reference to the precise spot where Greg's body was found was the only departure from her all-business orientation to Ebert Drugs.

There was a dark discoloration on the floor which was the only evidence that the store was a recent crime scene. "That mark, that burn or whatever it is, was it there before?" Vic asked.

"No. The cleanup crew scoured and waxed it. They told me our tile is extremely porous. We can replace that piece or live with it."

"Maybe we could use a floor display to cover it. Patients might be put off if they think the stain is blood," Vic suggested.

Claudia nodded and said, "I try to avoid clutter, especially if it could block the patient consultation area. We'll think about this some more."

Vic followed Claudia behind the prescription counter so she could finish his orientation before the first customers arrived. The computerized system for prescription filing, inventory control, and patient safety was QS/1; the one most widely used by independent pharmacies. Pharmacists-PRN charges pharmacies a 10% upcharge if they use any other system. Claudia explained what her roles were ... what Greg and Hal authorize her to do. Vic told her that he was only too happy to allow her responsibilities to continue as they had been under Greg even though he had the sense she wasn't asking for his permission.

CLAUDIA ADDRESSED THE FIRST SEVEN CUSTOMERS BY NAME. She acknowledged their comments about Greg's death, most of which included messages that one way or another conveyed their sorrow at losing such a wonderful and caring man. Greg's passing clearly represented a personal loss for many people. Their condolences were genuine.

The pace was more hectic than Vic had expected. Claudia reminded him that since the store had been closed for several hours Monday, normally the busiest day of the week, this Tuesday traffic reflected backlog from both Sunday and Monday. Vic got into the flow quickly and Claudia let him know the patients who needed the most thorough counseling on new prescriptions and the ones who didn't want to interact with a technician but only with "the pharmacist", even when they were deciding on things that weren't medical in nature. One lady that morning asked Vic to help her decide between ibuprofen tablets and ibuprofen capsules. He pretended that her query was worthy of his professional judgment. Successful small business owners have learned that patients equate their being coddled to an expectation of personal service.

Vic was deluged with phone calls, faxes, and occasional computer glitches, mostly of his own making. He still looked up in response to, "Good morning Dr. Fye."

Vic and Greg were members of the last class of pharmacists who could attain a bachelor's degree in pharmacy as their highest degree. At that time, pharmacy colleges were in transition toward exclusively granting professional doctorates when students graduated. Greg and Vic made no bones about the fact that they wouldn't stay in school any longer than the necessary five-year minimum required at that time to get licensed. Their mantra was "We're druggists, not doctors". Lynda must have shared their rants with Julie.

Julie wore a stylish version of workout clothes. Vic assumed from her perfect hair and make-up and the absence of any indication of perspiration that she was heading to, not coming from, some sort of exercise venue.

"I thought I'd better check on you, Vic. Good morning, Claudia."

"Hello, Mrs. Laine," Claudia returned with more formality than she had used with the majority of the clients she had been greeting.

"I'm glad that you're able to help out, Vic. I don't think Lynda has the energy to go through the hassle of finding someone else for a while. And I wouldn't want to have some pompous doctor of pharmacy try to take over here, would I Dr. Fye?"

Julie was no longer Julie mourning with her friend. Julie was back in character ... animated, playful, bordering on flirtatious. She slipped into that persona easily. She always had. Tracy had become angry the first few times she'd watched Julie go into her routine with Vic. Eventually she realized that Julie's implied shared intimacy spiel was directed at almost every male she encountered. It's not surprising that Julie had trouble forming strong, close friendships with other women ... especially with married women.

"I'll see you soon my druggist friend, I mean doctor friend."

"So long, Julie."

BY MID AFTERNOON, THE PACE HAD SLOWED. Other than Claudia, the cashier in the front of the store and Vic, the store was deserted. Vic took the opportunity to return a call.

"Hi, Tracy," he began with a questioning tone. He was never certain what she might want. They'd hashed out the financial issues of their dissolution in some detail but every once in a while there'd be a request for a DVD or a serving dish or something she wished she hadn't let him keep in their divorce settlement.

"I'm taking a late lunch. I think they missed me here at the hospital. The other RNs are saying they did, anyway. I kind of lost the continuity of the place but some of the patients are in and out of the oncology unit often enough that I know them anyway. This one gal is in here for the fourth time with a fever because of her low white cells."

Vic still wondered what Tracy wanted. "I'm kind of busy," he said.

"No, that's okay, I was thinking about you or I guess how you were doing. I know it'll be tough on Heidi and Pharmacists-PRN to have you out of the loop."

"I can handle lots of things for a while on-line or by phone. I'm assuming Heidi has figured out a way to cover the shifts that were supposed to be mine this week. It'll work."

"Sure, Victor. Oh, by the way. I picked up Sheldon. I explained to him that you don't love him anymore."

"I'll call you when you get home so you can put Sheldon on the line. Or maybe I'll Skype him when you're not there."

"Do that. Goodbye, Victor."

BETWEEN CUSTOMERS, CLAUDIA EXPLAINED TO VIC how Greg and she monitored the medications for their nursing home patients. Vic was soon able to assume a comfortable routine with her for checking each other's orders. He was impressed by the lack of medication duplications he saw for these patients. Most gratifying, not a single patient was on both an opioid painkiller and a Valium like drug, a combination that can make elderly patients forget to breathe.

Greg had lived up to his reputation as a conscientious consultant. Vic found no examples of unnecessary drugs or dangerous drug combinations. Patients enjoyed, often without knowing, direct savings on their drugs plus they avoided the potential costs of treating the consequences of medication errors.

"Is business always so slow after three o'clock?" Vic asked, once the nursing home order was finished.

Claudia said, "This seems worse than usual. Hal warned me that this might happen. He's been through the death of a pharmacist-owner at another store where he worked. Some customers are afraid to come in … afraid they won't know what to say, or afraid that they'll have to face a family member. Business has been dropping a little anyway. And Ali … you know Ali … has been trying to lure away our consulting business. She stuck her head in the door this morning but you were swamped at the time."

"Did Hal have any suggestions?" Vic asked. Hal had spent his 40+ professional years working for independent pharmacy owners. He moved to a different store if the competition from a chain or a Wal-Mart led to a closing. It wasn't that Hal lacked ambition. Rather he was content being able to comfortably support his family and his hobbies without the burdens of managerial or ownership responsibilities.

"Un-huh. Hal said that one store staged the equivalent of a 'grand opening'. They did it under the guise of celebrating the life of the deceased owner, reminding patients how he took care of them and how the new pharmacist would continue that tradition. Hal said it worked. They even attracted new business."

"How do you think Lynda would react to something like that?" Vic turned to Claudia and asked.

"We've already decided to do it. It'll be sometime next week. Julie, of all people, has agreed to do most of the work for Lynda in getting it organized."

"I detect that you're not fond of Julie," Vic ventured.

"She even hit on Rex," Claudia snapped. "I'm not saying she sleeps around. But, she doesn't worry about giving the impression that getting her into bed is always a possibility. I don't mean to sound like a preacher's wife, but being around Julie grates on me. She's what we call an e.g.r. ...extra grace required."

"That's okay. I know where you're coming from. I heard from her a couple of weeks ago. Completely out of the blue. She said that we should get together. She must have been trawling ... networking for her next in line."

13

HAL RELIEVED VIC MID-AFTERNOON. Vic had allotted time to make courtesy calls on other merchants who faced the square surrounding the courthouse. There were only a few cars parked in front of the businesses. It looked like a good time to approach the proprietors. Vic introduced himself and, after exchanging pleasantries, tried to determine if the owners had any insights on the revitalization that downtown Burgoyne was facing. Their reactions could be summarized as …"I wish I knew" and / or "I hope I can hang on."

His final stop was at what he deduced was going to be a bakery. He prepared himself for another contingency in case *Ye Olde Cookie Wench* turned out to be a tavern. The display cases and aroma that greeted him as soon as he opened the door confirmed that indeed it was a cookie shop. The diminutive, gray-haired proprietor bore no resemblance to the wench he envisioned.

"I'm Vic Fye, the new pharmacist at Ebert's. Do you have a few minutes to talk?"

She smiled and turned side to side as if she was making sure there were no customers lurking in her tiny store. She said, "Yes I can talk. That's terrible, what happened to Greg."

"Yes, it was."

"You're his brother-in-law aren't you?"

"His friend. His best friend."

The woman took charge of the conversation. "People are saying it was somebody high on drugs. I don't know. I had a customer as I was closing that day who freaked me out."

"How so?"

"He was a big ugly guy with a real deep voice. I didn't know him. He told me he'd like a cookie and when I asked him what kind he said 'the usual'. When I told him I didn't know his usual he said 'okay, make it assorted'. Then he laughed, picked up one of the prepackaged assortments of six. He started to pay with a Discover Card but literally ripped it out of my hand. Then he paid with a hundred dollar bill."

"Did anybody from the sheriff's office interview you? Did you tell somebody?"

"Yes. I explained it all to one of the deputies. He wrote it down in a little book and told me it might be helpful."

Vic couldn't keep from being intrigued so he asked her, "Do you remember anything else? Was he big as in fat or tall? What did he wear? Was he white?"

"Yeah he was white. He was dressed in denim like a lot of the men who work at the farms, except he was too big to be a rider or trainer. He was tall and looked strong, not fat.

Oh. I'm sorry did you want some cookies?"

"Not really. I just wanted to introduce myself and ask how you thought the revitalization project was going to affect you."

"I think it'll do great things for my business. I'm talking to people who can help me set up the equipment to make fudge. I've got space in the back I'm not using. My daughter has been out of work for a while and I think we'd have enough new business to support the both of us. Mr. Ryder told me that my shop was the kind of store that would do really well."

BACK AT THE MOTEL, VIC BACKED INTO THE LAST SPACE at the end of the rear parking lot. It was furthest from the entrance, well away from the dozen or so other cars ... the door-ding-free spot. Once inside, his key card elicited a red light no matter which way he inserted it into the room door reader. This was not unusual for him. He was cursed with an innate ability to mishandle cards in a way that demagnetized them. It didn't matter whether he kept the "plastic keys" in his wallet or in a pocket. The desk clerk didn't give him a chance to explain his affliction.

"We went ahead and packed up your things, Mr. Fye. I've got them over here. Thanks for staying with us. Do you need a copy of the bill?"

The clerk seemed proud of herself for a job well done. Vic's clothes were hung in plastic bags on a rack. His toiletries and laptop were in a white box with a motel logo and his suitcase, containing presumably everything else, was zipped shut and ready to go.

"I didn't know I was checking out."

The clerk gave him a questioning look and said, "But we had a phone call from your assistant. He said to check you out and box things up."

"This is bizarre. I don't have an assistant ... do you have another room or even the same room would be good?"

Now blushing, the clerk began typing on her computer keyboard with an intensity that demonstrated she would not be distracted until she corrected the situation. She promised to not charge for one night to compensate him for the inconvenience. Vic thought for a moment that she was going to shut down the desk to help him unpack.

The keycard for his new room triggered the comforting green light, giving him access to a room with the identical layout, dreary beige bedspread and mass-produced print of grazing horses he found in the previous room.

I wonder why somebody wants to mess with me?

14

VIC PICKED THE RESTAURANT WITHIN WALKING
DISTANCE. Like the other waitresses, Helen had
"always friendly service" embroidered on her
uniform. She seemed to interpret that to mean she
was supposed to be his friend not his friendly
waitress. Not seeking a friendship, he didn't
introduce himself. Consequently he became
"Sugar", the Woodford County equivalent of "Sir."

Coincidently there was another "Sugar" a
couple of tables away. He looked less like a "Sugar"
Vic thought immodestly. This "Sugar" sat by
himself at a table for four. He was too tall and too
bulky for one of the booths. Vic, sensitized to
grotesquely large males, became suspicious. He
decided it would be beyond bold for a criminal to
eat in a small town where he committed a
robbery/murder only a few days before. Besides
which, the guy wore a dress shirt and tie, he
concentrated on some papers, and he had an open
MacBook Air on the table. Given the national
obesity epidemic, there was bound to be more than
one enormous guy in this part of Kentucky. Vic had
seen several who qualified that morning at the 7-
Eleven.

The man was served a mound of onion rings
and a huge steak, cooked, if grilled at all, to blood

red doneness. Vic now understood why a 22-ounce T-bone was a menu item in a place that featured burgers and chili. The man caught Vic looking at him once but seemingly took no offense. He smiled and gave Vic a little wave before he picked up the bone to gnaw off the last fragments of fatty meat. Vic's side-salad, double order of steamed vegetables, and burger with only half a bun would probably have amused the guy if he'd been less preoccupied with his steak and had taken more than four minutes to eat it. Sugar became Earl when Helen, the hostess, and a busboy all wished him a "good night."

Helen wanted to chat. More so, Helen wanted to find out if Vic was a prospective suitor. The Cosmo feature articles that told her how men liked to talk about themselves must not have included caveats such as the all important "not while they're eating."

Since so many people in Burgoyne had an inkling by this time of who he was and why he was there, there was no reason to be duplicitous. Vic's undercover days were behind him.

"Oh, you're taking over for Greg," she gushed. "He filled all my 'subscriptions'. Are you buying the store?"

"No. I'm representing a business in Louisville. I'll be helping out until Mrs. Ebert figures out what to do."

"Greg was always my favorite. He never stared at me like the other guys in the breakfast group do."

She not so subtly threw back her shoulders to make sure that Vic understood the object of the stares. He decided not to suggest that her breast flaunting posture and her immodest decision to leave one too many buttons unbuttoned could have contributed to the men's down-blousing.

Instead he asked, "Are these some kind of service club meetings?"

"No they're all local business types though. Greg hadn't been coming for a while. Wendy, the other waitress who works mornings, said that he and a contractor had an argument. She said that Johnny Laine had tried to smooth things over but Greg never came back."

"Who was the contractor?"

"He's some hot shot builder who is trying to work with that group fixing up the downtown. He's a 'contractor' but when I dated him he was a carpenter's apprentice."

She abruptly smiled and walked to an adjacent table, thinking that maybe she had said too much about her love life. She had no way of knowing that Vic had been avoiding casual dating. In spite of his loneliness he'd been with no one since his divorce. His counselor had confronted him about this. She suggested to Vic that he was again letting unrequited loyalty dictate his actions.

She attributed Vic's responsibility for his divorce to a different misguided sense of duty. She let him know that she thought his dedication to the DEA had been over the top. He should have understood how exasperating it was for anyone to put up with a spouse who was so consumed by work.

Vic had thought it funny when Tracy told him, "I never have to worry about you having an affair. The DEA is your mistress." The counselor warned him that responding to his losing Tracy with post-divorce chastity was as emotionally unhealthy for him as avoiding Frisch's. Vic had texted the counselor to proudly announce "A fish sandwich!"

Vic turned Helen down when she suggested a homemade (probably frozen and commercial) dessert, even when she offered to warm one up (thaw in a microwave) for him. They both pretended to believe that these creations were concocted from a pastry chef's secret recipes and baked fresh on sight. It hadn't registered with her from his dinner order that he might be following a low-carb diet and that minimizing sugars and starches was a dietary priority.

ON HIS WALK BACK TO THE MOTEL, HE MULLED OVER THE PROSPECT that in case he needed to stay in Burgoyne for longer than he originally thought, he'd need to be more tolerant of all the "Helens."

He found it difficult to remain detached and treat Ebert's Drugs like the typical contracted pharmacist fill-in situation. He already was privy to some local political intrigues. Most of all he was deeply concerned for Zach and Lynda's welfare. But if he could manage to get Lynda and the store straightened away maybe she and Zach would be able to concentrate on getting other aspects of their lives in order.

The message light was blinking when he got back to the room. After decoding the less than

intuitive system for message retrieval, Vic was
greeted with a muffled, "Fye. I checked you out
once. Next time, you'll be checked out for good."

*I thought running me off the road and
checking me out of the motel were annoying pranks.
Not warnings. Not death threats in disguise. I get it
that I'm assuming Greg's role. I'm trying to
maintain a thriving pharmacy in what is likely to
become a sought after location. But should this be
a motive to kill somebody? Namely me?*

*Bastard! If you're trying to get my attention,
you've more than succeeded.*

15

WEDNESDAY WAS THE WEEKDAY WITH LOWEST PRESCRIPTION VOLUME for Ebert Drugs. To a large extent this was because the three physicians in Burgoyne clung to their tradition of taking a mid-week day off. Vic used the extra time to get to know those customers who did come in. He committed himself to linking as many names to faces and their health problems as he could. Greg's patients bought into what the sheriff was telling people. They hadn't entertained any thoughts that Greg's death was anything other than a random event, an unfortunate fluke. Unless an indisputable motive presented itself or a confessing suspect was arrested, it would take law enforcement personnel with more gumption and ability than Ralph Billings to solve Greg's murder.

About mid-morning, Special Agent Patrice Wilkins came in to complete her final inventory of controlled substances. Normally this would be a job for a DEA Division Investigator working with someone from the State Board of Pharmacy Examiners. The serial nature of the crimes and the fact that there was a homicide warranted special agent involvement.

Patrice and Vic had joined the agency at the same time and had persevered through the same mental and physical challenges during their demanding training exercises. She had been a high jumper in college and displayed a track meet level of intensity during her professional interactions. Her 5' 8" in bare feet height and upright posture gave her a commanding aura. Patrice's tailored dark blue business suit did little to disguise how fit she was. Patrice's face seemed paler than Vic remembered suggesting that her ongoing fitness activities must have been largely limited to indoor settings. Patrice's azure blue eyes, her most striking feature, were hidden behind a pair of Armani sunglasses. Since Greg was always meticulous in his maintenance of controlled substances records and the ordering and prescription profiles were computerized, determining the drugs stolen during the robbery would likely go smoothly.

When they shook hands Patrice gave him an extra squeeze and her version of a smile to acknowledge his personal loss. Vic didn't expect Patrice to waver from the unwritten protocol of "my crime trumps your business". He knew full well what was expected and would cooperate in any way that he could. She had already met with Hal and Claudia, the other two people who legally had access to the controlled drugs, before the store reopened.

Patrice worked quickly and within an hour and a half was closing her laptop and getting ready to leave. Before she could step down from the counter Vic asked, "What can you tell me? I'm having a hard time accepting that Greg's death was a robbery gone wrong."

"Vic, you know all too well that I'm not supposed to tell you anything as long as this remains an investigation in progress."

She slipped her laptop into a slim, leather brief case. She held up her empty Starbuck's cup as if to say, "What should I do with this?"

Vic took the cup and walked it to the trash at the end of the counter before saying, "Sure, I understand. For what it's worth, I've already figured out what's gone ... most of the stuff with the highest street value. I know that there was another robbery over in Blue Ridge. I don't know what was taken but it seems strange that nobody was killed or even shot for that matter. I can't imagine that Greg fought back. And if he had, why wasn't there more damage? Why weren't more shots fired?

On top of that, in the few days I've been here I've received a death threat by telephone, somebody claiming to be my assistant checked me out of my room, and a pickup truck ran me off the road and the driver managed to hit me with an orange."

"Now you're asking me to react to things that fall under the jurisdiction of the sheriff's office and the investigative team from Lexington. I'm not sure that there's another way for me to say that I won't compromise somebody else's investigation."

Vic persisted. "Patrice, I'm not asking you to compromise anything. I'm making sure somebody in authority, you specifically, knows that this could be more than an opiate addicted sociopath robbing pharmacies. You may or may not know that I requested a leave. I wasn't asked to resign but I had personal issues that made quitting seem like my best option at the time. I realize that my sob story doesn't translate into law enforcement authority. But I didn't turn in my brain with my badge. I might be able to help … probably a helluava lot more than Sheriff Billings who doesn't seem particularly excited about the fact that there was a murder under his watch or that drug abuse could be a bigger problem in Burgoyne than what he brags about during his re-election campaigns.

I don't expect you to react to this … I'm not begging you for crumbs. I do promise not to get in your way and if I learn anything, incidentally of course, I'll come to you first. I know how good you are and I'm in no way suggesting that you can't handle this alone. I'm offering a sounding board if you need it."

"Whew. Nice speech," Patrice said more gently as she put on her dark glasses to signal she was definitely on her way out. "You earned 'a crumb' which I'll deny ever telling you. The robber left an orange at both crime scenes."

Vic smiled and said, "I never reveal my sources."

"I'll come by with my preliminary report on what was taken. And Vic, remember what the speaker at our swearing in ceremony told us?" Patrice asked as she left the prescription area.

"I remember. 'Above all, don't do anything incredibly stupid'", Vic said. He gave her the okay sign when she turned and mouthed, "Be safe."

CLAUDIA AND VIC HAD ESTABLISHED A COMFORTABLE WORK ROUTINE. Like contestants on a celebrity dance show, he let the more experienced partner lead ... even though, metaphorically, it was still his right hand on her waist ... at least from the customers' perspectives. This was about more than filling in some shifts. Vic needed to be a surrogate for Greg in other ways, in ways that protected the future livelihoods of Lynda and Zach. Not to mention, none of the other Pharmacists-PRN associates should be subjected to death threats.

16

VIC'S KEYCARD WORKED. Two days in a row pretty much tied his record. The shades were drawn and the room appeared freshly made up but he smelled traces of smoke. Vic's room was on a floor designated as non-smoking with coinciding icons on the doors. It was possible that a maid or someone else from house keeping had selected Vic's room for a cigarette break. Maybe the bathroom exhaust fan wasn't up to the job. But that didn't explain why someone had taken his laptop out of its case. When he flipped his iMac open a sheet of the bedside notepad fell out. The message in large box print capital letters was simple enough … "Warning #3."

This must be the least security conscious motel in the state. If I had nothing better to do I'd figure out the leak. Right now it's easier to move to someplace else.

He had taken his computer down that morning. It was password protected so he wasn't concerned about his personal information and his Pharmacists-PRN files being compromised. Vic considered calling Ralph Billings, but even if the sheriff took fingerprints it was probably pointless. The dust on the keyboard looked like talc from disposable gloves. Handwriting experts seldom learn much from block printing. He saw no immediate need to notify the front desk. He didn't need another apology from a twenty-something receptionist.

Vic knew he'd experience more peace of mind by going on a run. Instead of a running shirt, he decided to wear a tomato red North Face bicycle shirt. His safety concerns had nothing to do with visibility. A pocket in the back of the shirt was big enough for his Kahr P380. The Kahr wasn't a DEA approved backup gun but Vic had opted to carry it for particularly dangerous undercover assignments. Of all the pocket guns he'd test fired, its action was most similar to that of his Glock. It not only was small enough to be easily concealed but also it weighed less than 12 ounces fully loaded. Right after he purchased it, Vic shot the factory-recommended 150 rounds. He kept cautiously aimed shots within a ten-inch target at 25 yards. On top of that, the Kahr didn't misfire once.

It was windier than Vic would have preferred but on the plus side there were at least two more hours of daylight. He selected the most direct way to the Kentucky River, specifically to Riverton. He was anxious to see the cottage and to start thinking about stocking the kitchen in anticipation of the fishing weekend.

The two-lane highway to the cottage grew more picturesque the further he got from Burgoyne and the closer he got to the river. Vic strayed away from the road onto its narrow shoulder when he needed to accommodate a car or a pick-up. After the earlier incident with the orange launching driver, he was inordinately cautious.

As he started down the gravel road serving as Riverton's single street, Vic experienced an eerie sensation … a combination of nostalgia and grief. He ran past Lynda and Greg's place and the other cottages and summer homes that comprised the unincorporated development. The road narrowed before it merged into a grassy stretch of trail that followed the river to what locals referred to as "the island".

A quarter-mile long trail led to a pronounced double bend in the river. The land encompassed by the river on three sides turns into an island when there are excessive amounts of rain. The resulting higher water levels, typically in late spring and early summer, create a temporary channel or water bypass to the east. But for much of the year, in agreement with county maps, the island technically is a peninsula.

Vic crossed over a dried-mud, rock-strewn area with occasional damp patches left over from the storm the week before. He was stepping onto Greg's and his favorite boyhood retreat. He hiked past an inlet on the north side where the two boys sometimes had been allowed to "camp out" on Greg's parents' pontoon boat.

Vic's ultimate destination was a flat limestone expanse, invisible from the water during the summer. There was sufficient space between the branches surrounding it to allow someone to sit on the stone and watch boat traffic on the river. Greg was convinced that this rock was one of the "secret meeting places" in the Hawkins books. Vic was less certain but usually went along with this and Greg's other flights of imagination

As Vic went up the bank toward the stone, he had no trouble seeing through the bright green, insect-free and still unblemished leaves that heralded spring. When he reached the retreat, he was surprised to find Zach sitting on the stone. Zach hadn't heard Vic approaching. He was listening to music on his smart phone. He looked mildly annoyed, when he first noticed Vic, but sighed, smiled, and removed his ear buds.

"Dad used to bring me here," Zach said, breaking their silence of several seconds.

"He and I used to spend a lot of time here too," Vic said, recognizing too late that he might have interrupted Zach from revealing some additional things he was thinking about.

After another long pause, Zach continued, "It never seemed like I belonged here when I wasn't with Dad. Funny, that's not true any more. I feel like the river is mine … that I've somehow inherited it. The stuff with these books is interesting, I guess, but I think a lot of what Dad believed to be the exact locations and even this rock were all imaginary in the first place. I shouldn't say this, maybe, but it is something of a relief to see things without imagining a bunch of boys chasing one another up and down the riverbank.

For my 16th birthday, Mom and Dad took me to London. I think they always wanted to go but they told me it was for my birthday. Anyhow, we went to 221 Baker Street and saw Sherlock

Holmes's apartment. Apartment B. I Googled 221B Baker Street when I got home and everything I could find said that there had been no such address. The Sherlock Holmes Society bought and razed a house, built a replica based on descriptions in the Holmes stories, and then convinced the city of London to renumber the houses in that block. I guess if you work at things long enough, you can always transform the imaginary into reality."

"Your dad told me that he'd discovered the entrance to the cave that his great grandfather wrote about. We were supposed to try and go there during the fishing trip. He didn't by any chance tell you that he found it or maybe where he found it?" Vic asked.

"No, he didn't give me exact coordinates or anything. But what he did say was that the entrance to 'a cave', he wasn't ready to call it 'the cave', was under water and that he knew it would take a lot of fast talking to get you to go with him."

"'Fast talking'? Knowing your dad, he probably would have contrived some sort of threat or bribe. Curiosity alone couldn't get me to venture under water."

"I've thought about trying to find it, but I can't see myself going there without Dad. I suppose eventually I'll look for it. I'll take you if there's anything worth seeing," Zach said.

"If it's the real cave it'll be worth it I guess. Especially if you happen to run across an entrance that isn't under water."

Zach stopped talking and looked toward the river. Vic eventually decided that it was his turn if they were going to continue talking. "I do get what you're saying. Your dad and I both dwelt a lot on our boyhood memories. I suppose at some level we wanted the stories to be true. I know you're not saying this but it's probably time for me to grow up too.

I don't mean to sound like a parent, but I missed you at Palermo's. Anyhow, you might want to know that people asked about you. You gave us a safe topic to talk about."

"I bet. I didn't come because I kind of needed to hang with Stephanie. She's been good about this. She's starting to move away again ... not 'moving' moving ... but not wanting to be with me as much. She tells me I can be boring in large doses. Well, it'll only be another year until college. Dad always told me that I'd make some of my best friends, women and men, in college."

"He certainly did, " Vic said. "We both did."

He knew by the way Zach was dressed that he had run there too. "Do you want to run back toward town together?" Vic asked. Zach got up without answering and led the way to the trail.

Vic ran fast enough to be respectable for a 42 year old, at least based on how he typically finished in his age group at road races. But he was no match for a seventeen-year-old cross-country runner and, during this spring season, a miler. Zach took the point and slowed enough for Vic to catch up four or five times. Neither of them saw any need for further conversation. In any case it would have been far too dangerous on the winding, narrow road to run side by side.

17

WHEN VIC GOT BACK TO THE MOTEL, HE SAW THAT HE'D MISSED TRACY. She'd reminded him of his promise to call. They had kept in touch several times a week since the divorce so her request didn't seem unreasonable.

"Hi Tracy. Sorry I didn't get back to you sooner."

"That's okay. I've been worried about Lynda and Zach. And you too."

"Thanks. I haven't seen much of Lynda but I had a long talk with Zach this afternoon."

"And?" Tracy liked details.

"And, he seems okay. He's a thoughtful kid when he opens up."

"What have you learned about the robbery? The Courier Journal says that it is connected to the other one 40 miles away. The same drugs were taken both times. At the other store he grabbed three cartons of cigarettes. I didn't know anyone still smoked Parliaments."

"You know more than I do, Tracy. The sheriff and Wilkins ... you remember Patrice Wilkins ... haven't been exactly overflowing fountains of information. "

"Really? Sheriff Billings was quoted in the Courier."

"That explains the details about the cigarettes. Now the robber will know to change brands. That damned Billings.

Changing the subject, how's the hospital? Are you completely back in the scheme of things or maybe I should ask how many of your patients cried when they told you good bye at the end of your last shift?"

"Come on, Victor. Don't exaggerate. Besides, I don't keep score."

Wanting to say 'since when?' Vic went on to ask, as if he knew or cared about him, "How's David?"

"I guess okay. I talked to him once since we got back from Boothbay but we haven't been able to connect."

"Weren't you guys supposed to start living together?"

"We talked about it. He has shared custody of his kids so he's worried that explaining my clothes in his bedroom and everything would be too awkward. At least this soon after his divorce. We exchanged keys and we keep some things at each other's places."

Tracy's tone was less than bubbly. She didn't sound upset, more resigned that things weren't ideal between David and her. Vic didn't want her to be hurt. At the same time, if interrogated, he'd have to confess that he wouldn't mind regaining favor in Tracy's eyes. He knew this was a selfish way to think when he hadn't decided whether he was interested in a full reconciliation.

"Will you be coming back to Louisville any time soon?" Tracy asked in a manner that Vic, still in his needy persona, interpreted as containing an implied "I hope so".

"Not real soon. There doesn't seem to be much progress in finding a permanent pharmacist replacement. Maybe I'm too convenient of a fill-in."

Tracy said, snapping him out of his self-pity performance, "C'mon. You know Lynda appreciates what you're doing for her. What choice does she, or you for that matter, have at the moment?"

"Yeah. You're right. Talk to you soon Tracy."

"Yeah. Bye, Victor."

VIC PAID A RETURN VISIT TO HELEN. He opted for the salad bar and a grilled chicken sandwich. She displayed her proclivity for names by remembering to call him Sugar before asking him how his day went and how many 'subscriptions' he'd filled. A woman Vic recognized as an Ebert customer at a neighboring table looked over and rolled her eyes. He winked in response.

Stephanie, Edwin and Mrs. Ryder were several tables away. They exchanged greetings with Vic. Given their brief time in Burgoyne, the Ryders seemed to be on speaking terms with a great many of the restaurant's clientele.

A husky busboy was solicitous toward Stephanie and she spoke to him in an animated way. Vic had difficulty imagining how a busboy could ever be less boring than Zach. Vic became more incredulous when the young man turned in his direction. It was Gus, the guy who Vic had dislodged from the hood of his car a few days before.

Gus glanced toward Vic. He rubbed his upper lip with a thumb and forefinger as he continued to stare. Then he scrunched up his face as he tried to think, tried to remember. His eyes widened and Vic could lip-read an "oh shit". Gus looked away and hurried toward the kitchen. He was able to avoid bussing tables on Vic's side of the restaurant for the rest of the meal.

When the waitress brought his sandwich, Vic stopped her.

"Helen, tell me about the busboy with the blond hair. I think I know him from a Frisch's in Frankfort."

"Yeah, that might be true, Sugar. I heard he works somewhere else, too. He's only here with us two nights a week."

"Does he live in Burgoyne?"

"Sure. You know Stoner's Pub don't you? He's Merv Stoner's boy. He's Merv junior but he goes by Gus. I think Gus still lives at home. You want to talk to him?"

"No, I wanted to make sure I wasn't imagining things."

Remembering Vic wasn't a dessert person, Helen left the check.

VIC PAID AND WALKED THE THREE BLOCKS BACK TO
THE MOTEL. Out of habit, he checked to make sure
his car was okay. The Ford ... the car that by rights
should be safely tucked away in its garage in
Louisville ... was far from okay. The hood was
open revealing a haphazard bouquet of disconnected
sparkplug wires. There were large looping scratches
across both doors on the passenger side. The
antenna was snapped off and was laying on the
blacktop. It was the probable source of the defacing
job. The gas cap on this model Ford was hidden
behind the rear license plate. Otherwise the
harassment might have been complicated by sugar
in the gas tank, a classic stunt employed by vandals.
Vic began rhythmically slapping the damaged front
door, increasing the intensity with each swat. He
stopped before he damaged either his hand or the
car.

*That asshole Gus, I bet. No, wait. I'm his
alibi. He may be an asshole, just not the asshole
who violated the Ford. Gus definitely seemed
surprised to see me and he's probably not clever
enough to check me out of the motel or gain access
to a room.*

*Whoever did this ignored the Lexus LC that
somebody parked back here tonight. Its hood is cool
to the touch. It had to be sitting here at the time but
it wasn't vandalized. This is personal.*

As Vic reconnected the wires, in the dim
lights of the parking lot and the glow of his smart
phone flashlight app, he reaffirmed his vow to say
goodbye to the motel and its staff's inability to

protect property. But it had to be more than a security question. Vic realized he had inadvertently contributed to his own harassment. Any time he was in the room he put out the "Do Not Disturb" sign. If the sign was gone, Vic was gone too. Any number of people would know the Ford was his car. When he checked in and registered, he had obeyed the request and filled in the vehicle information as "a black and white Ford Fairlane" with classic car plate "312 4BL".

VIC STOOD TO THE SIDE AT THE FRONT DESK OF THE MOTEL until a harried mother with a crying baby balanced on one hip and a toddler hugging the opposite leg was handed a complimentary toothbrush and disposable razor.

"Are you the manager?"

"He left but I might be able to help you," the college aged woman said.

"I hope so. Have you worked here long?" Vic asked.

"I'm finishing up my semester internship next week. I'm a hospitality management major."

Vic said, "Let me tell you my complaint. In the few days I've stayed here, somebody checked me out of my room without my permission, I've had a hostile phone call, two threatening notes left in my room, and somebody vandalized my car. The car was parked in your lot. I've never told anybody either of my two room numbers. So I'm thinking somebody who stays here or works here who has access to my information is the ... uh, the person who's responsible for all of this."

The woman said, "I'm working a twelve hour shift. I'll see the manager in the morning and relay all of this to him. No, I'll call him now. I know he'll recognize how serious this is. If there's anything I can do for you tonight ..."

"Not really."

Vic returned to his room. He got the Glock out of the room safe and put it on the nightstand before he went to bed. He was finally able to fall asleep a little after midnight.

18

VIC FELT JUSTIFIED IN HIS DISGUST TOWARD THE
MOTEL'S inability to protect his car and prevent
access to his room. Of lesser importance, he was fed
up with the breakfasts. He was tired of the
awkwardness of sharing pre-read sections of USA
Today with strangers. He craved something other
than over-cooked hard-boiled eggs as his best
breakfast protein source. And he'd be happy not
seeing people casually walking into the breakfast
area, attired in whatever unorthodox articles of
clothing they happen to wear as sleeping garb. Vic
was grateful that this motel didn't attract the 7% of
the population who purportedly sleep naked. The
single cinnamon-pecan roll Vic allowed himself
each morning scored slightly above moderate
tastiness on the palatability scale but even those
calorie bombs lost their appeal after having them
several days in a row.

He decided to force down one last
complimentary breakfast before confronting the
manager. He had an eating companion who
indicated he wanted to talk. The 'Hi there.' and the
'How are you this mornin'?' before Vic had a
chance to pour his coffee should have warned him
to fill a tray and head back to his room. Since the

man ostensibly had returned his attention to CNN,
Vic went ahead and sat down. For some deeply
engrained cultural reason he didn't want this
complete stranger to believe that he was being
unsociable.

The man was casually but neatly dressed.
His face was round and florid but not puffy. He
reminded Vic of someone he had apprehended in St
Mary's, West Virginia who he'd caught using his
niece's Diaper Genie as his stash.

The guy cleared his throat and announced he
was down from Wheeling. Vic took no comfort in
having guessed his state of origin. The man
explained how he represented some investors who
had sold their chain of radio stations and who now
had part of their holdings tied up in a horse farm.
He had been visiting a few stables to inquire about
stud services and had finished his business only the
night before.

Vic became interested when the man
became more specific. "The Laine farm. Isn't that
the one on the other side of the river?"

Happy to have sparked an interest that
would allow him to hold court, the man went on,
"The Laines have Peck's Pick and two other
stallions with credentials almost that good. There
doesn't seem to be too much trouble with
scheduling. It was about the cleanest place I could
ever want to visit. They must muck the place all day
long.

You ever met Mrs. Laine? What a looker!
She and that Timmy feller, I guess he's her brother,
run the show. They're not pushy. I'd like to give

them our business but my investors will want to investigate blood lines a little more closely."

Among Vic's most vivid post-childhood recollections of Timmy were watching him trying to impress people as a big brother at "brother / sister" college weekend at U.C. and then again at Greg's visitation. Aside from gaining fifty pounds or so, he hadn't changed much since he was that twenty-year old. He was still unaccountably arrogant. On Monday he had worked the room as methodically as his brother-in-law but he was not nearly as well received. He went from person to person, hoping to initiate any sort of interaction. He wore a form-fitting dress shirt showing people that his strength made up for his lack of height. It was as if he was saying, "Pay attention to me. I'm more important than you think."

"I'M VIC FYE. ARE YOU THE MANAGER?"

"Yes I am, Mr. Fye. I see that we comped you one night for the checking out mix-up but I'll see to it that you're not charged for the rest of your stay. I contacted all of the employees I could get in touch with last night and had them come in for a meeting this morning."

"And?"

"And, right after the meeting my chief maintenance man left. By left, I mean he got in his car and drove away. I called the sheriff's office but they said they couldn't do anything unless I could charge him with something. They said they couldn't arrest somebody for leaving work."

"I don't suppose you can give me this guy's name, address or anything can you?" Vic asked.

"Afraid I can't do that, Mr. Fye. I'm sorry but I did give all that to the police. If you decide to press charges, I'll cooperate. If nothing else, I can testify that the guy spent a lot of time hanging around the front desk between cigarette breaks. Two of my clerks complained about him."

Vic had stayed in worse motels but never one where he'd been a mark. If this man or the person giving him orders tried to make good on the threats, Vic would prefer not to be cornered in a motel room. Lynda previously had offered up the family cottage. In accepting her offer he reminded her that he'd stayed there a number of times before and he didn't object to its rustic ambiance and sparse furnishings. He saw no need to bring up his incident with the truck, the vandalism to his car, or the warnings he'd been getting.

Once he checked out, Vic stowed his clothing and other belongings on top of the blanket he used to keep his trunk pristine. He stopped at the Burgoyne Krogers before he moved into the cottage.

When the men went on their annual outings, they brought more food and drinks than they did fishing tackle and clothes. They treated the trips as opportunities for self-indulgent binging, unapologetically eating and drinking whatever they wanted. Their staples were snack food, cold cereal, and beer. After taking care of his personal preferences in those three departments, Vic's secondary priority was to stock the cottage with anything else he needed once the fishing weekend was over.

Greg's brother, Roscoe was in line at the adjacent fast service counter. He looked straight ahead. He didn't look at or otherwise acknowledge Vic.

"Hey, Roscoe. How's it going?"

"Oh, hey Vic. I'm down here to do a little painting."

And to the clerk, "Give me a pack of Marlboro Reds.

Lynda told me you'd be staying on the river. That's fine with me but I'll need to pick up a couple of canvases and some other supplies I keep at the cottage."

"Of course," Vic replied. He wondered whether Roscoe looked upon Catfishpalooza as encroachment. Greg and Lynda were the owners but Lynda insisted that Roscoe should be allowed access anytime. The cottage was a part of Roscoe's childhood too. Lynda couldn't resolve why there were lingering tensions between Greg and his younger brother. It was because of her efforts that they got along again.

19

VIC PROPPED OPEN THE WOODEN SCREEN DOOR WITH HIS BACK. He hesitated before unlocking the inner door as if going inside without Greg would somehow erase his memories of the times the two of them spent there.

Vic entered the largest room with its barn wood paneling and faux beams. This main living area, in a more luxurious structure, might be referred to as a great room. Except for the two ancient industrial-tan colored lounge chairs, his and Greg's bourbon sipping seats, everything ran to wicker. Even the entertainment center had a wicker finish on its doors. Those doors concealed a television and component set left over from Lynda and Greg's early years of marriage. Lynda had tried in vain to get rid of the hideous purple floral hide-a-bed, uncomfortable for both sitting and sleeping. An apartment model fireplace, with smoke-stained white tile and grout adorned the east wall. It was too small to adequately augment the output of the inefficient baseboard heating.

A belly-high counter with an avocado top separated the main room from the eat-in kitchen. This area was spotless, witness to Greg's compulsive cleanliness and sense of order. In one corner was a workspace with plywood cabinets that housed Roscoe's painting supplies and some fishing tackle. Greg referred to a shallow alcove as his second office. On a small desk, he kept copies of many of the Hawkins books and several notebooks.

Since Roscoe popped in and out during all seasons of the year, the electricity and water were left on. Vic stowed the groceries, refrigerating the perishables and the beer. He threw out a few eggs in a carton that showed them to be outdated but assumed that the wrapped slices of cheese, the mayo, and ketchup, since refrigerated, would still be okay.

Vic laid claim to one of the twin beds in the bedroom adjacent to the bathroom that had a modern white stool. That toilet had to be changed out because Greg somehow dropped its predecessor in the process of replacing the seal. Several pieces of broken pink porcelain, intended to be a permanent reminder of Greg's plumbing prowess, added a whimsical touch to Lynda's rock garden behind the cottage.

He filled half of the door-less closet in his room, selected the best pillow, and made up his bed, the one closer to the window. He put out towels and threw linens on the other beds. The hide-a-bed wasn't made up since it wouldn't be needed. Most of the windows opened without much effort and all of the screens were intact. Nothing smelled musty, but things seemed fresher once he opened the windows to air the place out.

Vic walked down the sloped backyard to the floating dock and to the adjacent boathouse. The

Ebert family pontoon boat with its faded canvas cover was out of storage and mounted on the manual boatlift. Greg had already serviced the boats for the season. The pontoon boat had a newer motor and better cushions than it did when Greg and he had been entrusted with this slow, and to them at that time, unglamorous craft. A three seat fishing boat occupied much of the limited space of the tiny boathouse.

Vic looked up to see Timmy piloting a small craft straight toward the dock. He stayed seated in his boat. Vic didn't object. He had no desire to be subjected to Timmy's ritual pectoral flexing as if his muscles were so strong they were out of his control.

"I heard you guys were going to be down here fishing this weekend. I hope you didn't put a taxidermist on retainer." He fancied himself to be the great outdoorsman. He looked for opportunities to imply that his hunting and fishing excursions outclassed those of Greg and his neighbors.

"Yeah, yeah. Keep it up and I won't invite you to any of our shore lunches," Vic countered.

"Julie sent me over to remind you that the river is more shallow than usual right now. We had that one big rain but that was about it. It's not supposed to turn chilly until Sunday night. You guys lucked out."

"Thanks for the tip, Timmy. I better make sure I've got some dry wood."

Timmy looked at him questioningly. He evidently didn't realize that Vic would be staying in the cottage for longer than the weekend. When Vic explained it to him, he shrugged and said, "Oh. Makes sense, I guess. I better head back."

Vic watched him steer his boat back to the Laine dock. The dock, like the house itself, overlooked the water at the first of two big bends the river made to accommodate the limestone cliffs. From Vic's perspective, there was no such thing as a bad view along this part of the river. Except for occasional dwellings, the areas between the small cliffs were overgrown with forest along both shores. The wooded zones didn't extend far from the water. Most property owners retained the foliage as an undeveloped buffer between their farmed and pasture lands and the river.

Vic had promised Lynda, over her protests, that he'd earn his keep. He found Greg's tractor mower in the shed. After trying various positions on the controls and priming it numerous times, he started Greg's ancient mower. He set the blade up as high as it would go since the mowing was already long overdue. Whatever government agency was responsible for mower safety would have praised him for mowing vertical swaths up and then down the hill.

As it happened, the second pharmacist at Ebert Drugs, Hal, owned the cottage next door. His wife Goldie walked down to their dock and waved. She changed directions toward Vic who obliged her by stopping the mower and stepping off.

Goldie smiled knowingly when Vic told her about his new living arrangements. Other than a look of skepticism when Vic explained how quiet the weekend fishing was going to be, Goldie seemed genuinely happy to have Vic staying there.

"Other than us, the Eberts are the last hold outs," Goldie said.

"What do you mean?"

"Hal and I had to make enough off this place to move into The Manor in Lawrence and still have money left to lease a lot and buy a big enough mobile home in Florida. We're tired of hauling our Airstream down to Clearwater every winter.

The sons of bitches cut the power a couple of times earlier this month but there hasn't been a disruption since we started negotiating."

"Which sons of bitches are you referring to?"

" Johnny Laine and his friends that run the development company. They're going to tear down all of these places along here and build some fancier, estate-type houses. We were told that we'd be given first rights to buy a lot. Most of us river rats sure as hell couldn't afford to put up the kind of house they're talking about."

"So you've sold?"

"We're close on price. Now we're trying to negotiate being able to stay until there's an opening at the manor. They're estimating it could be October before they'll have an empty apartment for us. It's kind of morbid waiting for other residents to die off or become incapacitated. We're second on the list. Hal wants to continue working at the store as long as he can. He doesn't want to leave Lynda in the lurch.

Well, I'd better head back. I need to drive over to Lexington for a cardiologist appointment."

Vic finished the mowing. His shift at the pharmacy began at 2:00. This gave him just enough time to check out the fishing boat. He donned a life jacket and tossed in a fishing rod Greg or somebody had left in the boathouse. It still had a soft plastic wiggler on its line. It crossed Vic's mind that no self-respecting fish should fall for anything that was neon green. After this weekend, he didn't plan on doing much serious fishing so bait selection wouldn't be a big concern.

For the second time that day Vic managed to start an engine when he didn't have step-by-step instructions. Tracy, whose Dad was able to build and repair almost anything, would have been impressed ... mildly so ... but impressed.

Vic made his way down river, remembering places where Greg and he used to venture ashore. There was the big tree that blocked the hollow place in the cliff. There was the little tributary and there was the island.

The cave was another matter. Greg was convinced that some day he would find the cave that was a hideout for various fictitious villains. Vic once told Greg, "Unless we find it in the next twenty years or so, the two of us will be like George Burns and Art Carney ... geezers looking for excitement in order to have something to do."

Greg and Vic had an ongoing dispute whether the books could be strictly interpreted ... the "Gospel according to Hawkins". Greg's argument was that everything else was like it was described in the books. Therefore, there had to be a cave. Vic contended that it wasn't "everything" else. There was no waterfall, no ruins from a round stone barn, and there was only the single shack across the river, not a row of cabins where a gang of "bad boys" plotted against the fictitious Hawkins and his pals. Besides, the two of them had explored as far as they could reasonably canoe in search of the cave, both up and down the river.

I hope I'm not deluding myself. First, I assume as long as I'm wearing a life jacket I'll be safe if I happen to fall in the river. Second, Ralph and Timmy haven't tried to beat me up for almost thirty years. Third, ecological issues aside, people with cottages here in Riverton have killed off almost all of the copperhead snakes. Seriously, it can't be any more dangerous down here than a motel with zero security, can it?

20

VIC'S PHONE PRODUCED AN INSISTENT BUZZ. He had forgotten to take it off silence mode. He didn't recognize the number but it was a Burgoyne area exchange.

"Hello, this is Vic."

"Hi, this is Julie," she said in a way that suggested Vic should be excited. "How's life in God's country?"

"Nothing to brag about but Lynda and the pharmacy tech Claudia have some ideas of how to keep the place financially afloat, at least one of which involves you, I understand. My only reason to show up at the store is to keep things legal."

"I hear that you're going to be staying on at the Ebert cottage once the fishing weekend is over."

"News travels fast. Yes, I guess so. Or at least I will until Laine Industries buys Lynda out and razes the place," Vic answered with forced pleasantry but with no attempt to hide his anger.

"I hear you Vic. But you should know that the riverfront enterprise is Johnny and his contractor's project. Johnny lets me oversee the stud farm; I leave him and his cronies to do their thing. Speaking of which, the partners flew out to somewhere near Lake Tahoe. There's a golf resort they all go to every year about this time. In case betting on their golf games isn't enough, they can take a shuttle into downtown Reno.

We ought to get together for dinner," she added in a matter of fact manner.

Vic wasn't sure whether Johnny being gone had anything to do with her invitation or whether the 'we' included all three of them. In either case his answer was a noncommittal, "Sure."

"Good to hear from you Julie, but I'm out on the river and I need to be at work in an hour."

He wasn't brushing her off. He'd be lucky to make it on time.

Lynda had warned Vic that the grass might need cutting. She hadn't prepared him for his next discovery. No one had turned on the water heater. The frigid water from the cottage's deep well almost made Vic nostalgic for the multifunctional showerhead and near instantaneous hot water at the motel. Rustic living has its pitfalls. He found an electric razor in the medicine cabinet, suggesting that the lack of hot water might have been a problem before. After a less than close shave, he wolfed down some baked ham and Swiss cheese fresh from the Kroger Deli.

HAL HAD EVERYTHING UNDER CONTROL WHEN VIC GOT TO THE STORE. That came as no surprise since Claudia was on duty. She informed Vic about pending refill authorizations and insurance company concerns.

"Hal, I appreciate your covering for me tomorrow."

"I'd already planned on taking over for Greg so it's not at all inconvenient. There have been Saturdays when it's scarcely worth turning on the lights. Besides, I've got a good novel ... a Grisham. It's his newest or at least the library's newest."

A FEW MINUTES LATER ROSCOE STOPPED BY. He walked straight to the prescription counter and said, "I can't remember whether I told you that you might see me around the river this weekend. I'm going to paint some landscapes for a show in Cincinnati later this spring."

He noticed Vic's hesitation but went on, "I'll be doing all of my painting from the other side of the river. People seem to like a little human interest so I thought having you guys in boats, fishing and whatever else fishing buddies do would be good. If you want to leave the boats tied to the dock or pulled on to the bank, that'd add some interest too."

Vic was rethinking his opinion of Roscoe as nothing more than a parasite. Roscoe took his art seriously. He might at some point be able make a living from it. As Vic recalled, the show in Cincinnati was refereed. With Roscoe's paintings of Kentucky River scenes he might be the one family member who could stand to benefit from the downtown revitalization.

"Good to see you. I think all of the beds are taken or you could stay with us. By the way, I like your painting of the chair and the fishing gear down by the bank. Would you be willing to sell it?"

"You better ask Lynda. She had me paint it for Greg. I picked a windy day. It was a challenge to paint, maneuvering from an anchored boat. The light off the water kept changing things and I had to face sideways to have room for my easel. It's kind of surreal now ... that empty chair."

"Yeah, I guess it is." Starting to again have regrets about being so judgmental, Vic added, "If you want to stop by for steaks and brews Saturday or Sunday night, you're welcome. Bring some cash for poker. I think you know all of the guys. Don't worry that it'll be too cutthroat. We still play for nickels like we did in college."

"Thanks anyway, Vic. I'll be fine."

LATER, A SOFT-SPOKEN, FRIENDLY MAN ASKED IF VIC HAD TIME TO TALK. Vic glanced at Claudia, and she gave him a stiff nod, letting him know that he definitely should make the time. Vic showed the man to the office located behind the pharmacy.

The man bore a strong resemblance to the solemn, distinguished-looking actor who played Winchester in the M*A*S*H television series. He wore a charcoal gray suit, a white shirt, and a conservative blue tie with small red dots. He refused Vic's offer of coffee but did accept a bottle of water.

"I'm John Sennett, the administrator at Fritsch Manor and McAuliffe Acres," he said by way of introduction.

"Hi. I'm Vic Fye."

"Yes, I know. Hal says that you're probably the person I need to talk to."

"Okay, I guess I am if Hal thinks so."

"We've worked closely with Ebert Drugs for many years. Our patients aren't required to use any particular pharmacy but it works better for those who require help with their medications if our nursing staff only needs to be competent with one packaging system and if the deliveries all come the same day. The patients and their families have appreciated what Greg has done for them."

"Yes. Greg always has taken his consulting seriously. I think he was an officer in the National Association for Consultant Pharmacists."

"That sounds right. I believe it's on his resume. Well, what I'm getting at is… or what I'd like to ask you are, uh, are you permanent? I mean will you continue to work here?"

"Well, Mr. Sennett, I wish I could give you an outright 'yes'. Unfortunately, I can't in all honesty make such a promise. I can assure you that I'm doing what I can to make sure that there's continuity in the services people have depended on from Ebert Drugs. My business, among our other services, tries to help stores with permanent pharmacist placement. We're searching right now for people who have expertise in consulting and who have an interest in relocating to a community like Burgoyne. I plan on being here until we find such a person."

"The reason I ask is that Ali Bourne has indicated that she's going to submit a bid. She left me a voice mail the afternoon after the robbery. In essence, with Greg's passing, the facilities I manage are no longer obligated to consider that Ebert Drugs has a valid contract for consulting services. Hal does a good job, almost as good as Greg, but he's gone so much of the time. We need to get something in place quickly or we'll jeopardize our accreditation."

"I understand. I'll try to expedite the hiring process, if I can."

"Thanks, Mr. Fye. I'll let you get back to your business here."

"I'll be in touch, Mr. Sennett."

John Sennett was unaware of two things. He didn't know, and it strained Vic's ethical tenets to their limits not to tell him that Ali Bourne had questionable practice standards in her consultant activities. She couldn't or, more likely, wouldn't make any drug therapy substitution that might reduce her own income stream. Mr. Sennett also didn't know that finding pharmacists willing to move to rural areas, whether they had consultant experience or not, was going to be challenging.

21

VIC FINISHED HIS SHIFT AND PICKED UP A SMALL
FILET BEFORE RETURNING TO THE COTTAGE. Having
learned his lesson with the water heater, he checked
to make sure that there was enough propane to last
the weekend.

Vic didn't want to do anything to upset the
fishing tradition but he'd have preferred to postpone
things so he could turn his attention to the future of
Ebert Drugs. He also needed to find out who wanted
him out of Burgoyne, seemingly dead or alive. He
believed the two problems were related. He
promised himself, that once the weekend was over
he'd dedicate several hours a day to figuring things
out. His vow and his resolve to honor it made him
feel better.

He finished the last bite of steak and was
thinking about opening a second Fat Tire. He called
Tracy first. Their worst arguments ensued when one
or both of them had drunk enough that it affected
their judgment, or at least their tactfulness.

"Hi."

"Hi, yourself," she answered. "What's up?"

"As of today, I'm staying at the Ebert
cottage. I got sick of the motel. They have some
problems with their help or I guess it's with their

security. The Ford got vandalized last night in their parking lot."

"Poor baby."

Vic wasn't sure whether she was referring to him or his car.

"We're a sad lot. It's Friday night and we've nothing better to do than talk on the phone with our exes."

"Sweet of you to bring that up. It's David's weekend with his kids. What's your excuse?"

"Touché. Anyhow, the guys will show up sometime after nine tomorrow. Pat is driving down with Will and Rex is bringing me their third car. One he and Claudia can't seem to sell. I've lined up a place to have the Ford's doors repainted, buffed out, and waxed and I've ordered a replacement aerial on line. I've installed one before. Anyhow, the guys will be here through Sunday night or early Monday."

"That'll be fun … having people around … your friends."

"The fishing weekends are fun but this one could be mostly awkward. Hey, I've got another call coming in. Should I call you back?"

"Maybe on Monday. Say 'hi' to the guys for me. Good night pathetic one."

"Ditto."

THIS TIME VIC IDENTIFIED THE NUMBER AS JULIE'S.

"Vic, hey. I'm two minutes away. Mind if I stop by?"

"Sure. What's up?"

Ignoring his question, she asked, "Do you have space in the garage. I'd just as soon not have any gossiping neighbors know that I'm visiting."

"Yeah. I'll go move my car into the carport."

"Okay. Bye."

Before he took care of the car, he cleared the table, rinsed the plate and silverware, and stacked them in the dishwasher. Like many pharmacists, he kept the workspace clear and cleaned up as he cooked ... but not as he ate. Without thinking he grabbed a couple of Tic-tac's from a container on the windowsill. *Julie must have been more than two minutes away. That's good.*

There was no need for Hal and Goldie next door to be alerted that Vic was having a visitor. He could hear their television when he went out to move the Ford. He was able to carry out his part of the subterfuge in the dark since no Ford engineer in 1957 envisioned headlights that automatically turned on in response to low levels of ambient light. *Tic-tac's? No lights? What do I imagine is going to happen?*

Julie maneuvered a new black Ford 150 pick-up, with lights on, expertly into the narrow one car garage. Vic met her on the breezeway, they exchanged a brief hug, and he led her inside.

She wore a flattering and somewhat revealing orange blouse that complimented her year-round tan. Vic couldn't tell whether she wore any make-up other than around her eyes. The skin-tight black slacks gave testimony to the benefits of her regular exercise regimens. She slipped out of her matching low-heeled sandals and, now barefoot, turned and expectantly looked up into his face.

She correctly interpreted his raised eyebrows and the pressure lines on his mouth caused by the restrained 'Wow'! She smiled broadly and said, laughing wickedly, "Don't get excited. I'm here on behalf of the Jehovah Witnesses."

She rejected his invitation to look around explaining that she'd been there a few weeks before with Lynda when they were trying to find Zach. She said, "This was the third time to my knowledge that Zach had taken off. He'd always come home before the next morning until the last episode. He had seemed agitated before he left. Like with his previous disappearances, he showed up, apologetic, and promised to call home if he stayed away again. Since he was gone for over twenty-four hours, Lynda took his car keys and cell phone. Greg convinced her to give them back the next day.

Can we sit out on the breezeway?" Julie asked. "I brought wine. It's in the truck."

"Yeah. It's a nice night for April. I'll grab some glasses. I think I saw a corkscrew somewhere."

Vic did better than that. He opened a package of sharp cheese … Kroger's finest … and put it on a salad plate with a knife and some Triscuts. He found the Swiss army knife with its corkscrew attachment in the drawer, checked the glasses for dust and dead insects, and finding none, carried everything outside.

"I thought you'd abandoned me, " she said from her curled up position on the porch swing.

"I considered it. I wasn't sure, though, how I'd explain your frozen body to Hal and Goldie tomorrow morning."

"I'd forgotten they were your neighbors. I see Hal sometimes. How's Goldie?"

"Well, for one thing, neither of them is happy with Johnny, and even less enamored with his negotiation henchman. I think they're resigned to selling their place but would have preferred to do it on their own terms. They also resented the condescending attitude of whoever told them that any house they could afford would prove to be substandard for the development."

"Believe it or not, Johnny is the soft hearted one of the development syndicate. The other guys were ready to have the neighbors' and this cottage condemned. They've got the votes in the council to do it but Johnny wouldn't hear of it. Don't ever tell Lynda this but Johnny offered to put up money out of his future share of the profits to pay Greg enough that he and Lynda could afford to rebuild down here.

Greg turned him down. Johnny ended up being frustrated with him. He always tried to take care of his friends, our friends in this case. Johnny couldn't understand anyone who put nostalgia or pride or any other emotional oddity ahead of a good, in this case, a very good financial arrangement.

Lets change the subject. This is such a nice view. Look at those stars."

They occupied themselves with opening and pouring the wine and slicing the cheese while balancing everything on the moving swing. They laughed when some of the Triscuts fell into Julie's lap. It felt natural to be there and to be laughing together.

"You seem to be getting along okay with Tracy," Julie said, Vic guessed she was referring to their sitting together at the funeral.

"Pretty good, I guess. She's been seeing someone she met at the hospital. I've gotten more and more comfortable with that. I think we're one of those couples who should have stayed friends."

"Friends with benefits?"

"I don't know about that. Realistically it didn't seem at the time there was any way that Tracy and I wouldn't get married though. I never questioned that I was in love. Which meant, I suppose, that I must have been. I believe she was too. In love with me, that is.

Does Johnny go on lots of golfing trips?" he asked in an attempt to extricate himself from his foray into the past before he became too melancholy.

"Golfing. Gambling. I'm not sure what else. We lead our own lives any more, other than social things at the club or when I help him campaign. We both enjoy our place in Vail. That's one thing we do together. We try to get out there several times a winter. We both like to ski. We used to mountain bike but we so rarely go there in the summer. I guess we like to be reckless together. Or not together."

"Reckless?" he asked.

"Controlled recklessness, I suppose. His impulsiveness can be exhilarating but some of his investments border on the insane. He likes to remind me that 'it costs a lot to be affluent'."

"You're okay aren't you?" Vic asked, knowing it was unusual for Julie to show this much vulnerability.

"Money-wise or are you asking about the two of us?"

She didn't wait for his reply but went on to say, "The answer's the same for both questions. Things are precarious. One of the curses of my background in accounting is that it becomes my job to keep track of the finances. He withdraws way too much money ... five thousand for this trip. And he must never win, at golf or gambling. We got tired of arguing about his spending so now we ignore it. Well, he ignores it. I deal with it."

"More wine?" they said at the same time.

"Lets finish it," she said, embellishing her answer by scooting up against him. It was her thigh-to-thigh routine. If it works, why change it.

"Remember when we were together?" she asked. Her inflection turned less conversational. Slower. Softer.

"As kids? In college?" he responded, conscious that he was surrendering to her verbal foreplay.

"When we used to make love."

"If used to, means in my dreams. I do remember quite a few times."

She laughed and said, "Was I good?"

"Which time?"

Julie sensed that their repartee was becoming more comical than amorous. She expertly returned to task.

"They say that dreams can become parts of your memories. My dreams concerning you seem vivid. I find that dreams and sex get better with some medicinal priming, I've got some high grade stuff in the truck."

"I gave that up for the most part after I became an agent. When I was trying to get on, I admitted to recreational use in college. That's the only history the DEA tolerates. I passed the lie detector test and wanted to continue to do so. Even though the DEA officially forbids drug usage, they gave me the okay to use a little when I was undercover. The stuff people smoke now is a lot stronger than I remembered from pharmacy school. By the way, please don't tell me what you have or where you got it."

"Excuse me," Julie said, moving to face him. She cocked her head back slightly and said, "You do know that 'Reefer Madness' was filmed in the '30s don't you? Besides, I thought you were no longer with the DEA. That you quit."

"I did. I have. It's hard to cut the cord. Not that the DEA has a great track record for reinstatement. I was told I'd be out for life. But also, there's an agent investigating the robbery. She's likely to be asking all of us what we know about drug activity in the area. I'd prefer to be ignorant in so far as you're concerned. That's all."

His cell phone rang. He saw that it was Pat and answered it in spite of Julie's scowl. She snuggled against him when she realized that he was only answering it to talk about the weekend fishing.

"Everything's ready. The fish are biting. No, I didn't say the fishing bites, I said the fish are biting."

Their bantering went on like this for several minutes. Julie sensed that Vic was losing whatever focus toward her he might have had and she edged back toward the other side of the swing. After her third sigh, she stood up. Vic quickly ended the call.

"I'd sort of forgotten about your fishing. I was hoping we could see each other. Maybe have dinner tomorrow night."

Vic didn't respond right away. He eventually said, "Sorry."

She shook her head and stooped to pick up the glasses. Vic grabbed the empty bottle, the plate, the knife, and the opener.

He speculated that Julie was unaccustomed to having her advances ignored. At the same time she probably didn't ordinarily include conversation about past and present spouses, capitalistic enterprises, or drug enforcement as seduction ploys. Vic preferred to assume that Julie didn't come on to men like this on a regular basis. Maybe Claudia's views of Julie were merely a product of her own unfounded jealousy over her husband Rex. Vic had no doubts about Rex's monogamy but then he wasn't married to Rex.

Julie returned to form. She hugged him a little longer than the first time. She took his hand and said, "Walk me to my car ... I mean my vehicle. I do know the difference between a car and a truck."

"I always did like mechanically inclined women," he said.

She squeezed his hand and said, "Help me up into the truck."

He opened the door and cupped his hands like a step.

"No. Like how you used to help me get on my horse when we were kids."

She lifted her left foot onto the running board and she let him push her the rest of the way up with a still-cupped hand on each cheek. Vic had been fourteen or fifteen when they'd walk to her pasture to go riding. Vic wasn't much into riding horses but he wasn't about to pass up the chance to put his palms on Julie Thompson's ass. He did remember. He was surprised that she remembered. He guessed she had known all along what she was doing to his adolescent libido.

In any case, Vic's ability to act on his lustful thoughts seemed more attainable now than they had twenty-five years earlier.

She lowered the window to say goodbye. It would have been awkward to climb up to kiss her. Vic resisted and watched as she backed out into the lane. She drove slowly with her lights off until she had gone several driveways beyond Hal and Goldie's cottage. He watched until he could see her lights on the highway.

"Good night, Vic."

"Is that you Hal?"

"Nobody else is staying down here besides the three of us. By the way, Goldie takes her hearing aids out of a night. You probably guessed that from our television being so loud. And I never needed HIPAA to make me mind my own business."

"Thanks Hal. Good night," Vic said, vowing never to risk even more serious damage to his car by driving it without lights.

It was a toss-up whether or not he'd have trouble falling asleep. He speculated that the wine coursing through his brain and the soothing night air breezes coming through the open window would offset his sexual stirrings. He chuckled at himself for his typical, as he'd been told, overly clinical perspective on things. The wine, augmented by the previous Fat Tire, prevailed. Vic fell into a deep sleep within a few minutes.

22

VIC WOKE UP EARLIER THAN HE HAD ANTICIPATED. Several exuberant robins, needlessly announcing that it was officially Spring, were the sleep-disrupting culprits. Melodious thrushes were better than a motel neighbor's flushing toilet any day. The robins served to remind him that many of God's creatures disagreed with the Eberts and their west facing bedroom windows. Songbirds prefer dawns to dusks. Vic was marveling at how majestic the twin cottonwoods looked against a neutral background. He was contemplating the early morning haze that shrouded the river and concealed the cliffs when he heard a noise in another part of the cottage.

Then a second sound ... the squeaking made by a floorboard readjusting itself in response to human movement. He had no weapons, no guns, in the bedroom. His handgun and backup gun were in a hidden niche that was tucked in behind the books in Greg's office. He tried to come up with possible intruders. He considered whether it might be whoever harassed him at the motel. Then Roscoe came to mind. Maybe he picked this morning to reclaim his art paraphernalia. Who else would have access and wouldn't bother to knock?

About the time he was weighing the advisability of crawling out the window to do some reconnaissance, he caught a whiff of brewing coffee. That sensation eliminated evildoers and was far too thoughtful to be attributable to Roscoe. He opened the door slowly and looked into the kitchen. Julie was at the stove, refreshing the musings of his imagination that had taunted him a few hours earlier.

"I didn't take you for a morning person," he said, announcing himself.

Julie turned and smiled. He had expected her to be startled but she reacted as if they were in the midst of a conversation and she knew he was there all the time.

"I didn't sleep very well," she answered with a coy grin. "I brought you some bagels and a newspaper. Tell me how you like your eggs. Or do you want everything to be a surprise this morning?"

"Scrambled. I'll clean off the table on the breezeway and pour the coffee that 'someone' made for us."

Vic wiped off the dew-covered table and the two chairs that he positioned at angles to let them look out toward the river. The haze was beginning to lift but he still couldn't make out the cliffs on the other side. He questioned whether this would be one of those mornings when they would be able to appreciate the full beauty of all that the river could provide in early spring.

He set the table. By the time he had poured their coffees and sliced the bagels, the rest of the breakfast … eggs and country ham … was ready.

"These eggs are perfect!" Vic announced with obvious enthusiasm.

"Don't sound so surprised. I can be domestic … if I have to be."

"Can't we all."

When Tracy and he went through pre-divorce counseling, Vic's willingness to do more than his share in the kitchen was one of the "good things" she came up with. Remembering their anniversary and always putting down the toilet seat rounded out her list.

Vic noticed that Julie hadn't served herself any ham or eggs. She nibbled on half a bagel topped by a nearly transparent film of cream cheese.

Her "natural good looks" do require effort and sacrifice. Her appearance gives her confidence without making her seem haughty. I'll be assigning her a numerical value, next. Why not? She was definitely a 10 in college. Still is, I guess.

"Well, thanks for breakfast. I'll clean this up and then I need to take a shower."

"Yes. You do need a shower and I can handle the dishes," she countered.

Vic grabbed a pair of boxers and a pair of jeans and went into the bathroom. The fiberglass shower stalls were modern upgrades in both bathrooms. He appreciated it more with a fully operational hot water heater. Vic shaved in the shower with one of the disposable razors he had picked up. Greg's cast off electric razor left a lot to be desired. When he stepped out of the shower, he remembered that he had thrown his towel into the basket in the kitchen that served as a hamper.

"Julie? Julie, can you bring me a towel? I think there's some in the bottom of the cabinets."

"First I'm your cook, now your valet. How do you ever get along without me?"

Vic heard a cabinet door squeak open and close. There was a delay before she tapped on the door.

"If you want to hand it in, ..."

"No, I think I'll deliver it," she interrupted and opened the door.

She was naked except for a towel neatly tied around her. Vic's initial response wasn't verbal but it was highly expressive.

"Here, take the towel. I won't look," Julie said, looking directly at his response indicator.

"Okay, I won't look either."

"Oh, that's too bad. I don't think you'll be disappointed."

Vic said, "The hell with this."

He ripped off the towel and dragged her toward the bedroom. He pushed her onto his bed and asked, "Do you want me to stop?"

"What are we, in college?"

Vic was too busy to answer.

They lay together, wet from his shower, wet from their strenuous sex. Vic thought how much he always enjoyed making love with Tracy. But with Julie it was the furthest thing from tender lovemaking. It was mind-blowing sex. *I deserve great sex. I've hurt long enough and maybe it's time I let myself get over Tracy.*

As if to signal, "so much for afterglow", she looked into his eyes with a satisfied smile and said,

"I thought that there might be one other little thing you might not want to do without me."

Back on task, he answered, between kisses, "This wasn't on the amenities list at the motel."

"Did you dial room service?"

"Should I have?"

"I don't know. How hot were the housekeepers?"

"Except for the two in the French maid outfits, I think you have 'em beat."

Pretending to squeeze him in a vulnerable spot she said, "It's 9:00. When are the guys supposed to start showing up?"

"Uh, at nine. I can put a tie on the door I guess."

"Right. Or I could say I was visiting Goldie and got the wrong cabin.

Think about me this weekend."

She glided out of bed, managing to give him a 360-degree view before scurrying into the other room. She was dry and dressed in a matter of minutes. She gave him a tender kiss before opening the door. She said, as if having read his earlier thoughts "If you ever want gentle, I'm good at that too."

"I never doubted it."

Finally, reluctantly it seemed, she said, "I'll miss you. Call me if you get the chance. I think your towel is still fresh, by the way."

With that, she went out the door to what had become her garage. He mused that the Ford could stay relegated to the carport. He recognized the sound of heavy tire tracks backing out onto the gravel as she drove past the cottage.

23

BEFORE HE WAS COMPLETELY DRESSED, VIC GOT A CALL FROM THE STORE. He was surprised that there was any situation that Claudia or Hal couldn't handle without him.

"Vic, I'm sorry to call you but Lynda is upset. This has been a terrible morning already. The revitalization plans were published in the paper this morning. There's a pharmacy in the plans but it's not ours. Two blocks down the street there's a new medical office building envisioned that includes a University of Kentucky sponsored clinic. There are eight office suites, a laboratory, and a pharmacy. U.K is supposed to staff everything and use the complex as experiential sights for their medical, nurse practitioner, and pharmacy students."

"Take a breath, Claudia. Is Lynda there?"

"Sure. I think she can talk. She's really upset."

"Hi."

"Hi, Lynda. Let me talk for a little bit. Claudia told me about the plans and I understand how it sounds. But I believe we're looking at a long time from now, if ever. Lots of things would have to change. The state budget is so tight it's hard to imagine that there would be funds to cover any of that in the near future. All government agencies, including the University Regents, are watching their pennies for everything except the basketball program. Building and staffing a medical clinic in Burgoyne can't be anybody's priority outside of a few delusional people in our county. There are too many under-served areas in Kentucky that could attract federal funds. Okay?"

"I guess I hadn't thought about how it would be financed. You're right Vic. I'm sorry. I've tried so hard to keep it together. It is uncomfortable being in the store. I keep thinking Greg will come out from the back room to pat my butt and pretend it was unintentional."

"Did he do that to you, too?" Vic tried to sound incredulous.

"Yeah, I know," Lynda, said, laughing a little. "He patted your butt long before he ever paid attention to mine."

"I think he used a rolled up towel on me. How about you?"

"None of your business. Anyhow, there's something else. Another reminder. There was a third robbery. They seem to be moving south."

"I haven't looked at the paper," Vic interjected without thinking. How would he explain having a paper?

"This sounds like it could be the same guy. The local police said that drugs and an undisclosed amount of money were reported stolen. The pharmacist was interviewed. I think he said more than he should have but he looked like he was Zach's age in the picture."

24

HIS FRIENDS WERE MORE SOMBER THAN USUAL …
sanctuary quiet … as they stacked fishing tackle on
the porch and put their extra clothes in the two
drawers each was allotted. The cottage and this
section of the Kentucky River had been sacred
ground to Greg. The men would ease into their
customary razzing.

Pat and Will had arrived first. Pat's Lexus
had more than enough space for their fishing gear
and the snacks their wives had packed. There had
been times when as many as five of them had made
do with Pat's SUV.

Rex had slipped in right behind them in the
Thurman's extra car he had promised as a loaner. It
was a Ford Fusion. Vic had arranged for his own
Ford to be picked up later that morning to repair the
door damage.

Within a few minutes the kitchen counter
tops were strewn with high calorie baked items and
marginally healthier cereals. The refrigerator was
fully stocked with beer, night crawlers, and leeches.

Vic uncapped four bottles of Beck's and
passed them around. Beck's was Greg's beer of
choice.

"To good friends," Vic said, trying to be enthusiastic.

"To good fishing stories, real and exaggerated," countered Pat.

"To good cards and gullible opponents," added Rex.

"To insobriety," they said in unison, anticipating Will's traditional toast.

They carried their beers outside. After they wandered around the property and evaluated the seaworthiness of the boats, they staked out chairs facing the river. They spent the rest of the morning on the patio, exchanging memories of past fishing fiascoes and bittersweet stories about Greg. The punch lines and conclusions were predictable. The laughs were anticipatory and as dependably forthcoming as if elicited from an audience at a sitcom taping.

The four went inside for a quick lunch of deli meat and cheese. They loaded a cooler, grabbed their rods and tackle boxes, and ambled down to the dock. They all wore jeans and lightweight jackets except Vic who wore his trusty fishing vest with flotation inserts. One of the earlier fishing stories recalled Greg asking Vic, "Do you stop to put that thing on every time you drive across a bridge?" Greg's assessment of the extent of Vic's water phobia wasn't too far off base.

At one time or another, each of them had piloted the pontoon boat. Unlike on the occasional fishing trips to other parts of the country, they didn't have to endure the cursory explanations from some sixteen-year-old marina employee about tricky chokes, where to fill up with gas, and where to dock the boat when they returned.

Vic eased the boat into the channel and steered it toward "the island". The cove would afford them shade and probably as many or more fish than anyplace else they might try during early afternoons. They could anchor there and not worry about drifting. For a while only the popping of beverage cans disrupted the silence. As captain of the day, Vic limited himself to a single beer. He rationalized that beer would taste better later in the afternoon. With no real strikes, in spite of partial losses of worms, they wordlessly determined that talking couldn't make the fishing any worse.

"What's going on with these robberies? Should you be working down here?" Will asked.

"Don't think I haven't questioned it. The robberies seem to be occurring closer together. The pharmacists who were robbed weren't given much of a chance to cooperate. It seems like it must be the same guy all three times. The robber hasn't exactly gotten away with gigantic hauls but they're big enough that this last interval of only a week seems short. He either has a serious habit or he's supplying several of his friends.

As for me working down here, right now it would be tough convincing anyone else to relocate to this part of the state. 'Looking for adventure? Work as a pharmacist in North Central Kentucky'".

"Greg's place looks about the same as when we were here four years ago. But the rest of the property down by the river looks ratty. Doesn't anybody own a mower?" Pat asked.

"Everyone except the neighbors to the immediate south and Lynda has moved out. Those neighbors told me they are about ready to close on their place. Greg was being pressured to sell too. The development company creating this forced exodus hasn't bothered Lynda about it recently out of respect I suppose. But I know Johnny Laine and the other land developers are getting anxious."

"I guess the property is too valuable for a bunch of cottages, huh?" Will continued.

"I wouldn't have thought so but the developers envision a luxurious compound down here. You don't suppose the four of us could buy a place together?" Vic asked.

"Is this your way of telling us that divorce isn't all that bad?" asked Rex.

Only friends this close would know that they could safely tease each other about such sensitive topics. Vic reacted to the question in the spirit Rex intended it.

"Sure. I'd be living in a waterfront bachelor pad in Burgoyne. Every single man's dream!" Given the sex he'd had with Julie, Vic mused that life in Burgoyne might have a lot to offer after all.

Several times they moved the boat to different spots with no improvement in luck. Pat and Rex each caught small channel cats that they tossed back before they chugged their way to the dock. For the group, this was a typical day's fishing.

The afternoon on the water made them hungry even though it was barely five o'clock. Vic grilled rib eyes and served them with baked Ore-Ida steak fries, and a three-bean salad he'd picked up at the deli counter. He didn't have to worry about supplying a dessert. The brownies that Claudia packed for Rev, the ones with the Symphony Bar middle layer, came close to sending all four of them into hyperglycemic comas.

By ten thirty, they had filled a good-sized trash container with empty beer cans and had finished their obligatory single malt scotches and evening cigars. They knew that the fishing would begin in earnest the next morning and that card playing only disrupted the reveries of their first night of drinking and reminiscing. They toasted Greg one last time and headed for bed. Vic told them that he'd go put the cover on the pontoon and lock their tackle in the boathouse.

He got out his phone to call Tracy. He couldn't come up with a good reason why he felt compelled to do so other than baseless guilt. They were divorced after all but Tracy seemed unhappy and after his early morning sex, Vic wasn't. Growing up with a Lutheran mother wasn't always a good thing. His Cincinnati friends had reminded him from time to time that he was no worse off on the guilt spectrum than if he had been raised Catholic like they had.

Before Vic made his call, Julie rang in. "You were supposed to call me."

"The phone was in my hand," he sidestepped her comment without lying.

"I'm at the Club, she said. "The boys, not my boy Johnny, are playing pitch. The girls, not Johnny's girl, are drinking and pretending to like each other. I'm supposed to be looking for something in my car."

"Looking for love in all the wrong places?" he asked.

"Come on. That was cruel. I'm lonely enough."

"Sorry," he muttered.

"If the guys are asleep maybe you could drive around to my house."

"Yeah, they're probably asleep or getting there but if I could legally drive, which I can not, I can't leave, no matter how plausible a story you can come up with."

"Oh yeah? How about I got a call from a gorgeous woman who told me that she was horny and that she wanted only me?"

"Yeah, like that'd happen."

"I thought it just did," Julie parried.

"Sorry, it's the wrong night. I'll try to call you tomorrow."

"Goodbye. I guess I'll have to find a willing lifeguard or golf pro or bartender."

"I got it. Good night, Julie."

Vic had lost the impetus to call Tracy. It wasn't all that late and she'd probably be watching some late night rerun, but he lied to himself that the guys would be wondering why he was taking so long. Vic locked up the tackle and tightened the tarp over the boat. A motorized fishing boat shot up the river in the general direction of the Laine dock. Maybe the pilot was one of the employees staying there coming back from a little night fishing.

25

EVERYONE WAS UP EARLY. They were on the water by 6:30. Will, who had the best fishing instincts of any of their foursome, took over as captain. They headed upstream along the eastern shoreline, expecting to find fish in the areas shaded by the bluffs. There were a couple of deeper pools and a few spots close to fallen trees, not yet drifting with the stream thanks to root systems that clung defiantly to the bank. These conditions made the group optimistic. Their only chatter was to make fun of Will who, in his eagerness to leave early, had forgotten to relieve himself of his three cups of coffee. A portrait of him, facing the shore with no elbows in sight, was the subject of their first candid photo of the morning. They cruised up and down the shore. Each of them caught several fish, a few of which were big enough to keep and to provide enough for lunch. Their count exceeded the previous year's total catch, although this wasn't saying a great deal.

They boated past the area that was the most likely site for a water entrance to the cave, based on Greg's estimates. The water level was rarely, if ever, much lower than it was that morning. Still, Vic saw no opening in the limestone cliffs.

WILL PILOTED THE BOAT BACK TO THE DOCK FOR THEIR TRADITIONAL SHORE LUNCH. Across from the cabin, they saw Roscoe, with sketchpad in hand, sitting mid-river in a small rowboat. Vic thought the light might have been better in the afternoon but decided photographers might view light differently from other visual artists. They all waved and Vic shouted to him, "Roscoe. You want to join us for lunch?"

"No thanks, Vic. I've got my artistic groove flowing. I might catch up with you later."

The guys were satisfied with the morning catch. Will caught the most, as he always seemed to do, but only landed two big enough, barely so, to keep. The others promised Will to let him eat some of theirs if he'd do the cooking. Since his wife often worked night shifts, by necessity, he knew how to cook well enough to satisfy his finicky kids. This made him the closest thing the foursome had to a chef.

Vic lit charcoal in the dockside fire pit and lightly greased an iron skillet. Rex rushed to clean off and set four places on the dilapidated picnic table. Pat didn't let it go unnoticed that this left him the job of cleaning the fish. Will thick sliced several potatoes and onions and fried them in liberal amounts of canola oil. He breaded the fish in his own concoction of corn meal, cake flour, and spices and fried them in the same onion-flavored oil. The guys thought that they were being served too much to eat. Will's cooking and the outdoor air proved them wrong.

"I'm not sure why I bothered to clean these. You guys would have devoured them whiskers, fins, and all," Pat said after ten minutes of all of them grunting, moaning, and making other primitive sounds of satisfaction.

"I wondered why mine were so chewy," Rex answered.

"Whiskers add roughage," Pat added.

Given that Will had done the cooking, the other three assumed the job of cleaning things up. Will took advantage of the end to his responsibilities and said, "I think I'll try my luck by myself if that's okay. There should be some shade on the west bank by now. I'll take the small boat so you guys can go out once you've finished K.P."

"Sure. Then you'll be able to lie about the big ones you almost landed," Rex answered.

Will smiled, picked up his rod and tackle box. Before he headed out he asked "Okay if I borrow your vest Vic? It's getting too hot for my jacket."

"Fine, Will, as long as you don't piss into the wind," Vic said.

"I thought all that cork you had sewn in was supposed to absorb urine."

Once they heard the chugging of the small outboard, Pat suggested they play a few rounds of cards before going back out. They played Red Dog, one of their favorite versions of poker. It was after three o'clock before they thought to see if any big catfish were feeling suicidal.

"Will must be having better luck than he did this morning," Rex said.

"I could repeat that lunch again tonight. I hope he's caught his limit," Vic said.

"And ours, too," Pat added.

They crossed the river toward where Will had told them he was going. When they didn't see his boat, they assumed he must have moved on. There were mostly open fields further to the south. These didn't offer much shade and so they boated toward the island. Pat called Will's phone to let him know they were on their way. There was no answer.

WILL'S EMPTY BOAT WAS ANCHORED IN THE COVE. The three shouted greetings but determined that Will wasn't close enough to hear. As they maneuvered through the lily pads they realized Will's line was still in the water and his tackle box was open on the seat.

"He's not averse to pissing in the river so why'd he leave the boat. Try his cell again, Pat," Rex said.

An answering ring came from nearby. Will's cell phone was resting face up on the bottom of the boat. They retrieved it and checked when he made his the last call. He'd made, or tried to make one at 2:17 to Vic's previous mobile number. Will must not have programmed in the number for my new one furnished by Pharmacists-PRN.

26

THE THREE OF THEM SCRAMBLED TO TIE OFF THEIR
BOAT BEFORE JUMPING ASHORE. Pat started circling
the island to the west and Rex went toward the
eastern side. Vic took the path through the center of
the island, going slowly, looking on both sides of
the rocky trail. He could hear Pat's and Rex's
shouts "... Will! Hey Will! Where are you? Will?
..." They were all yelling the same things,
sometimes in unison.

Suspecting that Will might have fallen, Vic
only needed to look to his left. The path abutted
limestone that was anywhere from waist to head
high on the other side. He shouted to the others
even knowing that they would have already said
something, "Have you found him? Have you seen
him?"

"No!" answered Rex.

"Hell, no. How about you?" asked Pat,
desperation in his voice.

Vic replied, "No, I haven't either. Wait!
Over here! Oh, shit! I think I've found him."

Will was lying face-up on the path at the
base of a large rock. He looked like he could have
fallen. His leg was twisted under him. His head was
resting in a small pool of drying blood. He wasn't

wearing his fishing hat …the hat they accused him
of wearing to bed. Will's donning and removal of
his hat defined the beginning and end of the fishing
weekends. There'd be no more fishing this year.
Will was dead.

Pat came crashing up the steep slope from
the water joining Rex and Vic. He knew from Vic's
reaction that Will was gone. He kept muttering, "I
should have gone with him. I should have gone with
him."

"What? Did he fall?"

"Maybe. He looks posed to me, like
somebody tried to make it look like he fell."

"Where's his hat?" Rex asked.

"Who gives a shit? Maybe it's in the boat."
Vic was starting to let his anger get the best of him.
"I didn't see it on the way up here.

We better call the sheriff's office. Tell
whomever you get to park as close to the trail as
they can. Tell them they'll need a gurney. I'll stay
here with Will while you guys go back to the
trailhead to wait for Billings."

Having little faith in the thoroughness of
local law enforcement's investigative methods Vic
wanted to examine the vicinity before the
authorities showed up. Will's billfold, some change,
and his keys were in his pockets. Vic retraced the
path down to the boat but saw no evidence that Will
was dragged. The foliage was undisturbed. It looked
like all of Will's tackle was in the boat. The night
crawler carton was left open and it hadn't been
shoved under the seat to protect any remaining
worms from the heat.

Vic returned to where Will was laying. He shivered involuntarily before walking past Will down the trail in the opposite direction from where they'd searched. Nothing looked out of place. He returned to sit beside Will and to wait. He gently patted Will's unfeeling wrist and turned toward the river. That was when he saw two cigarette filter tips. He picked up one, carefully wrapped it in a tissue, and put it in a pocket of his jeans.

Zach hung out near here on the island but Vic couldn't imagine that he smoked ... definitely not during track season. Several of Roscoe's paintings through the years appeared to have been made from this general viewpoint. Vic recalled from the previous day's encounter that Roscoe still smoked. It shouldn't require sophisticated science to determine what brand matched the filters. DNA analysis could be run on residual sputum. Teenagers from the area are reported to come here to drink and have sex but there are no cans, bottles, or condoms. Only the two filters.

Vic heard the sheriff directing the EMTs up the hill. Billings emerged first.

"Sheriff."

"Fye," he answered. "Your friends tell me he's Will Lounsberry and that the four of you are staying at the Ebert cottage. Is that right?"

"Yes, that's right."

"Why was he here by himself?"

"He was disappointed with what he caught this morning and he didn't like fishing from the pontoon boat."

"What do you think? Is this an accident?"

"I don't think so. Will had no reason to get off the boat. And why would he leave his phone? What do you think, guys?"

One of the EMTs shrugged his shoulders, as if it to say, "It's not part of my job description to think." The other man, known as Bob, had checked for breathing and pulse, had recorded Will's temperature, and had noted the time. In response to Vic's question, he carefully lifted Will's head.

"From what I can see, this guy either was wicked walloped or he hit his head on some big rock. Did you find blood on any of these rocks? "

"There's some blood on the one he's lying on. Otherwise, no," Vic said.

Vic saw from the sheriff's frown that he was angry that Vic had moved Will's head. Vic had little choice but to defer to Billings. He'd try to sort everything out later.

"I'm sure that the sheriff will want to search the area more thoroughly. I've mostly been sitting, waiting for you guys. The only thing I found was a cigarette butt over here," Vic said, pointing to the other side of the rock.

Billings asked, "Is stiffness starting to set in on the, er, uh the deceased?"

"Slightly, from what I can tell," said Bob.

"Well, after I take a few pictures lift him and carry him out of here as carefully as you can."

"Okay, Sheriff."

The two men had maneuvered people, living and dead, from awkward locations before and had done so together. Their actions were respectful as well as efficient. Indeed, they treated Will's body with more dignity than it would eventually experience during an autopsy.

"Reverend Rex says you're the one who found Lounsberry, is that right?"

"Yes."

"Is there some reason you sent two guys to wait for me and you stayed here?"

"Not really. I didn't think about it".

"Tell me again why Will was by himself. "

Vic answered, "He only caught two this morning so wanted to hit his limit if he could. A lot of times we split up."

"Didn't he know how to swim? He was wearing a vest?"

"That was my vest. He said his jacket was too hot."

"I see."

The sheriff photographed the area and the boat from several angles. He put on latex gloves when he bagged Will's cell phone and fishing knife, as he had earlier with the cigarette butt. He asked Vic to not move the boat or disturb anything else and told all of them to consider the island as a crime scene. They were to stay off of it until further notice. He did give Vic permission to remove the pontoon boat and to take it back to the cabin. He said he'd meet everyone there and he'd take down statements then.

Once Vic had docked the boat, he joined Rex, Pat, and Billings in the cottage. Billings asked Vic to verify what he had told him earlier and then said, "I realize how close you men are and after Greg this has got to be tough. I'll need your contact information, Pat. I know how to reach you other two guys."

Once the sheriff drove away the three of them sat silently on the breezeway, looking out over the river. They didn't speak for several minutes.

Pat spoke first. "I'm ready to go. I think I can be home in an hour."

"Can you drop me off, if an hour and ten minutes works?" Rex asked.

"Yeah, of course."

Pat finally addressed the rest of what they'd all been thinking, "Vic, this was no accident and that sheriff isn't going to do shit. It's up to you to figure this out. We'll help you any way we can. I'm not sure how exactly, but you've got to work through this. It would be nice to accept that Greg was killed because he resisted or because he recognized the robber. And it would be comforting to think that Will getting killed was a freakish accident. But none of us believe that, do we?"

Rex added, "It's possible that somebody mistook Will for Vic but we don't know that. If so, why is somebody out to get Vic? And, we can't know but what all of us are targeted for some reason. We all live public lives but I don't think anything that's happened would warrant us getting police protection. Am I blowing this out of proportion? Vic, what do you think?"

"I don't believe it is all of us. I've had a couple of telephone threats and you know about my car getting vandalized."

"Why are they out to get you?"

Vic answered, "Obviously, I've thought about it. Here's what I've come up with. There are people who want the pharmacy gone from the downtown renovation area. There's at least one person who wants Lynda's nursing home business. There are people who want this cottage bulldozed so a new development can commence. And who knows what else."

"There must be legal shenanigans that can accomplish most of that without killing you," said Rex.

"Yes, and killing Greg doesn't seem to have been necessary either. I guess I need to determine who is the greediest, or maybe the most sociopathic.

I'll work with the sheriff as much as I have to but if he doesn't made any progress or if he's not been forthcoming. I'll do whatever needs to be done to get the bastard who's behind this," Vic promised.

27

ONCE THE OTHERS LEFT, VIC CALLED LYNDA. He asked if he could stop by. She promised him a grilled pork chop and whatever else she might be able to throw together.

"That's okay Lynda. I already ate," Vic said. Eating was the last thing he wanted to do.

Lynda met him at the door with a hug. She backed away, frowned, and said, "I can tell. This isn't good, is it?"

"No. It's not. I wanted to be the one to tell you. Will died this afternoon. We found him on the island. He might have fallen. He might have been killed. We don't know yet. I don't want to lay anything else on you. But I didn't want you to learn from a neighbor or somebody."

"Oh, God. This is one endless nightmare! This has got to be tied to Greg getting shot doesn't it?"

"I wish I had an answer for you, Lynda. I don't know anything for sure."

"How are you coping with this? Did you find him?"

"Not so good," he answered sidestepping any conversation about finding a person dead whom you care about so deeply.

"Is there a remote possibility that it could have been an accident?"

"There's a chance. I'm not ready to rule it out but I really don't think so. There'll be an autopsy, and the sheriff is taking the precaution of treating it like a crime."

Lynda brushed away a tear, but they continued to flow as she spoke, "People really want us to go away, don't they?"

"Go away?"

"They want us out of downtown. They want our business. They want us away from the river. Yeah. They want us to go away. I'm going to settle things with the cottage. Even the river's not safe. You probably shouldn't be staying there either."

"I can see why you feel that way. You'd mentioned to me that you've seen police cruising your neighborhood for the first time ever. Deputies have been dropping by the store somewhat randomly, too. I honestly believe the threats to you are financial and probably resolvable even though the changes may not be to your liking. If I was concerned about your physical safety I'd be helping you move out of Burgoyne tomorrow."

"I know you would, Vic. And the financial difficulties, as you know, are getting steadily worse. Claudia tells me that a number of customers, town counsel members, development committee members, almost everybody but Johnny and Julie, have transferred their prescriptions to other stores. A few people who work for them have, too.

Julie and I had lunch on Friday. We always have lunch on Friday. She probably said too much but she told me that the river front developers had made a deal with Hal and Goldie. I guess you know they're our last remaining neighbors. She claimed she didn't like the developer's tactics and that she'd told that to Johnny in no uncertain terms. I guess I'll be hearing from the developers with an offer soon. She thinks it'll be twice the assessed value plus they'll pay all of the closing costs, even next year's taxes.

If that's what they come across with, I might have to take it. It'd be so hard going there without Greg anyway. I kind of think Zach would like me to keep it but the money would be enough to pay off the mortgage on this place and cover some of Zach's college expenses."

"I hear you. But I still want to help out with the pharmacy if I can. Not that I have any great ideas yet. But if you can delay the sale of the cottage for a month or so I think that would be wise. This is a major decision. You might want to move slowly right now."

"I'll try to hold off but it's going to be harder now with every thing going on. I assume you still have a gun of some sort. If you're going to continue to stay at the cottage, I want you to be safe. I can put in an alarm system. Install more outdoor lights."

"You're trying to up the assessment value … make Johnny pay double for your improvements. And yes, I have a gun or two."

Lynda forced a smile and chased Vic out the door. She was already starting to make supper for Zach who was studying with a friend, a different friend. Stephanie had, as Zach had said, drifted further out of his life.

VIC WAITED UNTIL LATER THAT NIGHT TO TELL TRACY. There was no need to interrupt her at the hospital.

"Vic. I can't believe this. I feel terrible for his family. This is like some cheap horror film. It's like none of you should leave the cottage by yourself."

"I know."

"With Will gone, I'll bet Susan and the boys will move to Texas, closer to her family. She never did like it in Cincinnati. She could never understand how living in Cincinnati seemed more like being in the south than it did when she lived in San Antonio. Not that I have any basis to disagree," Tracy said.

"I'll be going up for the funeral. I imagine it'll be Tuesday. Lynda says she doubts whether she can handle it just yet. I don't blame her. I'm not sure I can either," he said.

"I think I can get off, too. If you were in Louisville, we could drive over together. You might have been filling in somewhere else if you weren't in Burgoyne, I guess."

"Right. I might have been in Paducah. No one else wants to go there."

"I understand," she said. "We've been there. Remember?"

"I remember. Good night."

"Bye, Victor"

Vic didn't have the energy to try and analyze Tracy's interest in having him in Louisville. He wanted to get in touch with Roscoe.

"Roscoe. This is Vic. Any chance we can get together?"

"What's up?"

Vic thought a second about how forthright he wanted to be and then said, "Will is dead. We found him on the island. Just wondering if you saw anything?"

"I passed Will in the fishing boat before I headed north. I had no idea he died."

"I'd like to talk to you. Where are you?"

"I'm up the road having a beer. If you're at the cottage, I'll come by in a few minutes."

Vic wanted to either affirm or refute his suspicions that Roscoe might somehow be involved. He put his loaded Glock under a pillow on the end of the sofa. If Roscoe killed Will, there was no reason to assume he wouldn't kill again.

"ROSCOE. WANT ANOTHER BEER?" Vic asked after Roscoe walked in without knocking. Roscoe technically had no ownership privileges but knowing that it had been his family's cottage for most of Roscoe's life, Vic managed not to act annoyed.

"I better not. I already had a couple."

"Sit down and let me know if you change your mind. I've got quite a selection. The guys didn't want to haul any of it home."

Roscoe, acknowledging that Vic wasn't seeking to become his new best friend said, "You told me what happened. I'm not sure that I can be much help. And I've got to tell you, it pisses me off. It sounds like you're accusing me. How stupid do you think I am? You saw me this morning. And I suppose you find it incriminating that I happen to be a damned good shot."

"I'm not accusing you. And, incidentally, Will wasn't shot. If I wanted to get you in trouble I'd have told Billings I'd seen you."

Roscoe gave him a closed-mouth smile, nodded, and said, "What if Billings finds out I was on the river today? How are you going to explain not mentioning me?"

"I'll say that I forgot."

"Forgot?"

"I was being flippant. It's not like Billings is going to pursue this if he doesn't have to. Where were you painting this afternoon?"

"North of here, above the double bend. There is some wild honeysuckle in bloom on the eastern shoreline."

"Did you see anyone or did anyone see you?"

"If you mean, can I prove I was there, hell no. But I've got the painting I did up there in the back of my van and it's still a little wet if you want to see it."

"No. I'm good. How come you and Greg didn't get along?"

"Whoa. So now we're into motive."

"Consider this practice, in case Billings does find out," Vic said.

"Right. Practice."

Roscoe sighed and began, "We used to get along okay, or we did when we played sports together. We were both good at baseball. I was his catcher. But Greg gave it up when he got into high school. That's when he started working a lot at the store. Mom for some reason didn't want me to work there. Anyhow, I think he got tired of defending me."

"Defending you?"

"I took art classes all through high school and several of the guys in those classes were gay … flamboyantly so. Greg warned me. But these guys were talented and funny so I didn't want to shun them or make fun of them behind their backs. That was all it took in small town Burgoyne to be labeled a 'queer lover'. There are still some people who I went to school with who go out of their way to avoid speaking to me. Wonder why I hate Burgoyne?

Greg and I got jumped one night his junior and my sophomore years by some guys who wore Ninja suits and masks. We were sure that they were Ralph and Timmy and a couple of their friends. Anyhow one guy knocked me down and kicked me a bunch of times. But the other three pounded and kicked Greg really bad. Anyhow, I guess Greg felt, and rightly so, that it was my fault."

"How could that be your fault? No one deserves to be assaulted. And if the tables were turned and someone jumped Greg, you'd have wanted to be there," Vic said.

Roscoe paused for a few seconds and then began again, "Yeah, you're right I guess. But Greg did have to loan me money a few times when I didn't want to admit to Mom and Dad that I owed the kid who supplied my weed. I guess the clincher was when he had to bail me out of jail when I got a ticket for O.W.I. He told me to never ask him for help again although he eventually apologized.

We'd gotten along better lately, mostly because of Lynda, I suspect. It did seem to get tense any time Mom was around, though. Our final reconciliation came when I told him if Mom gave me preferential treatment it was because she felt guilty."

"Guilty about what?" Vic asked.

"Those were Greg's exact words. I'll tell you what I told him: 'Who the fuck names their kid Roscoe?'

But back to your original question, God's truth, I didn't see anything."

28

VIC UNDERSTOOD WHY PHARMACISTS FIND THEIR PRACTICES FULFILLING. He was in a zone, handling the routine but being able to stay on top of the details that mattered: telling the patients what they needed to watch out for and what they could do to minimize problems. At the end of the day, the goals of pharmacy and drug enforcement were the same … ensuring the health and safety of people. Maybe being denied reinstatement as an officer was what made the DEA seem so much more attractive.

Many customers expressed their sympathy and acknowledged that Vic had gone through a tough week. He knew that if he had been undercover in Louisville or Cincinnati the criminals he'd have been associating with couldn't have cared less about his losses. Violent deaths were a given in the lives they led.

Customers who were older men, at least the ones who came in the pharmacy almost every day, spreading out their errands to keep busy, were especially solicitous. As a group, they had diminishing numbers of friends, if any at all. Even the younger Buzz, who got his antidepressant and sleep medications refilled that morning, made a point of shaking his hand and telling Vic how sorry he was that he had lost another friend.

Mid-morning there was a call from a Burgoyne Town Council member.

"This is the pharmacist. How may I help you today?"

"Hi. This is Bernice Lamont and I, er ... I want to have my prescriptions transferred to another pharmacy. My husband works in Lexington and it would be more convenient if he could pick them up at Walgreens on the way home. And I think they'll be cheaper, too"

"I have your profile here. Oh you're on Foster. You must be Lynda's neighbor. Okay. We're looking at hydrochlorothiazide and phenformin. Both generic drugs. With your Humana, your copays add up to $7.00 a month. Walgreens can't discount copays but I understand the importance of convenience. And I appreciate how hard this must have been for you to make this call."

"Why do you say that?"

"You're on the Town Council and so, well, I thought promoting businesses owned locally is ... you know. But let me assure you, I adhere to the same HIPAA guidelines of confidentiality that physicians follow. No one will know. Which Walgreen's should I contact? I think they have five stores in Lexington."

"I'm not sure. I'll have to get back to you."

"Okay. Anything else I can help you with this morning Mrs. Lamont?"

"No. Goodbye."

During their first breather, about 1:30 or so, Claudia seized the opportunity to acknowledge what he'd done. "I'm glad you said what you did to Bernice. Maybe you saved us a customer. I've wanted to tell these people what I think for a long time. Several of them go to our church, so I dare not say anything.

Like it or not, people change churches the way they change pharmacies. Rex can only save souls if he gets them through the door. Spirituality. Health. Consumers rule in both cases."

"I guess you're right. But I'd like to believe many people aren't that way" Vic said supportively.

"I've been meaning to tell you," Claudia began, "my friend and I go to state association meetings together. We techs hang out in our own little groups. Anyhow, she's a tech at a ScriptCoMart, one of those franchised pharmacies. She says their business seems to hold up no matter what competition moves in. Lots of the customers believe that their stores are part of a chain. The franchisees do have buying power and advertising that allows them to compete. I wonder if Lynda would consider something like that."

"That's a good idea. I should have thought of it. As it turns out, I've been negotiating with ScriptCoMart on behalf of Pharmacists-PRN. Each store is responsible for finding its own back-up pharmacists. Heidi and I aren't ready to take on relief for 300 pharmacies but we think we can start small ... maybe Louisville, first."

AGENT WILKINS GOT CLAUDIA'S ATTENTION. She asked if this would be a good time to interrupt. Claudia motioned for her to come behind the counter, indicating she could handle things while the two of them retreated to the office.

"I took you at your word and assumed that you'd come in today. I brought you something. I think it might help."

"Might help what?" she asked.

"These cases, okay?"

Vic handed her the plastic bag with the remains from the cigarette. He explained to her what had happened the day before, what he'd seen, and how he'd left a second cigarette butt for the sheriff's investigation.

"And, how exactly do you want me to label this evidence? Let's see, I'm investigating these robberies and I think the DNA we find here in the traces of saliva will give us our answer. Oh, yes this was found five miles away from the scene of one of the robberies by an anonymous tipster."

"Works for me," Vic said. "I hope this demonstrates though that I still have good investigative instincts. I know reinstatement as an agent is complicated and it isn't something that I'm ready to pursue even if I could. The other possibility is that you could bring me on board as a consultant. I'm here all the time and, it's not your fault but there seems to be no progress being made on solving the three robberies. Since you've got eight other investigations going on maybe you can justify hiring me for this."

Patrice smiled. "You win. I'll talk to my boss. She says she knows you. I'll let you know tomorrow."

Vic was anxious to contribute to the apprehension of Greg and Will's killer or killers. Even restricted DEA affiliation might help. Leaving the organization did nothing to make things better with Tracy. If relapsing to a life of Frisch's fish sandwiches didn't lead to dire results, maybe he could tolerate a taste of the DEA.

29

AFTER HIS SHIFT, VIC WENT FOR A RUN AND GRABBED A QUICK DINNER. He was ready to unwind. Thinking about the robbery and murders was frustrating given that he had no access to any of the evidence or reports that Patrice had promised. He turned his attention to Greg's obsessive search for the cave. He justified the diversion by hypothesizing that thinking about the cave might get his problem solving and investigative juices flowing. He grabbed Greg's third notebook and sat down in the ancient recliner that was closest to the cottage's only floor lamp. Vic usually avoided caffeine at night but decided that half a Mountain Dew could provide enough stimulation to keep him alert. And its effects ought to wear off in time for him to get to sleep.

Greg, in one of his notebooks, described a trip he had taken by himself to Hannibal, Missouri for a week. He had rented a boat and had spent several days and nights on the island in the Mississippi where Tom Sawyer and Huck Finn had gone when they ran away. Greg took four guided tours of a nearby cave, the model for where the characters Tom and Becky Thatcher had gotten lost. Greg took detailed notes and hundreds of pictures.

He concluded that a young Sam Clemens had spent many hours on the island and in the cave.

In another section of the third notebook, Greg documented every instance in the Hawkins books where the cave was mentioned and wrote down every reference to twists, side passages, the three openings, the chasm, the water below the chasm, and the paths to the bottom. He tried a few imaginative drawings and maps but acknowledged that they could be misleading.

If Vic didn't know better he would have concluded that Greg had given up because the final entry at the end of this notebook was made early last summer.   That made no sense. Greg had insisted that he had something new. Maybe there was a fourth, more recent notebook that Greg kept hidden somewhere.

A business-sized envelope addressed to Greg was stuck in the back of the third notebook. The letter was postmarked March of that year and had a return address to the Kentucky Spelunking Society. The envelope was thick enough that it required two "Forever" stamps.

The cover letter explained that the society had looked into Greg's query and that indeed there was a file verifying the presence of a cave along the Kentucky River, WNW of Burgoyne. After the good news validating the cave's existence came the statement that the cave was deemed as hazardous to public safety and was sealed shut in early 1958.

A photocopied description explained how there was a large entrance in the side of a bluff. The passages, some mile and a quarter in length, were for the most part tall and wide enough for a person to comfortably walk through. The hazard mentioned was a wide, deep chasm with shallow, rapidly flowing water at its bottom, with numerous protruding sharp boulders.

A FRAMED PHOTOGRAPH OF LYNDA AND GREG THAT STOOD ON THE MANTLE EXPLODED spewing glass fragments into the room. This was followed immediately by a jarring thud into the back of the lounge chair where Vic was sitting. Retorts from the shots followed a fraction of a second later. Vic rolled out of the chair and, staying low, ran into the laundry room. He pulled open the electrical box and flipped off the master circuit breaker. After retrieving his Glock and an extra clip, he slipped out through the side door.

Once Vic's eyes adjusted to the faint light supplied by stars and a glow from Hal's bathroom window, he shifted into a crouched position and headed slowly toward the river. *Why does trouble always come from the river?* He assumed with the security lights turned off he would be next to invisible. A rapid burst of gunfire tore up sod a few feet in front of him, refuting his premise.

He crouched lower and dashed the last twenty-five yards, wanting to use the boathouse as cover. Once he had squatted in place, he fired three rounds in the general direction he believed the shots were coming from. All that accomplished was to draw another burst of automatic weapon fire.

He heard several loud shots coming from up the hill. *Shit. They've got me in crossfire.* He quickly ascertained that Hal was the new shooter and he was firing across the river from behind a tree in his side yard. Hal had been one of the first personnel with "boots on the ground" in Viet Nam. Besides his background as a U.S. military "advisor", Hal was an avid hunter.

There was no return fire from the other side of the river. A boat sped rapidly away heading to the north with no lights.

"You alright, Vic?" Hal shouted.

"Yeah. Thanks to you. I'm sorry you got drawn into this," Vic answered as he trotted back up the hill.

"Wouldn't have missed it. I'd have joined you sooner but I had to get Goldie hunkered down behind our couch. Who was it? Do you know?"

"Wish I did.

What kind of gun were you using? It sounded like a cannon."

Hal answered with a reverential tone, "It was a rifle that Dad called his "varmint gun". It was my grandpa's before that. Both of them told stories about killing coyotes. The stories got better over time. The coyotes ran faster, they were further away, and the missed shots were fewer. By my reckoning though, it's got a range of 250 yards and is damned accurate when it's light enough to see."

"Unlike tonight, huh? Well, again I'm grateful you were here. Don't say anything to anybody. I don't want Lynda getting more upset than she already is."

I could just go back to Louisville and get on with my life. It's me they're targeting. But Reverend Rex and I talked about this. I'm here for a purpose. No other relief pharmacist would have the resources to deal with this. This is mine. I've got this.

30

VIC WENT BACK INSIDE AND RECONNECTED THE
POWER. He swept up fragments of glass from the
picture frame, recovered both slugs, and put them in
a small baggie. One was deeply imbedded in the
paneling above the fireplace. The other barely
protruded from the front of the chair, not far from
where Vic's right shoulder had been. There were
two tears in the window screen that he patched with
a couple of small strips of duct tape.

He briefly considered whether or not to
contact Billings. In the end, he saw no advantage to
doing so. Like he'd said to Hal, Lynda and Zach
didn't need to know. It wasn't because they might
be upset. But if they found out, it could cloud
Lynda's decisions about keeping the store and any
urgency she might feel about selling the cottage.

*Whoever is responsible for these last two
attacks must be familiar with this part of the river.
That doesn't limit things much. Boat traffic is never
heavy but between people fishing and pleasure
boating from other cottages and public ramps, I'm
never surprised to see boaters. There are also a
growing number of people who are trying to canoe
every navigable segment of the Kentucky River.*

Besides Roscoe, we saw a couple of dozen boats and canoes the Saturday Will was killed.

VIC HEARD SOMEONE PULL INTO THE DRIVEWAY. When the sound continued on into the garage, he knew it was Julie. He was unsure whether to be grateful or angry. He would have preferred being able to digest what had happened a little longer. No such possibility. She tapped on the door before coming in.

He hadn't realized that a hug could be so expressive. When they pulled apart, holding each other's hand, Vic could only assume that she was acknowledging how much Will had meant to him and not how he had survived a gunfight. In any case it was therapeutic. He felt foolish that he'd been angry or considered her visit to be intrusive.

"I thought you might need to talk. I thought you might need me," she said. For once Vic saw no indication she intended a double meaning.

"Lots of things seem to be ending," Vic began, editing out allusions to what just happened. "It's almost like that final scene in 'Deliverance,' where Ned Beatty says after all of the tragic things that happened that he wasn't sure he wanted to see Jon Voigt again for a long time. I'm trying to process how I'm going to handle being with Pat and Rex. I'm not sure we'll ever go fishing together again or if we'll want to. And like you, I want to help Lynda and Zach, but it's hard to know how to do anything when they don't know what they want. And this all happened in the face of the proposed changes for the downtown and likely changes down

here along the river. I want to believe it's all a
coincidence. I want to support them but I'm not sure
where to start. Lynda says you've offered to help.
What do you have in mind, Julie?"

"Maybe Lynda's already told you. I wasn't
sure it was the right thing but I thought if I could
somehow help her negotiate down here, to keep her
away from some haggling, not with Johnny, but
with some other guys who are going to be less
sympathetic. These guys have a lot of money tied
up. Believe me, Johnny does too. They've got
people who are ready to put down money on
properties but no one is going to do that until they
see streets and lot lines that currently go through the
middle of properties, and so forth. Right now
money is going out and nothing is coming in.
Johnny thinks the whole project could be at risk.

I know this sounds like I'm helping me and
not Lynda. I don't have as big a conflict of interest
as it might seem. With our farm and stables, we'll
get by. We always do. And for once, Johnny didn't
go all in. Well, nothing has a second mortgage, at
least.

If this makes you uncomfortable, let me
know."

"No, Julie, it's okay. I need a break from
obsessing about dead friends and feeling guilty
about what I could have done differently."

"I want to talk about something else, if
that's okay" Julie went on.

"Sure, I guess so."

"Johnny and I have an open marriage. It's
more of a partnership than a marriage. I think we

love each other. I know I love him and he tells me that he loves me. But as long as each of us can be discreet we've agreed that we can see other people."

"I suspected you had sort of a Bill and Hillary thing going on," Vic said. "Maybe that's not a good analogy unless you've got a bunch of pantsuits in your closet."

"Hey. I'm trying to be serious here. Anyhow, when you and I were younger, I know I kind of messed with your mind and I took you for granted. I thought you'd always be there. Then you married Tracy and I sort of tossed that idea aside. Eventually, after Eugene, my first husband, I met Johnny."

"Is there a question in there somewhere or why are you telling me this?" I asked, not sure I was going to be ready for the answer.

"Seeing other people has become less pleasurable than it used to be. Either men have gotten worse at screwing or vibrators have gotten better. But being with you is different. You don't act desperate or try to be all macho. You act like being with me is fun and that sex is a bonus, not our only reason for being together."

"So I'm better than a vibrator."

"Yes, on the test drive. But it's scarier. I don't want to leave Johnny. It would hurt him and his political career. I have to be extremely careful seeing you here around Burgoyne, at least as often as I want to see you and in the way I want to see you.

I want us to be together, and, yes, intimate without always having to look over our shoulders. I want us to see each other here in Burgoyne but it'll be easier in Louisville or wherever you go. I have the money and the freedom to come to you and spend hours or days or even a week now and then. I know you're who I need and I'd like to believe you'll eventually feel the same way."

"I can give you my initial reaction. I'd rather react more later when I'm not so distracted by all this other shit going on. Is that okay?"

"Okay," Julie agreed.

"I'm still sorting things out. I'm getting closer to figuring out how things went wrong between Tracy and me. What I should have done and areas where I shouldn't have had to compromise. It's complicated by the fact Tracy and I did NOT have an agreement to see other people while we were married. I guess I betrayed my vows by not putting her needs first. But there's betrayal and then there's …" .

Vic had apparently said the right things. Her shoulders dropped into a more relaxed position and she gave him her best smile and said, "Fair enough. I'm hoping all of this serious talk hasn't dampened your fun-loving nature. Oh, I bought these jeans for you."

"Well lets hang them up," he said, as they turned toward the bedroom.

31

AT WILL'S VIEWING, MOST OF THE PEOPLE WERE FROM CINCINNATI. Will had switched his major to actuarial science after three years in pharmacy school. This, and the introverted nature of actuaries, explains why many of his friends were pharmacists.

Of the many seating options for Will's mourners, Vic selected a chair a respectful distance away from Will's family but not so far away that it made him appear aloof. Apparently, he succeeded in the non-aloofness department. He was an unintentional magnet for Will's pharmacist friends until Pat showed up near the end of the viewing.

Because of his DEA affiliation, Vic had always been something of an odd man out among his college friends. He later thought that their pointed questions ... many assumed that he had been fired ... and their earnest attention to his answers ... gave them excuses not to talk about Will.

Angela Wray, who never relinquished her student role as class organizer, interrogated him so intensely that he began to suspect that his comments would show up in the alumni newsletter that she single-handedly produced and distributed.

For the third time in the past hour he found himself explaining, "I quit the DEA because so many of my assignments were undercover and, necessarily, each new assignment meant temporary periods when I needed to be away from home. When a case broke, somebody inevitably figured out that I was the undercover guy, the plant. Or we had to assume that was the case. So Tracy and I were forced into a life of anonymity. Everything was unlisted. Social media was out of the question in case someone recognized a picture of me."

"It sounds scary," Angela said.

"It was scary. The people I associated with were dangerous. They'd have been dangerous even if they weren't high most of the time. Plus, they were paranoid like all criminals. It's how they survive. I felt like I was on stage every waking second," Vic continued, while thinking that repeated explanation didn't bring him peace of mind.

"I can't imagine trying to have a life, turning it on, turning it off."

"Exactly. The undercover work took over my life, became my life. I became part of a criminal "we". I found myself plotting with them against rival drug gangs. I became more aggressive. Meaner. I had to. But it spilled over into the rest of what little life I had left."

"Sounds like you needed a support group."

"Yes I did. It was too much to ask of Tracy. You knew Tracy and I got divorced?"

"Yeah, I heard. I'm sorry, Vic."

"No, that's okay. We never had kids and we're getting along. We almost came here together but she couldn't get a full day off."

Our other classmates had drifted away and Angela continued to probe, "Why did you go into relief work? I thought you were tired of travel?"

"I'm not as noble as this sounds but it's one way that I can pay back the profession. There were too many cases early in my career when I was the bad guy. Pharmacists were often my targets. Anytime we believed physicians were diverting drugs, we'd scrutinize the purchasing records of all the local pharmacies. Most of the time they were innocent and I'd be elated for them but I'm not sure they always believed that. So if I can help someone take a vacation or have an afternoon off every week, that's one way of paying my dues."

"It must seem dull after what you did before."

"Change of pace would be an understatement. But every store has its own unique problems. I challenge myself daily unless it's someplace I've been to regularly. At the same time, I can leave the job behind at the end of the day or at the end of the week."

"That sounds like a 'non-answer answer' if I ever heard one," Angela said.

"You got me. Yes. It is dull. I do miss my former life. Pharmacists-PRN keeps me busy and I guess that helps. And pharmacy practice isn't without its own rewards."

"Could you use somebody else? What I mean to say is, uh, are you hiring?"

"Always."

"I'm so sick of working for a chain. I'm on my sixth district manager in four years. They all come in forgetting that they were ever in a store and ... oh you know all of this. Plus, I need to be closer to Lexington."

"Why's that?"

"Dad has non-small cell lung cancer and Mom isn't coping at all well. My brothers are no help other than cutting the grass and doing that sort of thing and I understand ... they do have families."

"I don't mean this to be flippant, but would you consider Burgoyne. If you live on the west side of Lexington it'd be a short commute."

"If you, if they I guess, catch whoever's behind this ... you know. Yes, I would be interested."

"Good. I'll be in touch."

"Pat. Rex. How've you been?" Vic asked in a low solemn voice.

"About like you, I imagine," said Rex.

"This may sound selfish. Rev and I have been talking. You don't suppose that we're all targets while we're here, do you?"

"No, I can't imagine why we would be," Vic said, trying to set their minds at ease. "We're the kind of fishermen the authorities love. We always buy licenses and we rarely catch fish. I think the Department of Natural Resources will leave us alone."

"Okay. Okay. Don't make fun of us. We don't carry guns like you do," Pat said.

Vic did have his back-up gun in the ankle holster. His friends wouldn't be reassured if he admitted it. Evasion seemed better.

"Like I did. Like I might start doing again. But, seriously, if I'm in Burgoyne for a while, it might be a good idea for you NOT to come and see me, Pat. And we probably ought NOT hang out together, Rex. Who knows?"

"So what are you saying exactly, Narco?" Pat sensed that he was back peddling.

"What I'm saying is that I don't think there's any reason that we'd all be targets. Will and I are roughly the same size. And he was wearing my vest.

As you know, I've had several warnings to leave Burgoyne, some not so subtle. Somebody doesn't want me there. I'm thinking whoever it is doesn't want me helping out Lynda and Zach but that doesn't fit in with the pharmacy robberies. I don't know but I'm sure nobody is gunning for you two. Still, other than me attending your church, Rev, I want to avoid you and make sure neither of you is collateral damage. If this was a bunch of guys waiting for me after school to beat me up, I'd tell you to 'man up' and help me out. Now what I'm telling you is 'this is my fight'."

"We understand. You know I'll be praying for you," said Rex.

"In spite of what you misguided Protestants think, my Catholic prayers work too," Pat said.

"Thanks, guys."

Vic took his leave from them and from the family members who were beginning to decompress

after having to console all the people who
theoretically should have been there to console the
family. He was asked, not for the first time, in this
case by Will's widow Susan, why there had to be an
autopsy and if he knew anything yet.

"I wish there was a way to streamline things,
Susan. Anytime a person dies of a traumatic wound
and nobody witnesses it, there has to be an
autopsy," he explained. Strictly speaking that was
the truth.

"I doubt that the coroner will conclude that
there is anything to suggest that Will simply didn't
take a nasty fall," Vic said as convincingly as he
could.

Susan and the others may or may not have
suspected what Vic believed to be true. He was
convinced that Will had been bludgeoned to death.
Those suspicions would probably be confirmed or
refuted within the next forty-eight hours. The sheriff
had told Vic that he would wait until after the
services to interview the family, should that be
necessary.

Protestant Hell, what could different and equally well-meaning interpretations of body and blood do to them. She patted his arm after they returned to the pew. They hadn't taken communion together for over a year. Nothing about how they handled it had seemed unnatural. Vic thought he saw Julie's jaw tighten a little but maybe it was because he anticipated she'd react.

The four of them filed out together. Vic kissed Julie and Lynda goodbye. Julie, accustomed to such subterfuge, offered him her cheek, anticipating that Vic might be confused. He and Tracy walked to their cars that were parked behind each other. Tracy also took the lead. They kissed on the lips, sort of a first-date goodnight kiss and agreed to talk later.

VIC STOPPED FOR GAS BEFORE HE MERGED ONTO THE INTERSTATE. Gas was always cheaper in Cincinnati than in Burgoyne and most other parts of rural Kentucky. He opened the glove compartment of his newly appointed Ford and set the extra clip and the holstered Glock on the passenger seat next to his tie to remind himself to take them into the cottage. He needed to start carrying both guns any time he was near the river, maybe at other times too. Vic had two dead friends whose murders needed solving. The killer wanted him and maybe others dead as well. Vic was accustomed to thinking that arrests and convictions meant closure. If at all possible, he'd settle for nothing less than revenge.

33

VIC WAS AWAKENED BY UNEXPECTED NOISE: the
sound of several trucks rumbling past the cottage.
Thursday was trash day for Riverton. It wasn't
Thursday and it wasn't a garbage truck he heard.
Vic could make out the clanging of large chains and
two loud squawks and thuds ...sounds of ramps
being released. Another engine roared to life and a
backup warning signal beeped repeatedly. The
mechanical sounds stopped long enough for a man
to shout orders.

The next engine noises were followed by the
screech of nails being pulled from boards and the
clattering of falling timber, shingles, and bricks. Vic
stepped outside to see which structure, which
cherished part of a family's memories of vacations
and weekend getaways, had been reduced to rubble
by not one but two relentless bulldozers

Before leaving for work, Vic closed the
windows in an attempt to block the clouds of dust
and mildew that emerged when each structure was
razed. Vic knew that his efforts would fall short of
complete success. The musty odor of old wood
deprived of circulating air had already begun to
permeate the cabin.

A man glanced at papers he was holding and
pointed at a house that looked starkly isolated after

the demolition of dwellings on either side of it. He then looked at Vic from under his hard hat. He grinned. Vic fully expected him to make a mock throat-cutting universal signal with his hand. Instead he waved and looked, again at his papers.

PATRICE WILKINS HAD ARRANGED TO STOP BY THE PHARMACY BEFORE IT OPENED. She was polite and direct.

"Vic, I want you to do as much preliminary investigating as you can. I know this sounds unorthodox but I'd like you to use several of the on-line commercial systems to see what you can find out about your suspects. The non-government systems often reveal things that government records lack. You'll be reimbursed for subscriptions required for background checks, criminal records, property records, and all of that. I haven't been successful yet in getting you access to Agency databases as a temporarily reactivated consultant. In any case I'll give you summary statements as they become available."

"Happy to give it a try," Vic said.

"Share anything you believe to be evidence or pertinent information with me first," she said. "I'll decide what needs to be passed along to the sheriff and the crime unit in Lexington. I can't have you compromising either of their cases or mine for that matter. I assume you'll notify me immediately if you unearth anything that sounds unethical or, more so, might be a criminal violation by any of your subjects. In other words, act like you'd want a consultant, a consulting detective, that you'd hired to behave."

"Will do," Vic said.

"I have no results from the DNA analysis. If something turns up that's definitive I'll e-mail you the information. You've told me that teenagers and others hang out in the area of the crime scene. We can't arrest someone for smoking in an area with public access. When the analysis is complete I will give you any identifying information that I have.

Oh yeah, no one knows that you're working for us do they?"

"No. In this town, telling anyone anything is tantamount to a public announcement."

"In order that I can coordinate our efforts with yours I need to know who you're investigating. I assume you have your suspicions about some folks?"

"The people who I'm considering as possibles don't have motives that seem compelling enough to commit murder. I'll tell you my initial thoughts and send you a list with addresses and other identifying information later. Right now, I'd say they're persons of interest, not suspects."

"As you know Vic, that can be a fine line."

"Johnny Laine and others who I'll list are backing a development along the river. They're anxious to begin getting things platted with streets, water, utilities and sewers in place so that they can begin building. Lynda is one of the last holdouts and the Burgoyne Town Council is prepared, if necessary, to condemn her property.

Similarly, the downtown redevelopment project is progressing, even without Ebert Pharmacy capitulation. As street parking disappears, the pharmacy may be forced to close its doors or at least to relocate. Some of the same people redeveloping along the river are involved there, as is Edwin Ryder. Again, there's motive to eliminate Ebert Drugs, at least at the downtown location, but murder seems extreme to me. Murder is seldom a rational act, though.

Ali Bourne is and has for a number of years been trying to lure away Greg's nursing home business. This might increase Ali's revenues by $100,000 and her profit by $10,000 at the outside. Ali is already one of the wealthiest pharmacists in the state. This shouldn't be that big of a deal for her.

Greg's brother Roscoe theoretically might stand to inherit more money from their mother. But I can't imagine that Zach if not Lynda and Zach are not contingent heirs. Roscoe has to know that the cottage will soon be gone and he's not an especially materialistic guy. If he has cigarettes and art supplies he seems contented. He's never been what you'd consider a warm person. But as far as I know there wasn't any festering rivalry between Greg and him.

And as to bringing Will's incident into the picture the only thing I can come up with for motive is that somebody mistook Will for me. As I told you, I've had threatening messages that not so subtly suggest I ought to leave Burgoyne. Nobody knows this but some shots were fired at the cottage the other night."

Her body tensed and her hands curled into two tight fists. "When were you planning on enlightening me? Even frigging Lone Ranger, and I put the emphasis on 'Lone', kept Tonto in the loop. What do you mean by 'some shots'?"

"Two initially. And some more directed at me when I went outside. I'm still not sure why I'm being targeted. My living at the cottage or helping at the pharmacy only delays development and other inevitable changes by a week or two if that."

"I don't know why I'm bothering to ask but did you happen to report the shooting incident to the sheriff?"

"If I didn't notify you why would I tell Ralph Billings? Actually I didn't want Lynda or Zach to find out and I can't trust Billings to keep things to himself."

"Point taken. I need you to remember that I'm Lone Ranger in our relationship. Understand?"

He thought about calling her 'Kemo Sabe' but instead said, "Yes."

"Okay. Go ahead and see what you can dig up on your possible suspects. Include names of their associates with your list if you have them. You know the drill. And try to be discreet. If you use *Classmates* for example as one of your tools, people can pay to find out who has looked at their information.

On another but related note, I've seen the report from the medical examiner. It differs from what you told me. The official cause of death is a concussive blow to the base of the skull. As to that cause, the medical examiner classified the origin as inconclusive but noted that there are many large rocks in the area, that the trail is steep, and that some rocks are well worn and slippery. By my way of thinking, there was enough hedging that if other evidence is brought to light, Will's death could be reclassified as a crime. Oh, and there was no suggestion of drugs and only a trace of alcohol in Will's blood."

"What was Billing's take on this?" Vic asked.

"I asked him if he concurred. He didn't answer me directly. What he said was that he was glad that the community didn't have another major crime that needed solving," she said.

"Translation: his re-election campaign doesn't need another crime. The Riverton housing project doesn't need another crime. The downtown redevelopment committee doesn't need another crime," Vic answered, making no effort to hide his disdain.

"I'm merely telling you what the sheriff said. I didn't say I went along with it but that's his official stance. We can work within that. You have to work within that. You can not refer, at least openly, to Will's death as a murder nor will you call the island a crime scene."

34

VIC REHASHED THINGS AS HE DROVE. He couldn't imagine why there would have been a conspiracy to kill Greg but it seemed to be in lots of peoples' best interest to not make too much out of it. It was as if it had become politically incorrect to say Greg had been murdered, as if unknown killers had rights superseding those of their victims. Realizing that his cynicism would accomplish nothing, he resorted to his default emotion-stabilizing cure ... running.

He vowed to turn it into a long run, longer than he'd been able to work into his schedule for a while. As was now his habit, he made sure he had the Kahr P380. Once he ran past the devastation of Riverton's demolition, he let his mind and legs go into autopilot. All the trees were leafed out and even the weeds had turned green. The humidity was low, the temperature was a tolerable 68°, and he had a reason not to push his pace. He had been in the process of gradually altering his running stride over the past few months. He knew the changes needed to be incremental. His feet already had become accustomed to pointing a few degrees more inward, more straight ahead, and that day he worked on leaning forward slightly from the waist. The idea was to let gravity pull him forward. He thought of a song his fifth grade teacher liked to play with a lyric about how Egyptians walk. Vic wanted to run like a Kenyan not an Egyptian. Maybe he could run like an older, taller, heavier Kenyan if not the elite distance runners. The run was working. He was thinking about Steve Martin rather than the murders.

Tracy's car was parked in the driveway of the cottage when he returned. His run had been exhilarating and mind clearing. Now, he'd need to start policing his thoughts and words. He wished that he could be happy she was there. This would have been a good night to be alone with his new assignment and to run background checks.

Sheldon met Vic at the door. He rested his paws on Vic's shoulders, managing to avoid bare skin. Sheldon delayed several seconds before responding to the down command as if to remind Vic that his obedience doesn't relinquish his alpha male status.

"Hi Victor, I brought us dinner."

"You won't want to come any closer until I take a shower," returning her greeting in the most upbeat tone he could muster.

"I remember," she said. "Go ahead. This'll all keep."

Not all joggers extend the same courtesy. Some running apologists contend that sweat from exertion doesn't smell as unpleasant as sweat caused by emotion. Vic suspected that non-exercising significant others were not consulted prior to making that declaration.

"I made your favorite," she yelled from the porch.

Vic joined her, thinking how he thought of himself as a good cook but in reality when it had been Tracy's evenings to make dinner, her offerings were far better.

"You weren't kidding about my favorite! Enchiladas! Your enchiladas reheated are better than most restaurants can serve fresh," Vic said.

"Yes. You've told me that before," she said, seemingly not unhappy that he still believed it. "It was hectic down here when I first pulled in. Trucks kept hauling boards, shingles, plumbing fixtures, all kinds of stuff away. There were fleets of them. All the cabins are gone except for your cabin and the place next door. I hope you appreciate my cleaning off the furniture out here. It was a mess."

"I can imagine. Thanks, and thanks for dinner. You even brought real sour cream and refried beans. I could make margaritas except I don't have the glasses, or the mix, or the coarse salt, or the tequila. I've got a bottle of Woodford Reserve, though."

"That's okay. I didn't want you to be hungry and lonely. If it's come to sitting here by yourself, drinking the local bourbon, that's sad."

"It's sort of mandatory to own a bottle of Woodford County's finest. Everyone is expected to be a staunch supporter of the Bourbon Trail. I've seen more unopened than open bottles. I hadn't indulged since the last time we had mint juleps with the Eberts but I've been enjoying having a sip now and then.

By the way, you know, that thing I told you about being a consultant. I wasn't supposed to tell anybody. You can't say anything."

"Whom would I tell?" she asked with a defensive tone, then lightened things by turning to Sheldon and saying, "Victor must mean you big fellow."

"I know. Agent Wilkins made such a deal about it."

Sheldon snorted in response.

"You always used to be able to talk to me about things. Victor, you still can."

"I know I can. I'm out of practice with this stuff."

"What stuff? DEA stuff? Or being with me stuff?" Tracy asked.

"Both, I'm afraid."

"You don't have to be afraid," she said, almost sounding seductive.

After dinner, they cleaned up. Vic was assigned the glass casserole with the twice-baked cheese. Enchiladas could be the test-kitchen standard for spray-on oil substitutes. He didn't need to shower again but the kitchen needed to be wiped down. He was surprised by the amount of dirt on counters he assumed would be clean until he remembered all of the cabins, sheds, and boathouses that had been torn down in less than nine hours.

"Red or white?" Vic asked before they went back outside.

"Red, it's getting a little chilly," she decided.

After a few minutes, Vic reappeared on the porch with two glasses and an uncorked bottle of pinot noir. Carrying their glasses, they walked Sheldon down toward the water. He established a new territory for himself as if there might be rival dogs showing up to detect his scent. All of the neighborhood pets were long gone with their displaced owners. Vic tied the end of Sheldon's lengthy leash around a porch pillar before Tracy and he settled into side-by-side chairs. Sheldon managed to squeeze between them. Other than a couple of deep sighs, sighs that sounded like satisfaction more than regret, all three of them were quiet for several minutes.

"Do you think we'll ever get back together?" Tracy said like she was afraid of being overheard.

Passing up the obvious and the certain to be provoking "we are together." retort, Vic said, "I can answer related questions more easily. Not that you asked but, yes, I still care about you. Do I still love you? Well I must because somewhere I read that the opposite of love isn't hate. It's not caring. But, I'm not ready to answer the question about getting back together."

Tracy was quiet. It was dark enough that he couldn't judge whether she was angry or upset or relieved or what.

"I understand," she said. "That's what I would have wanted you to say. If you'd given me an outright 'yes' I might not have been able to ask you my next question."

"What's that?"

"If I promise to leave early tomorrow morning, can I stay over?"

"I knew I washed the sheets for the other bedroom for some reason. Let's finish our wine before I try to locate the biggest pillow," he answered.

They continued talking for a couple of hours and managed to get half way through their second bottle of wine. Sometime after midnight, Tracy and he went to their separate beds in their separate bedrooms. Sheldon busied himself trying out everything softer than the wood floor as his potential bed.

35

THE SQUAWKING OF ANCIENT PLUMBING JOLTED VIC INTO CONSCIOUSNESS. It took him a moment to remember that Tracy was sleeping over. He hadn't heard Sheldon and Tracy leave or return from her ritualistic morning power walk. While Tracy was showering, an exhausted Sheldon had settled in for a nap on the couch he had staked claim to the night before. Apparently the forced march had rendered him too tired to grant Vic his usual over the top, jubilant morning greeting.

After refilling Sheldon's empty bowl with the mandatory flavored water, Vic heated the counter-top grill and proceeded to meticulously follow the directions on the Aunt Jemima pancake mix. He was preparing half of his repertoire of guilty secret recipes, the other being the one for fudge on the back of the marshmallow cream jar. He timed the pancakes, eggs over-easy, and slices of microwaved bacon to coincide with Tracy's emergence from the shower. She joined him at the two-stooled counter. She had a pink glow and Vic recognized the scent she always wore ... some kind of floral combination he couldn't identify. Even in one of

Greg's castoff robes, Tracy reactivated stirrings, some of which were feelings of regret.

"What did I do to deserve this?" Tracy asked.

"You wore out Sheldon and let me sleep in. Breakfast seemed like the least I could do."

"I'd prefer it if you were in my debt," she answered.

"I'm afraid to ask but why is that?"

"The national society's biggest breast cancer meeting I go to every year starts tomorrow and before you ask once again, 'No, there is no difference in cancer treatment based on boob size.' Since you're no longer staying at a motel I was thinking Sheldon would prefer staying with you rather than the kennel for the next few days."

"Getting to keep Sheldon makes up for stealing my joke."

"After five years in a row, I think your so-called joke is supposed to become part of the public domain."

On her way out, Tracy dropped off a half-case of raspberry water, a supply of Sheldon's custom food, and a spare leash. The final whiff of her perfume bothered Vic to a greater extent than her departing kiss, validating that men's sensors for seductive smells are more erogenous than their left cheeks.

Vic took Sheldon outside for a final bathroom break before locking him in the cottage and leaving for the pharmacy.

CLAUDIA AND HE BOTH ARRIVED EARLY. This was the morning of the special sale. Claudia told him not to pour a coffee but to head for the clinic because Zach was in an accident.

Lynda greeted Vic outside the curtained area that surrounded one of two hospital beds in the room that served as the equivalent of an E.R.

"Zach was out on a run. It was barely light when he was forced off the road. He's okay I think. He's covered in scratches and he had to have four stitches behind his left ear. I'm hoping he doesn't have a concussion. He says that as he was falling he saw an orange rolling by. That seems strange. Anyhow, Stephanie is with him now."

"Did he see enough to know who did it?" Vic asked.

"He's not sure. It was somebody in an old truck. Zach says he was running right along the edge of the road but that the truck swerved at him. He says he was lucky that it was a place where there was a drop off. It was at the long stretch of limestone right before South Fork Road."

Stephanie came out from behind the curtain. She was crying. Seeing the look on Lynda's face, she said, "It's okay. Zach is fine. It's just me."

Lynda went in anyway. Vic stopped Stephanie and asked what was wrong.

"I don't understand why everyone has decided to hate Zach. I'm not supposed to be his friend anymore. I'm not supposed to talk to him or anything. There's some sort of unwritten rule. No one is allowed to go into the store even. Should I go see the principal about this, about this morning, I mean?"

"Why don't I do that?" Vic volunteered.

She seemed relieved and rushed off to try to make it to her first class. Lynda and Zach emerged from behind the curtain. Zach seemed in better shape than she did.

"The nurse practitioner said that Zach shouldn't go to school until tomorrow. I'm taking him home. Or maybe he'd be safer if I drove him to my folks," Lynda said.

"No Mom. What would I do all day at Grandma's? I'll go to the store with you. Maybe I can help out with the sale."

Lynda looked at Vic helplessly as if she expected him to argue with Zach. Instead he smiled, shrugged his shoulders and shook his head 'yes' indicating that he thought Zach had a good idea.

"Oh, all right," she said. "We'll see you at the store."

Vic drove to the school. A student receptionist helped him find the principal's office.

"Thanks for seeing me Mr. Cox," Vic said.

"How may I help you?" he said in a crisp manner.

Vic speculated as to how many times a week Mr. Cox said those exact words. He further wondered how often the people he said them to received help. Vic hoped to be one of them.

"I'm here concerning Zach Ebert. I'm his uncle."

"Oh, I heard he got hurt this morning. How is he?" Mr. Cox asked, abandoning his authoritarian tone.

"He's doing okay. He's recuperating with his mom who had to work today at the pharmacy. He'll be back tomorrow. He has a note."

"Sure. I'm glad he's okay," Mr. Cox said, folding his hands in front of him on the desk.

"I learned from one of Zach's classmates that he's being ostracized … shunned, if you understand what I mean, by the other students. The person I talked to didn't know why and I don't care why. Shunning is hurtful. But trying to hit him with a truck is by definition attempted murder."

"I'd heard rumors. Unless there's bullying, our office can't get involved. I will try to do something about this, though. Have the police been notified?"

"Zach refused to let his mom call them. I think he thought that it would make matters worse here at school."

"Of course. Can you share any details with me?"

Vic told him what he knew.

"Wait right here if you've got a few minutes," Cox said.

The next thing Vic heard was a harsh screech and then static coming from a speaker somewhere behind him. Then there was a perfunctory throat clearing. Cox began to speak.

"This is Mr. Cox. It has been brought to my attention that an unidentified person or persons in an older model truck forced Zach Ebert off the road this morning. Zach was taken to the hospital but is okay and should return to class tomorrow. If any of you have information concerning who might have done this, you should notify me. He'll be back in class tomorrow but is able to see people if they stop by Ebert Drugs after school."

"I'm impressed," Vic said when Mr. Cox walked back into his office.

"I know. I'm young enough that I still remember how useless my principal seemed to be. There were kids who needed his help but he was invisible. The only time students heard from him was if there was a candy sale or if an ice storm or something was going to cause us to dismiss early. I'll be on the lookout for even subtle bullying, should anything continue. There are always students who act like prison 'trustees'. Plus, if there's anything else you think I can do to help, let me know."

"I will. Thanks a lot," Vic said.

BY THE TIME VIC GOT TO THE STORE, THE SALE WAS IN FULL SWING. Julie had organized the displays and had designed and paid for the signage. Much of what was on sale was overstock, but a wholesaler provided some new gift items, candy, and cosmetics, all on approval, that the store priced at just above cost. The customers later that day seemed to welcome the chance to speak with Lynda in this informal setting. Some of them had been dreading the awkwardness of their first interactions with their recently widowed acquaintance.

About mid-afternoon, Stephanie and a couple of her friends came in. They surrounded Zach in a tight triangle. He entertained them by insisting that they each needed to buy an atrocious neon green backpack or, if not, some other equally gaudy piece of merchandise. The three giggling girls each made a point of hugging him as they headed to the register to make their obligatory purchases. Stephanie earnestly kissed him before showing him the ugly backpack she would buy.

As if a floodgate had opened, for the rest of the afternoon, Zach seemed never to be alone. He used his guise as salesman to approach many of his fellow students. Their presence suggested that the shunning might be abating. It remained to be seen whether the parents of the teens followed suit.

36

VIC HAD A MESSAGE FROM JULIE. She arranged to meet him at the Steak 'N Shake in Lawrence. He was told to be there at 6:30 and was supposed to pretend to be surprised to see her. The message was directive but he wasn't resentful. Her life was centered in Burgoyne and she was in her marriage for the long haul. She had more to lose.

He went back to the cabin to let Sheldon out, feed him, let him out again, shower, and change. An oversized dog and a white pharmacist's smock might make Vic's arrival at Steak 'N Shake too memorable. He was trying not to assess the impact of his continuing to see Julie on what might or might not happen with Tracy. It didn't help that Tracy had left him a note, detailing how he should move her washed sheets and towel over to the dryer, telling him that he'd find the coffee carafe in the dishwasher, and reminding him, with an accompanying smiley face, that she preferred creamy Jif not crunchy Skippy.

Tracy ended her three-Post-it epistle with a promise that she wouldn't have time to call.

VIC ARRIVED AT THE RESTAURANT EARLY. He went ahead and got seated at a booth that was visible from the hostess area. Julie, equally adaptive, saw him and feigned surprise before asking if he minded her joining him.

"I thought about objecting," Vic said once the hostess had left them.

"That possibility had crossed my mind," she answered with a tight smile.

They politely described their days. Vic talked about Zach's experiences at the store after she left and the reaffirmation that the youth of Burgoyne, at least many of them, weren't dragging the town down the road to perdition. She recounted the rest of her day after she left the sale in the hands of others. She then insisted that he inspect the results from a new manicurist who had worked her in. They each ordered salads with dressings on the side. He also asked for their steak burger ... a meatier version of a hamburger, at least taste-wise.

He had just taken the first bite of his salad when Julie said something that affirmed where he suspected this rendezvous might be headed, "I thought about coming by last night. It looked like you had another visitor. A Tracy-person, maybe?"

"Yes, the Tracy-person, " he said.

"So are you ... have you ... are you getting back together?"

"You know as much as I do. I think we'll remain friends. I suspect she believes that there's some possibility we'll eventually be together," Vic explained.

"And why exactly would she believe that?" Julie interrupted.

"We did not have an acrimonious divorce. We are not mad at each other. On the other hand, we both know that there are reasons we shouldn't get back together and that some of those may be insurmountable. Let me put it in present tense. We have not gotten back together."

"I guess I thought we'd be exclusive, you and I," Julie said.

"You, me, and Johnny, you mean?"

"I think you know what I mean."

"As to exclusivity," Vic began again. "Tracy and I are not intimate. In case you don't already know, Tracy spent the night. I didn't kiss her good night. I didn't tuck her in. We didn't make love."

Julie said, "All good."

HE LEFT HIS CAR IN THE 24-HOUR WAL-MART PARKING LOT. She took back roads, asking Vic to slouch down whenever her Jag met oncoming vehicles. She explained that Johnny had a meeting in Bowling Green with a group of political cronies who always drank so much that they had to stay over. The Laine's front gate responded to the programmed signal and they drove directly into the garage attached to the sprawling, two-story house.

"First, let's ride," she said.

"Of course. Riding horses. That explains the clandestine meeting," Vic answered.

"Well, let me show you my horses. I'm afraid we're not dressed to go riding."

"I know I'm not," he said.

Hand in hand, they followed a brick sidewalk to the nearby stable complex. It was a

large building, much too big for the ten or twelve
horses that he saw. It smelled mildly stable-like and
to Vic the mixed aromas of horse manure, leather,
and straw were not at all unpleasant.

She reminded him how her brother Timmy
managed the whole operation. She further told him
how they were in the midst of negotiations with
another horse farm that would add three more
promising stallions.

Without warning, Julie pulled off her jeans
to reveal thong panties. She climbed the wooden
fence of a stall and adroitly swung onto the back of
an obliging horse all the while looking directly into
Vic's eyes. She leaned slightly forward and rocked
back and forth. Her mouth was open and her eyes
were half shut as she seemed to pleasure herself.
She unbuttoned her blouse, one button for every
four rocking motions

She said, "Are you here to watch me play
sexual solitaire or are you willing to join me over on
that inviting pile of hay?"

"Why should the horse have all the fun? Get
over here," Vic said trying to avoid some of the
prickliness by spreading his jacket, shirt, and pants
on the hay.

Whether or not Julie was trying to make him
forget about Tracy, the outcome was the same. They
both received some small scratches but he couldn't
blame the hay for tooth marks on his right shoulder.
She suggested they clean up before going back for
his car. She slid into the shower. When it was his
turn, he indulged himself to the point that he began
to worry about the capacity of the Laine water

heater. The towels were considerably softer and more luxurious than the ones he was accustomed to at the Ebert cottage.

He donned a heavy robe that Julie had left for him and went into the large family room with sliding doors that provided a view of the river. Julie walked into the room and set two glasses of wine on the kidney-shaped glass-topped table. He was seated on a long white sofa. He paid no attention to the arrival of wine. Julie saw that he was distracted by a telescope mounted on a tripod by the window so she invited him to try it. He focused on the cottage's outdoor light across the river and nearly a mile away.

"Not bad, huh?" she asked.

"So this is how you keep track of me?"

"That wasn't my intent last night," she said. "I was lonely and thinking of coming by. I checked to see if you were home ... if the cabin lights were on. Please let's don't get into this again."

"Okay," he agreed. "Are we talking or drinking?"

"How about we smoke a little something before we do either one? We can go through the sliders onto the balcony."

She expertly rolled a joint and handed it to Vic. He looked at it as if she'd handed him a turd. That didn't deter Julie from lighting it and taking a puff. She pulled the smoke in deeply, waiting ten seconds before exhaling.

"I think we ought to share this," she said.

"It's been almost a year. I'm not sure my lungs and throat are up to it."

"I doubt you'll notice," she said, handing him the joint.

He surmised that the anti-nausea effect of the marijuana must have overcome the irritating harshness of the smoke. He was soon reminded what a "high" was like, and as they passed it back and forth he muttered, "Oh, wow."

She giggled and said, "I can't believe you said that oh cliché master."

"I'll come up with something more profound but less spontaneous later."

"I hope not. I'd rather we enjoy this, banality-laden or not."

He pulled her closer and kissed her gently on the neck. Then he kissed her not so gently on the lips and moved his hands beneath her robe that was a smaller version of the one she'd loaned him.

"Fishing cottage single beds are nice. Hay can be romantic. But how about we try a real bed for a little variety," she whispered between kisses and caresses.

"Yeah, variety would be good. This is getting boring," he said as they held hands and walked toward the bedroom she shared with Johnny.

"Let's create a few more 'oh wows'" she said as she turned off the light.

37

JULIE AND VIC AWAKENED BEFORE SIX A.M. They laughed and nuzzled and poked each other like teenagers during the drive to pick up his car from the nearly empty Wal-Mart lot. She waited and watched as he cleaned off the overnight dew from his windows, blew him a kiss, and roared away.

Vic drove as fast as the Ford could manage on the curvy two-lane roads. It was not engineered for grand prix handling. He took every shortcut he knew back to the cottage. Sheldon was prancing with his leash in his mouth when Vic, who changed into running attire in under two minutes, emerged from his bedroom. Sheldon impatiently allowed him to attach the leash before he pulled Vic, stumbling toward the porch. Once outside, Sheldon relieved himself against an ornate birdbath, announcing to the robins and their brethren that the territory wasn't theirs alone.

Vic didn't have time to go long so it was a perfect day to run with Sheldon. Like all greyhounds, Sheldon was hard-wired for short bursts of speed. Fifty yards at top speed was pushing it. Three hundred yards, much slower, was Sheldon's limit. This would be speed training for Vic.

Sheldon loped by Vic's side as they ran up the lane to the paved secondary road. At the intersection Vic pulled him toward the left where the road's shoulder was not restricted by limestone cliffs unlike the southern route toward town. One large rock outcropping they passed had a graffiti marred entrance that led to a tiny grotto. A four-foot deep cavity does not a cave make but Greg and he used to pretend that it did. As kids they huddled inside it once for most of an hour to wait out a thunderstorm. The boys left, unmolested by the twenty-three spiders they counted, grateful that the shelter had been rendered both fly- and mosquito-free.

Sheldon made Vic run faster than race pace. This would translate to performance benefit but significant soreness. Microscopic muscle tears, he'd been told, produce both phenomena. "No pain, no gain." has a scientific basis.

They turned around at the limestone cavity. If anything the dog seemed to pull harder on the way back, like a horse returning to the stable. When they reached the cottage, both were panting.

Once they'd caught their breath Sheldon pulled Vic down toward the river. He yanked his master toward a small pinkish mound, nestled next to the dock. "Sheldon. Stay," Vic said with an authoritative voice Sheldon rarely heard.

The greyhound obeyed, cocking his head as if to indicate he was supposed to be in charge when the two ran together. Vic took one of the plastic bags he carried to collect Sheldon's poop and cleanly scooped up a fist-sized ball of raw hamburger. Sheldon looked longingly at the prize before providing an equally massive deposit of his own. There was no logical reason for uncooked meat to be left in the yard. The demolition crew ate their lunches on site. There was no evidence that they'd done any cooking. Besides, hamburger left there overnight wouldn't look that fresh.

PATRICE RESPONDED TO VIC'S PLEA TO MEET HIM IN THE STORE PARKING LOT.

"Do me a favor and have the lab do a toxicology screening on this meat. It could be nothing but I found this behind the cottage. It's almost like somebody hoped Sheldon would get into it."

"Sheldon? Who's Sheldon?"

"Sheldon's my greyhound," Vic said.

"I see. And exactly how do I justify my request this time?"

"I suppose you could tell them the truth and say that a paranoid friend believes that evil forces are out to kill his dog."

"I'd be better off saying it was sitting out on a table next to some drugs I confiscated."

"Lie if you must, Agent Wilkins. Stick with me. You're getting good at this."

"Do you want me to do this or not?" she asked with a wink, reminding him that their friendship could at times overcome her "by the books" approach.

"Yes I do, Patrice. And I do appreciate the favor. And thanks for meeting me outside the store."

"What are you doing with ... with Sheldon, is it?"

"I have a customer who has business in Louisville. She's agreed to take him to our kennel."

THE PREVIOUS DAY'S SALE WAS A SUCCESS. Nonetheless, Lynda and Claudia were having a pity party when Vic walked through the back door. He suggested a SWOT analysis ... a process he learned in the mini-MBA that the DEA required every in-charge agent to complete. Even if SWOT doesn't help in decision-making it can show people the worst things that can happen. Sometimes even worst-case scenarios are events that many businesses can survive. Furthermore, Lynda and he would have the time to go through it when they made their trip to Lexington to visit a ScriptCoMart franchise. Hal was to come in at noon, a carry over from when Greg used to go to Rotary Club luncheons.

Lynda and he quickly went through the exercise and came up with the following on their drive to the west side of Lexington:
"S"...Strengths: Claudia; the business is running in the black; the family name is a recognized brand; there is a loyal but slightly shrunken customer base.

"W"…Weaknesses: There is no pharmacist who is in charge over the long term; there are no financial resources to be able to draw on nor is there any inclination to expand; there are no known potential buyers if one wanted to sell out.

"O"…Opportunities: The pharmacy could become an affiliate of ScriptCoMart; the pharmacy proper could be converted to a soda fountain-sundries shop.

"T"…Threats: Wal-Mart, Walgreens, and other chains with full service and convenience are siphoning off business; Ali is aggressive in usurping the nursing home business; there is an ostracism by the revitalization leaders and their allies.

Lynda and he had no sooner finished their SWOT exercise than they pulled into the parking lot of the small stand-alone pharmacy. The pharmacist was a perky second-generation Vietnamese woman with the requisite straight-black hair and sparkling eyes. She had a commanding presence inconsistent with her five-foot two-inch height. She warmly welcomed them to her ScriptCoMart store and immediately gave them an abbreviated version of her life story. It ended with, "My husband is a medical rep for a pharmaceutical company and with this arrangement, we're both off weekends."

"Are you familiar with the Burgoyne area?" Lynda asked.

"Oh, sure. I've lived in this part of the state most of my life," she said.

"There's only one other independent pharmacy in our county, and it's not in Burgoyne. There's a Wal-Mart and many people work in

Lexington or Frankfort and use pharmacies there, " Lynda said.

"Yes. I think two patients had their scripts transferred to me from Ebert Drugs last week," she said, her expression displaying the next best thing to an apology.

"That's another story," Lynda said. "This is a lot smaller than our store but maybe I can do something else with the space."

It was apparent that the pharmacist was satisfied with her situation and was a good spokesperson for ScriptCoMart's compromise between chain and independent pharmacy practices. She explained the services and costs of doing business as a franchisee to Lynda before saying, "You know that the problem in finding a pharmacist won't go away. Most of the new graduates want to live in big cities. But other than that, this sounds like a good fit for you.

Are you going to be the owner of record Mr. Fye?"

"No. Lynda will be."

"That won't work. ScriptCoMart requires that franchisees be pharmacists."

"Any exceptions?" Lynda asked.

"None. Sorry to say."

As they got into the car Lynda said, "Scratch ScriptCoMart from 'opportunities."

She was quiet for a few minutes as they left the outskirts of Lexington before continuing, "Yesterday, in spite of the way his day and my day started, was the happiest I've seen Zach for a long time. I wish he was a senior. It would make the decisions easier. We could just move."

"How so?" I asked.

"Zach is unhappy but he's reluctant if not adamant about our not moving."

"Even after yesterday? I sort of assumed that somebody's parents were behind the shunning routine … I mean, given that he and the store were supposedly off limits."

"That was a part of it. Zach shared with me that some of the other students think he's an informant, his dad having been a pharmacist and all. Greg used to give drug talks at the school. And, Zach doesn't use drugs, or that's what he tells me. So right away, you know, students who are druggies don't trust people who aren't fellow users."

"What kind of drugs are we talking about, " Vic asked.

"I asked the same question," Lynda said. "Zach told me that the kids have no trouble getting some high grade pot. There's some coke use among the richest kids, but it's mostly marijuana and, as you'd imagine, alcohol."

"Really? Burgoyne isn't on the DEA radar screen. Not that we didn't assume kids will display anything other than normal rebellious tendencies but the drug distribution networks that we knew about didn't include this county."

"Zach says that lots of kids regularly drive up to Cincinnati. They buy enough for themselves and a few friends. I guess the stuff is so potent that kids have no trouble staying within the one-ounce limit for their personal use. They're sophisticated when it comes to the risks involved. Risks of going to jail, that is."

"And Zach doesn't use anything?"

"He says he tried vaping it once but that his asthma kicked in", she said. "He generally has no breathing problems when he runs or does anything physical as long as he remembers to use a puff from his bronchodilator. For a couple of days after his marijuana experimentation, he says he needed two puffs and he didn't dare try to work out. I think the idea that anything would keep him from running scared him."

"That's not a bad thing," Vic offered. "So the kids are vaping oil with THC or what exactly?"

"I'm not sure but whatever it is doesn't have the marijuana smell or cause the kids eyes to turn red. The parents who find the pens assume their kids are vaping nicotine."

Lynda continued, "You ought to know that Zach, well both of us, but, anyway, Zach is worried about you."

"About me?"

"He says you've been vague when you talk about Will. He's afraid that somebody's out to get all of Dad's friends," she said.

"I can't say that the thought hasn't crossed my mind but I'll be fine. I guess we're worried about each other," Vic said.

38

VIC ANNOUNCED TO HAL HE'D TAKE OVER. Hal had filled in a lot during the shortened weekend of fishing and for Will's funeral. Vic wanted to make up some of the extra hours so that Lynda wouldn't need to start paying overtime. Besides, Hal valued his time off more than the money. He had dropped Lynda by her house and before driving to the pharmacy.

"Vic, I'm glad you stopped back early. I've had a hell of a time. Some kid or somebody turned off a bunch of circuit breakers. I didn't think, nobody thought, that there was a row of these at end of the alley inside a big grey box. The circuits are there with all the meters. They're coded by address. Whoever did it flipped every breaker. We each thought it was only our own store for a while."

"I suppose the computers all went down," Vic said knowing that they had but still wanting to be sympathetic.

"Yes, the computer and the registers. We had cash but couldn't run charges. Our clerk got short changed. A couple of other stores did too. Maybe it was the woman who scammed us who shut off the breakers," Hal continued.

"I'll finish out your shift if that's alright. It sounds like you could use the relief," Vic said.

"Great. I'll stay with you until we get caught up. Claudia's not here this afternoon and it took me a while to remember how to reboot the computer. I think we'll be okay in an hour or so," Hal said.

"Thanks, but I hope you'll feel free to go once we're on top of things."

"Sure will," Hal said. "Oh, you might want to look at this. I'll let you pass on the 'good news' to Lynda."

He handed me a notice from the town council. It announced that later in the summer the segment of the courthouse square in front of the pharmacy, the principal business access, would be the first phase designated for repaving. Parking would be eliminated permanently on both sides of the street and a wide bike-path would be created. Parking would be available on parallel streets and in a city lot that was supposed to be completed before the repaving began.

"This might be great for tourists, assuming there will be any such folks. What about the parents of a sick kid needing an antibiotic in a hurry? They're not going to wait for us to deliver. We might as well shut the place down." Vic said, loud enough for the whole store to hear. Fortunately there were no customers, but the clerk got a worried look.

"That was my take on it too," Hal said.

It was almost five o'clock before Vic had a chance to check for messages. He had two that had arrived minutes apart. The first was from Tracy.

The second was from Julie. This reminded him of a time when he was in high school. He had written inside a history book cover the names of two girls, each name in its own heart, each followed by a question mark. A friend who borrowed the book thought it would be funny to show it to both of them. Vic got the book back with big lipstick 'X's' across both hearts. One would think that after twenty some years he might have figured out how to avoid such conflicts and the potential for subsequent regret.

"Hi Julie, I assume it's always okay to call you on your cell."

"Yes, but let's be careful, Vic. I am talking to the same Vic who left his sunglasses on the nightstand, aren't I. That would be the nightstand on Johnny's side of the bed that I'm talking about. "

"Okay. Okay," he said laughingly, assuming that she'd found them before Johnny returned.

"Would you like me to drop off your glasses tonight? It's a special service that I provide for all of my friends."

"I don't think that'll work. I'm here until 7:00 and then the sheriff is going to drop by the cabin."

"The sheriff?"

"It's something to do with the fact that I found Will and he has some sort of long report that I need to read and if necessary make corrections and then initial or sign it several times. I'm a little worried that he's going to try and prolong his visit. He said he'd bring the beer."

"I'll put your glasses some place for safe keeping … maybe on top of my nightstand," she said.

"Okay, bye."

Vic hoped his conversation with Tracy would be as uncomplicated. She seemed increasingly lonely and seemed to be requiring more of his attention. He knew, without her saying so directly, that David might not be making her the center of his life. She wasn't likely to complain to her friends at work, many of whom were both their co-workers, about his breaking off an affair. And a few of her other friends were married to guys Vic still saw in Louisville. Vic wanted to be supportive but not a surrogate girlfriend.

Obviously relying on her caller i.d. Tracy answered, "Hi Victor. Why are you calling so late? I though you were off this afternoon."

"I was but I filled in, I am filling in, for Hal. What's up?"

"I'm doing fine. I needed to hear your voice. I'll be pulling a twelve hour shift, seven to seven, and was finishing up my patient assessments."

"Sounds tiring, Tracy. How do you keep it up?"

"Yep. Tonight … I'll be queen of vital signs, i.v. pump alarm resetting, and urine volume measurement. Tomorrow … I'll take over for Dr. Oz and explain how TLC cures cancer, heart disease, and tennis elbow."

Vic told Tracy about Lynda and Zach and the store and the upcoming meeting with the sheriff. Then he said, "I had a customer who was going to

Louisville drop Sheldon off at our kennel. I figured I'd save you the trip."

She said, "I guess that means you weren't thinking of coming to Louisville this weekend. There's an art show Sunday."

"Probably not this weekend. I'd planned to …"

"See Julie?" she interrupted.

"See Julie?" he repeated.

"You don't have to pretend. I saw the way she looked at you at the funeral, the way she looked at us. I have no right to judge, but Flavor of the Month Julie? Come on."

"What makes you think …?"

"Stop it," she said. "The other night I suspected there was somebody else. You were acting distant or maybe overly cautious. Please don't ruin things by lying about it. Okay?"

"Okay," he said.

"Back to why I called you, I need something for my coffee table. Sure you can't make it for the art show?" she asked.

"I'd like to but I can't. It's got nothing to do with her," he said.

"You can say 'Julie'. It's alright."

He laughed and said, "I need to start closing up."

"And I need to help check on a patient they just wheeled in. You know I'm not mad don't you?"

"I didn't think you were," he said.

39

Vic contacted Patrice Wilkins before his appointment. He could always give her a debriefing later, on the off chance he learned anything of relevance from the sheriff.

"Patrice?"

"Vic. The meat tested positive for warfarin. Probably anticoagulant from d-CON not medical sources."

"Did they give you any indication of how much?"

"They estimated that there was enough to kill a horse, if horses were carnivorous."

"Whoever planted this stuff must have hoped I'd get to see Sheldon salivating and peeing blood, fading away as he bled out internally. As if finding him dead wouldn't have been bad enough."

"It'd be tough to track d-CON sales. Every farm and stable in the county uses it to control the rodent population."

"I know, Patrice. I know."

"And there's something else, but I'll let you go ahead," she said.

"First, I guess, is the DNA. Was there enough dried saliva on the cigarette to make an identification? I know results take a lot longer than what people think from watching TV crime shows."

Patrice said, "As it turns out we got reasonable results. Unfortunately, we weren't able to make a positive match with anyone we already have in our system or with data from the FBI, Interpol, or our other law enforcement sources.

Given your lack of official authority, I doubt whether any thing we might have learned would even be admissible anyway. Most defense attorneys would make sure that we couldn't introduce it. I can hear it now. 'So this private citizen took the evidence from the crime scene because he thought the sheriff wouldn't take care of it properly.'"

"I thought of all that later," Vic said.

"Wait, I do have more. The tobacco varieties and the filter are consistent with all of the brands manufactured by Phillip Morris. That's not definitive but at least we're on the right track. The cigarette could be a Parliament like the cigarettes taken in that one robbery. Or it could be from an L & M, or a Chesterfield, a Marlboro, or a Benson and Hedges or a... I'm sure you get the picture. It was too thick to be a Virginia Slim. Like that'll narrow things down a lot. Maybe Sherlock Holmes with his microscope and chemistry set could identify criminals by tobacco fragments but our lab usually can't. Most of the time the best we can do is to corroborate evidence or rule out certain brands."

"Any suspects for the robberies?" he asked, hoping the DEA had uncovered something helpful ... something he didn't already know. Vic treaded gingerly, being careful not to overstep his role as a consultant.

"Not really. The only insane thing we noted from the inventory we took was that some phenobarbital was missing from the third robbery," Patrice said.

"Jeez. So our suspect either has epilepsy or he doesn't have a clue what he's looking for other than the oxycodone," he said.

"Yes. That's our take on it too. Maybe we can pick-up on something more useful with the next robbery," she said.

"I don't think there's going to be a next robbery. I contend these so-called robberies were all staged as a cover up for Greg's murder," Vic said, announcing a premise he'd been reflecting on for the last few days.

"Interesting. You could be right. But the DEA isn't prepared to assign motive yet. You probably ought to keep your 'grassy knoll' or any other speculative hypotheses to yourself. Not that I would rule out something along those lines but we seem to be a long way from having evidence to back us on any of that."

"I know. Here's what I've got for you," Vic said. "Everything that I remember about the DEA take on Woodford County still seems to be true. That is, I haven't come across any strong evidence of organized drug traffic. Drugs, mostly marijuana, are easily available to anybody at the high school. Vaping seems to be big. I understand that kids make road trips to the Cincinnati area to get what they need. It sounds as casual and risk free as driving to Tennessee for fireworks."

"What about alcohol?" she asked.

"Woodford County isn't dry. Sales to minors don't seem to be a law enforcement priority. I doubt that parents lock up their liquor. Yes, most kids have no trouble getting alcohol."

"Opioids?"

"Nothing extraordinary that I've been able to pick up on but come on, these three robberies wouldn't have much impact on supply on the street," he answered. "My technician tells me that she can't remember being presented with altered or forged prescriptions."

"I guess neither of us has anything new. Keep plugging along. Sorry I can't help more but I am working on it," she said as she hung up.

40

VIC WENT INTO THE ALCOVE OFF THE KITCHEN. Greg's hand drawn map of landmarks up and down the river was lying on the desk.

It was his cave. Hope he found the damned thing.

THE SHERIFF RAPPED ON THE SCREEN DOOR. Seeing Vic sitting in the desk chair, he let himself in. He delivered the promised beer and the two of them moved to the ancient, creaking lounge chairs in the living area. They shared President Obama's presumption that beer and comfortable chairs could make conversation between potential adversaries less awkward.

"What's going on Ralph? What can I help you with?"

"Not a lot. For openers, you can go back to the island anytime you'd like. My men and I combed every square inch out there. There are worn down areas ... old paths. I think kids go out there sometimes and I know people fish out there. We found a couple of lures snagged up in a tree, an empty disposable lighter, some other cigarette filters that hadn't degraded. I'm not sure they ever break down. And that's it. Nothing suggesting a crime. So, officially, there's no reason to treat it as a crime scene.

Oh, and the lab couldn't get prints or anything for a DNA sample off that cigarette you found. We're still going with 'accidental death,'" the sheriff said.

Vic waited to see if Ralph would say the words ... "This case is closed."... but they weren't forthcoming. He saw nothing to gain by arguing or otherwise leaving Billings with the impression that he knew of DNA data to the contrary.

"Well, that's good, I guess. You said 'for openers' when you started talking. Is there something else?"

"Do you know about the man in Lawrence who was reported to have died from carbon monoxide poisoning ... a suicide in his own garage?"

"Todd somebody." Vic said. He hoped Billings had a point to make.

"Yes, Todd Ertz. Anyway, the county coroner has informed me that she found a needle mark and lethal levels of an opioid in his blood. There were no other needle marks. The blood levels were low enough that he didn't show tolerance. Somebody wanted his death to look like a suicide."

"And why are you telling me this?" Vic asked.

"Todd Ertz was the maintenance man who worked at the motel where you stayed. The one who left so suddenly that morning. Possibly the guy who was harassing you."

"You're not thinking I killed him, are you?"

"It crossed my mind. Hal confirmed that you were here at the cottage that night. He told me you had company. After the company left, he talked to you. About ten minutes after that your lights went out. Nobody came or went until morning."

"Thanks for letting me know. I never thought that whoever was doing it had picked me at random to harass. Somebody was orchestrating all the crap he was pulling. I guess I'll never know who was giving Ertz his orders."

Neither spoke for several minutes. Rather than breaking the silence, Billings handed Vic another beer and took one for himself. Vic knew there must be something else.

"How's Lynda doing?" Ralph finally asked.

"About how you'd expect. She's still processing things. The incident with Zach is troubling her a lot, as it would any parent.

I hope she hasn't driven out to where it happened. A few seconds earlier or later and Zach would have had no room to get himself off the road and out of the way."

"Zach wasn't very cooperative with us. He didn't report it in the first place. When I did talk to him, he couldn't tell us anything about the truck or whomever he thought might be driving it. I talked to several of his friends from school. No one admits to knowing who did it," Billings said in a fruitless effort to let Vic know what a capable law officer he was.

"Do you in all honesty think it was kids that time of the morning? It happened about 90 minutes before their first class period."

"Well if it wasn't kids it was probably somebody headed for work who didn't see him ... or maybe they saw him but were too scared to stop. People who don't stop in those situations are people who have a history of driving infractions ... maybe an OWI, or several moving violations, or no insurance, or something along those lines," the sheriff explained.

Vic decided the sheriff either hadn't put in a lot of time on the investigation or he knew more than he was willing to let on. In either case, he decided it would be useless to keep pressing. So he said, "I'll let her know you're working on it if it comes up."

"Are you planning on staying on or is she hiring someone else or is she even going to try to keep the store going?" he asked, turning to his real reason for asking about Lynda.

Vic wondered exactly how much of anything he said was going to be relayed to Ralph's Burgoyne cronies the instant he left. Vic continued to be as obtuse as he could get away with without sounding uncooperative, "She's still upset. I think she's trying to figure things out. I'm able to stay here as long as she needs me."

"Any chance that you'll have to stay down here in the Ebert's cottage much longer? It might be wise to move some place else. It's going to get busy down here. There'll be lots of workmen coming and going. I'm not sure we, uh, the department, can guarantee your belongings will be safe down here."

"Am I missing something? Lynda still owns this place. As far as I know she hasn't sold it," Vic said, trying to keep the agitation out of his voice.

"I probably shouldn't be telling you this (interpreted, I was instructed to tell you this) but the Town Council, as you've heard, has decided to condemn the place if they have to," he said.

"I didn't know it was official with the Council?"

"Well, some of their members," he answered. "They're thinking that soon you'll have some outages and some temporary disruption of services. The contractors and the utility companies are running new gas, water, and sewer lines out here within a couple of weeks."

"The water and sewer lines should have nothing to do with the cabin's well or septic system. I can get by with interrupted electric for a few days. There's no air conditioning in this place anyway. Let the Council know that I appreciate their concern."

"No need to get angry. I'm trying to give you a 'heads up'. I probably need to be going."

"Hey, Ralph. I'm not blaming you. I would hate to see Lynda forced into anything. And I know that's not your intent."

Vic accepted Ralph's half-empty bottle, shook his hand, and walked with him to his cruiser. Vic waited until the sheriff had driven away before muttering. "What a joke! Billings will be calling in his report to his politically supportive friends before he hits the highway."

41

IT WAS 9:15 AND VIC HADN'T EATEN SINCE NOON. The not-so gourmet Stoners Pub was still open in Burgoyne. Instead, he elected to walk the half-mile to what was affectionately known as the DunT, the Dunphy Tavern. Walking to the DunT on moonlit nights was a tradition among people like the Eberts with cottages in Riverton. The tavern was small but upscale. Areas not carpeted revealed wide-planked flooring. The walls were covered in red velvety fabric. The tables were dark and heavy. The matching chairs and barstools were upholstered with rich tan leather.

The Dunphy Tavern kept its kitchen open late … something about being licensed as a restaurant with a bar. Fortunately they didn't specialize in Irish cooking like the owner's name might indicate. Instead they had the county-wide reputation for having great steaks and generous pours of bourbon and a loyal clientele with those tastes. Vic's slacks and pullover shirt would more than satisfy their dress code.

He seated himself at the bar, ordered a glass of Ruffing Chianti, and told the bartender that he needed to see a menu. The bartender said, "The kitchen is still open so long as you're interested in a steak."

"That's what I've been thinking about on my walk over. I'll have the small sirloin, medium rare, steak fries, and a dinner salad with house dressing on the side."

As he was keying in the order the bartender said, "I can't guarantee the salad. The cooks close down the cold table first. But since you've been here before, you know the steak's worth it, with or without anything green. My friend and I used to say that potatoes are technically a vegetable and wine comes from fruit."

Vic took a sip of his wine and turned away from the bar to survey the room. There were four or five couples, either having desserts and coffee or having drinks. In the far corner, Johnny Laine was holding court with several of his business associates. If Johnny had been his usual boisterous self, Vic might have seen them earlier. He assumed that their discussion must have been a serious one, maybe one based on a report from Billing's.

Johnny noticed Vic looking toward his party and him. He got up and walked toward Vic with his hand outstretched. He told Vic that his dinner meeting was winding down and asked Vic if he might join him in a few minutes. Since Vic was alone and waiting for his food, he had little choice. He smiled and nodded yes.

As Johnny pulled out a stool and sat down ten minutes later, he said, "''Bout the only place you can count on a late dinner that's cooked to order around here. Convenient for you, I'll bet."

"It's close enough that I walked over. All the people who used to live or who summered along the river would walk over so as to not worry about who would have to be designated driver," Vic said.

"I remember some of them doing that, especially on Friday nights. Many of the folks could have used a designated guide ... one person sober enough to find everybody's way back without wandering in front of a car.

"I think I know some of those people from when I'd visit Greg," Vic said.

A tossed salad, a fresh-looking tossed salad, showed up so Vic turned the conversation over to Johnny by asking him about his current campaign for the state senate. It took Johnny until about half way through the main course to complete the full explanation of why it was "a lock". If Vic hadn't known better he might have concluded that Johnny was running unopposed. Vic then asked him about the riverfront development. Johnny answered more cautiously.

"It's a done deal. We have preliminary contracts for ten of the twelve homes we're going to build over there. There's only two sold to people around here. The other people are from Frankfort or Lexington. We're bringing new money into the area, new business. These are people who will probably do a lot of entertaining. I've agreed to sponsor any of the new home buyers at the Club. Since we don't have a waiting list, the board of directors is willing to waive half the initiation fee. We want to get these people to be part of the community, even if they're only here weekends."

"So I'm going to have some upper crust neighbors in a few months," Vic joked.

"Yes you will," he said in the same spirit. "We've applied to have the cottage be a historical site. Maybe we can have you dress as a moonshiner and give tours."

They both laughed. If Vic lived in the Woodford County district, he'd probably vote for Johnny. Vic speculated that lots of people who didn't belong to his party or even particularly trust him, voted for him based on his charm.

"You know that I'm not going to hurt Lynda, don't you?" he asked. "Like with all of the previous owners, I'd offered Greg to rebuild at a reduced cost. I've sweetened the deal for her. I don't know how well off Greg left her but I'm not going to take advantage of 'widows and children', so to speak. Besides, her and Julie's friendship goes way back. If I took advantage of Lynda I'd probably be building a new place for myself down there, in Riverton Heights."

"How did Lynda react?" Vic asked.

"She's thinking about it but I believe she's leaning in the direction of selling," Johnny said.

"Here's a wild idea, Johnny. I haven't thought it through but let me put it out there. What if she sold you the property? Give her whatever deal you offered. But you sold me the building rights. I'd love to have a place down here. I could keep a condo in Louisville and run my business electronically …e-mail, phone, internet, fax. As it turns out, I'm doing some of that already."

"I'd let her sell the building rights," Johnny said smiling, "but not to you."

"Okay," Vic responded, with a quizzical look on his face.

Johnny looked around and even though they were the last people sitting at the bar, he lowered his voice.

"Okay? No, not so okay. Let me explain.

Julie is usually discreet with her affairs. I typically have a good idea of who her 'man of the month' is at any given moment. I became suspicious of the two of you when she stopped seeing Neal. You wouldn't know Neal. Neal lives north of Frankfort. I'd arranged for them to get together. I knew he'd not get any crazy ideas. Neal is on my campaign committee.

I can't abide having the sort of rendezvous the two of you had at Wal-Mart. A shirttail relative of mine is in charge of security there. One of the people who works there showed him the tape of the two of you. He had me come over to examine it before he erased the incriminating part.

I can't allow there to be a scandal. My likely opponent isn't as well connected as I am but I can't assume anything. He may have a relative who operates security at Dollar General. I don't know. But you get what I'm saying, right?"

Vic shook his head yes and maintained the close-lipped smile he'd adopted during this revelation. Johnny was being more civil to him than he necessarily deserved. Johnny's civility, given Vic's moral disadvantage and Johnny's connections, political and otherwise, put him in command of the conversation. It was not a time for Vic to act indignant.

Johnny continued, "This has nothing to do with Lynda or your connection to Lynda. I'm going to give her all the help she needs. But there will be no scandal. As far as you're concerned, there will be no Julie.

Don't react. I know this is awkward and no man wants to be told what to do. I'm not going to tell you what to do. I am going to tell Julie what she's going to do, or rather who she's not going to do.

Julie wants to be the governor's wife, probably more than I want to be governor. She's not exactly a historian but she does have a handle on the legacy of governors from Southern states ... Carter, Clinton, the Bushes ... why not Laine?

I'm trying not to take any of this personally even though it's crossed my mind that you and Julie were doing this to defy me. I've rejected that idea but if I hear about anything else that goes on between you, I'll be forced to consider otherwise. Here comes the bartender."

"Can I get you gentlemen anything else," he asked.

Johnny looked at Vic and then answered for both of them, "I think we're about ready to go. Add this man's bill to my account, Mike."

It didn't seem like the right situation for Vic to make an issue over who should pay the check. It wasn't going to be his night to win any pissing contests. Johnny looked toward the door and they walked out together.

Apparently Johnny had said all he wanted to say. They talked about how nice the evening was and how good the steaks were at the DunT like two old friends. Johnny gently punched Vic in the arm before he said, "Let me drive you home."

Before Johnny let Vic out at the cabin, he made sure that they shook hands. It was a "we have a deal" handshake. Vic understood they had a deal but they both knew there was another party involved who hadn't shaken on it. That did not mean that Johnny wouldn't expect him to abide by their unwritten contract.

42

VIC WOKE UP EVERY HOUR FROM 1:00 A.M. ON. He finally gave up at 6:30. He talked himself out of running and opted instead for going into the pharmacy early. Since it was Saturday, Claudia wouldn't be there to establish the workflow pace or to solve the inevitable problems associated with not being able to immediately access all of the health care providers who take weekends off. He recognized that his idea of getting on top of things might be thwarted when Lynda greeted him as he unlocked the door.

"It's your lucky day," she said. "I'm going to be your cashier."

"What happened to Zach? I thought he was my Saturday right hand," he answered.

"Zach tried to go full steam after his accident. He came home from school exhausted yesterday. I forced him to go to bed early and told him I'd fill in. Oh, and you'd better get used to me," Lynda said.

"Used to you?"

"Yes. Jo Ellen's husband made her quit. She'd been with us twelve years. They don't need the money but she liked being out with people. She'd have lunch every day with somebody or other who works here in town. We'll miss her but this might be good for me if I need to understand the business. I can give up some of my social and charitable involvement. More and more of the meetings for those groups take place at night anyway."

"Okay, you'll be an asset for the store and business in general but let's back-up. Why did Jo Ellen's husband 'make her quit'?" Vic asked.

"He is a contractor negotiating with Edwin Ryder to oversee some of the Downtown Revitalization Project. Poor Scott stood to lose potential contracts recreating our downtown area into an idealized village that oozes quaintness. Jo Ellen was to stop 'consorting with the enemy'. Can you believe that?"

"Any more, nothing surprises me," he said.

"Are you ready for another one then? The nursing homes are close to going with Ali. She agreed to pay for the buy out of our contract ... our consulting contract. We wouldn't lose the patients who get their scripts from us. Well, we wouldn't right away. There's not much Ali wouldn't say about us to take away that business, patient by patient."

"Who makes the final decision?"

"They've got a board of directors. We've been invited to make a presentation along with our contract offer. The contracts are annual with perfunctory renewal procedures for the subsequent four years."

"I can help you put that presentation together, Lynda. I suppose we have to make some big financial concessions," he said.

"No, not really. We're close on fees. Otherwise the homes wouldn't want to hear from us. The facilities need to have some evidence that we'll still be in business for the next five years."

"Assuming that's your plan, that you plan to keep the store long term, I can put a good spin on that too," Vic promised.

"Zach has said the same thing. Not that he understands the business but I believe that there are times when he thinks in Excel and PowerPoint. But you've asked the right question."

"What's that?" Vic asked trying to remember a question.

"Do I want to be owning a pharmacy five years from now?"

"Oh yeah. That question. Well, do you?"

"I'm not sure whether I want to stay ... that I want us to stay ... in Burgoyne. The thing this week with Zach ...if something would happen to him because I make the wrong decision about staying, I couldn't live with myself."

"Lynda, listen a minute. Didn't we go through all of this on the ride to Lexington? We didn't come up with an answer but we listed a lot of the weaknesses and threats, and discounted many of those, didn't we?"

"That's just it, Vic. We keep getting new threats. Not just new but worse threats. Or maybe they seem worse. My accountant gave me the month-end report yesterday. Greg hadn't told me that customers had already started drifting away, a few in late March. It's not like we have this untapped population base of potential new customers that we can go after.

And then there's the little matter of finding a pharmacist. I can't expect you to stay here much longer. And I recognize that you're charging me a 'family and friends' rate. I'm costing you a lot."

"Don't forget, you're putting me up at a river resort with a private yacht at my disposal," he said, in an effort to change the downward tone their conversation was headed.

"Then there's the cottage," she said, ignoring Vic's attempt to lighten the mood.

"I'd try to keep it or a new place on the river for Zach, keep it in the family, and I talked to him about it. Sometimes he's 17 going on 38. He reminded me that young people tend to leave Burgoyne at their first opportunity. He admits that he loves the cottage and loves being on the water but that in a few years he'd probably only be able to visit the place once in a while."

"Did Johnny ever formally draw up what Julie suggested would be his buy out offer?"

"More or less. The contract, in some of its wording, is close to what Julie said. He's not as generous as she indicated for building rights or maybe I misunderstood her. It would cost more than I'd get for the cottage to build down there."

"So which way are you leaning, Lynda?"

"Today, I see myself in one of those free standing villas east of town. I'll work part-time somewhere and only think about another move if Zach gives me grandkids."

"I'd label these plans 'first draft'. Try not to jump too quickly," he said.

As if to announce that their conversation had run its course, the first customer of the day, the first customer most days, came in. He greeted them both, and set two dollars and twelve cents on the glass checkout counter. He showed them the three Kit Kat bars he'd picked up, demanded that we "have a nice day", and headed for his car. The only time this ritual varied was if he needed diabetes test strips or one of his medications. Those would be six Kit Kat days. He's one customer Ebert Drugs can count on.

Vic quickly ascertained that the prescription area was in good shape. That wasn't a surprise since he closed the store the previous night. He'd have plenty of time to outline a presentation for the board meeting should Lynda opt not to surrender to Ali and to fight for the consulting business.

Business was slow so he was able to take several personal calls. One was a Louisville number but otherwise, as the message reminded him, an unknown caller.

"Vic, this is Angela. I thought I better get back to you about our conversation, the conversation about me possibly taking the job in Burgoyne," she said.

"Oh, Angela. Good to hear from you again. What are your thoughts? Would you like to come down and visit?"

"No. That's not going to be necessary. I did some inquiring. One person who's active in the consultant pharmacists group said she understood that Ebert lost all of its nursing home contracts."

"I don't have to guess the source of that 'fake news,'" Vic said. "And by the way I'm working on a board presentation to go along with our biggest contract renewal offer as we speak."

"Well, anyway, it's not the right time for me to make another job change. If we buy in Lexington, I can commute if I have to. I appreciate your offer but my answer is 'no'."

Vic knew that it would be pointless to argue. He knew the source of the misinformation she'd been fed. He imagined diabolical ways to take Ali on if Lynda decided to keep Ebert Pharmacy as a going concern. As if she'd been telepathically transported, Ali walked through the front door. She glowered at Vic but waved as she barged over to talk with Lynda.

Ali spoke with rodent-like nervousness. Her head moved as if her eyes were fixed in their sockets giving her no peripheral vision. She was annoying to watch and Vic didn't even know what she was saying. When she left, Vic poured a coffee and took it up to Lynda.

"Ali asked me to come up with a price for our prescription files," she said. "I told her that I'd contact her if and when I decided to sell. The woman is nothing if not brazen."

"She is that," he said as he returned to the prescription counter. He decided against telling Lynda about Angela and her reluctance to move to Burgoyne.

HE HAD A MESSAGE FROM JULIE. She got to the point quickly. "Johnny knows about us. He says that it's a matter of time before people … meaning voters … find out. I'm sure that he has ways of knowing if we see each other again. I want us to stay 'friends with benefits'. I'm guessing if we're far enough away from Woodford County, he'll let it go. Text me."

Vic complied, texting her "Any suggestions?"

She answered, "Johnny's out of town. I propose something less hazardous. Game?"

"Sure. Things are getting boring in Burgoyne."

She answered, "My cure for boredom is the Frankfort Hilton, I'll be in room 359 from 7:00 on."

"Presuming a lot, wouldn't you say? See you at 7:01."

The store closed at 4:00 since it was Saturday. As he pulled down the lane toward the cottage he saw a United Van Lines truck in front of Hal and Goldie's. The two of them were sitting in dilapidated lawn chairs, facing the river.

"Hey Hal. Hi Goldie. Thought you'd be here a while longer," Vic said.

"We did too. The development corporation is paying for everything until we can move into the retirement center. We're getting a full pack. They'll pay for the furniture to go into storage. Our clothes and personal things will be waiting for us at the Residence Inn. Goldie and I were saying that we wished that the full pack included this view."

"I know. I guess if there wasn't this view, everybody would still be living here," he answered.

Goldie shook her head and said, "And we'd be living here for what other reason?"

"Fellowship?" he ventured.

"Yeah, that's an issue too. We already miss our neighbors."

Vic shook Hal's hand, kissed Goldie on the cheek, predicted a life of loneliness for himself after their departure, and walked to the cottage to shower and change. He hated it that they were being forced to leave. Hated it too for all the other displaced people they represented.

43

VIC'S FORD WAS ACCUSTOMED TO FREQUENT
SERVICING. Since the car was in the Jiffy Lube
database, he stopped at the franchise on the
outskirts of Frankfort. He liked being able to stand
by the waiting room windows to monitor what was
going on. The technician eventually accepted that
Vic wanted nothing checked, only an oil change and
filter and that, yes, the oil had been changed only
757 miles before.

As he made the short drive to the Hilton he s
analyzed how well he'd done since coming to
Burgoyne. Ebert Pharmacy was still operating but it
was rapidly losing business with no turnaround in
sight. He'd been unable to find a replacement
pharmacist or come up with a survival plan. His
consultant job with the DEA and his involvement
with Julie were jeopardizing any reconciliation
possibilities with Tracy, assuming he wanted there
to be any. Being with Julie was great. But that was
bound to change given that their relationship was
destined to be long distance. Will had been killed,
Zach could have died, and somebody tried to kill
him twice. Plus he'd made no progress in solving
the robbery or the murders. His pangs of self-

flagellation ended abruptly, though, when he saw
Julie's Jaguar parked outside the Hilton.

He knocked on the hotel-hollow door of
room 359 at 7:03. Momentarily he wondered why
they weren't on a non-smoking floor until he
remembered their recent chemically enhanced sex.

"Room service?" Julie asked through the
door.

"Only if you're a big tipper."

His remark was apparently the Hilton's
counterpart to "sesame" because the door was
pulled away from him. He saw Julie. He saw most
of Julie although he was vaguely aware of some red
lacy swatches artfully placed to direct his game plan.

Apparently they had nothing else to say to
each other ... at least for the next twenty minutes.
With that, they eclipsed their "all time shortest lack
of restraint" record. They pulled the sheet and one
blanket up over themselves and lay in each other's
arms, still wordlessly, until a yelling child and
slamming door in the hall disrupted their reverie.

"Have you had dinner?" she asked.

"I started with dessert, I think."

"Nice of you to say so Sweetie. It's always
good to cleanse our palates with a little bread and
cheese. Would you mind taking care of the wine?"

As he handed her the glass of pinot noir, she
said in a matter of fact manner, "Johnny made it
clear that he wants you out of my life. He sounded
almost combative about it."

"That's what I assumed from your text
message. I thought the two of you have an
arrangement," he said.

"Apparently, you and I were too careless. At least one person he knows saw us. Johnny says we were on a security video at Wal-Mart. So I think this is more than a hunch on his part. I'm not sure that Frankfort is far enough away. Johnny's political ties cross the entire state but this is his home base.

I'm not so naïve as to believe that you're sticking around so that you can have your way with me on a regular basis. I know that Greg getting killed is still bothering you. You're going to have to let it go, Vic."

"Letting go seems to be my mantra today. Johnny wants me to let you go. It looks more and more like I'll oversee Lynda letting the pharmacy go. And now you're asking me to let the murder of Greg go unsolved or at least uninvestigated."

"Sorry, Vic, I followed you up to the part about Greg. I thought Ralph Billings and that chick from the DEA were doing the investigating."

"We've got a robber who, with the exception of Greg, likes to hit people in the head. He's good at it. The two times were violent and deliberate, almost elegant."

"What's this 'we'? Are you still with the DEA?"

"No. Of course not," Vic lied. "It's hard to give up old instincts. Especially given the episode with Zach."

"I'm not a criminal expert but I've got one opinion I need to share. I don't want you to react if I say something contrary to your instincts, okay?" she asked.

"Sure," he agreed.

"I know Johnny has a lot riding on the development and the downtown revitalization. But you don't know Johnny as well as I do. I can't imagine him doing anything violent. He and Greg were as close as their differing lifestyles allowed."

"I suppose you're right," he said as earnestly as he could.

You may be right but I'm not about to write him off as a suspect. Johnny's got partners and he and his partners have people who work for them. I'm sure Johnny didn't rob three pharmacies or kill my two friends but I can't rule out his involvement altogether.

"Let's change the subject," he said.

"Okay. But I want to get any unpleasantness out of the way. How about you and Tracy? How are things on that front?"

"I thought we'd been through that. I worry that her doctor friend jilted her, if indeed he has. I don't like it when anything hurts her. And she says she's worried about me. She didn't like how dangerous my DEA assignments had gotten and now she doesn't like the fact that I could be the pharmacist working during the next robbery."

"Do you feel guilty about us? I mean if you're talking to Tracy or with her do you worry about what's going on between you and me messing up any future reconciliation?"

"Well it does cross my mind but guilt, if any, is fleeting," he said with what he hoped was another convincing job of stretching the truth.

"So are you going to feel guilty if you run into Johnny?"

"Probably not," he said.

"Does it make us being together any less fun?" she said.

"Oh, are we supposed to be having fun? Right now, what we're doing isn't my idea of fun or foreplay for that matter. Now earlier ..."

"Yeah. I'm ready for a replay of when you first came in."

GIVEN THEIR CONVERSATION THE NIGHT BEFORE they knew it would be foolish to have breakfast together at the Hilton cafe. Julie told him he should leave first and that she'd check out in a few minutes. Before he could kiss her goodbye, for the fourth time, his cell phone vibrated.

"Vic, this is Lynda. Wherever you are, you better come back. There's been a fire down at the river. No one was hurt. No one was there to be hurt."

"I'm in Frankfort," he said

When Julie scowled, Vic mouthed 'It's Lynda'. Julie raised her eyebrows but decided that he probably did know how to be discreet.

"I'll be down there in half an hour. I still need to check out and the Ford is low on gas."

"Zach and I will wait for you. By the way, it's not the cottage. It's the boathouse. Plus somebody smashed up the outboard on the pontoon boat. Be as quick as you can. Goodbye."

"Bye," he answered as they disconnected.

"The boathouse burnt down and there's damage to a boat," he explained to Julie.

"You better get back. I'll text you."

"See you, Julie."

44

VIC THOUGHT THINGS THROUGH ON HIS DRIVE BACK
TO BURGOYNE. Even though Johnny had an alibi his
associates might not. There are so many of them
and those associates have their own associates.
Besides, there are others who would just as soon
chase him out of Burgoyne since he was making it
possible for the pharmacy to stay up and running. If
Ebert Drugs closes its doors that could be pivotal
for other existing businesses to follow suit ... the
florist, the cleaners, the insurance agent, the realtor,
and even Stoner's Tavern. Speaking of which, its
possible Stoner's boy Gus might be getting even for
their earlier confrontation. And Ali. Ali would be
ecstatic to see him gone.

Lynda had said that it was not the cottage.
There was little if anything of value in the
boathouse. Some fishing gear was the only thing
Vic remembered seeing. Anything else, he'd
classify as junk. The pontoon boat was right beside
it on its lift by the dock. One of the deputies had
dropped the fishing boat off next to the cabin when
the sheriff declared that the investigation was over.
Vic hadn't gotten around to hauling it back down to
the river so maybe it was spared.

Lynda and Zach were sitting outside the cottage when he drove up. So was Ralph Billings. Zach took Vic aside and confirmed that the only losses were to the boathouse and pontoon boat. He reminded Vic that he'd taken his kayak up to the island where he liked to keep it in the summer.

Billings spoke, "Mind if I ask you where you were?"

"I had business in Frankfort. I spent the night at the Hilton."

"And you'll be able to document that?" Billings asked.

"If you're asking about an alibi, I can corroborate I was there all night if it comes to that," Vic said.

"You might need to do that but this isn't the time."

"Out of curiosity, Sheriff, why would you think I'd burn down the boathouse and disable the pontoon boat? Like maybe I wanted to NOT take a boat into the river. But oops, I forgot the fishing boat wasn't in the boathouse."

"No need to get sarcastic. I need to consider every possibility. You know that. By the way, was it you who moved the other boat up here by the cabin?"

"No, your deputy left it there when he brought it back from the island. He's the one down there with the camera. Let's go verify this together shall we?" he said as he took a step toward the river.

"Calm down, Fye. Not necessary. I remember telling him where to leave it. And before you ask, I'm not sidestepping the investigation of

Greg's death by making this into something it isn't. Okay?"

Vic nodded yes and only half listened as the sheriff finished up his report and information for Lynda's insurance company. He did get it. Billings rarely had to cope with any serious criminal activity in his jurisdiction until Vic showed up in Burgoyne. Vic was unable to provide Billings with any concrete evidence that contradicted the findings of the department's search of the island or the land surrounding the river. It would be out of line to infer that Billings missed something or botched the investigation when Vic had nothing to contribute beyond his experienced hunches. So in Billing's mind, there was only the one murder.

When the sheriff left to take photos, Lynda looked at Vic. After some effort she managed to give him a smile. She looked tired. Zach turned his eyes back and forth between his mom and Vic, waiting for a forthcoming discussion that might clarify everything that was going on.

Zach said, "You better tell him, Mom."

After a long sigh Lynda began, "I'm going to sign the papers with Johnny tomorrow morning. It's probably more money than the place is worth. If there was no development, I still might have tried to sell it. Greg used to spend a lot of time keeping this place up. It's a lot of work. Johnny and his friends want possession in two weeks."

When Vic turned to Zach he added, "I don't think Mom can do anything else. Besides, it already doesn't seem the same. Not bad. Just kind of eerie. An empty feeling maybe."

"This is hard for both of us and I know it's hard for you, too, Vic. The cottage is where you and Greg used to play when you were kids. Not to mention how you two would sneak down here every time you were in Burgoyne. Hardly anything ever changed over the years. It's time we all let it go," said Lynda.

"I know," Vic said. His shoulders slumped and he gave her a tight-lipped grin. "What can I do to help you close the place up?"

"Once you move out, Zach and I will come down and clear out the desk and take the pictures and things like that. Our church will pick up most of the rest. We sponsor needy families. There's always somebody who needs dishes, or a chair, or linens, or something. It's not like anything down here is likely to show up on *Antiques Roadshow*."

"I'd still like to spend more time looking through Greg's papers," he said.

"Of course, Vic. You know this isn't all he's got. Sometime you ought to look at the stuff he kept down in our basement. He finished off a little room down there," Lynda offered.

"Tell you what. I'll box up some of the materials and bring them by. I'd definitely like to take you up on that offer to see his basement stash," Vic said.

"Tomorrow afternoon would work for me," she said.

"Unless we can come up with a pharmacist who wants to be a co-owner, the franchise thing isn't going to work" he said, returning to an earlier topic.

"I've given up on that, too. Hal could retire any time. He has no interest in owning a pharmacy. It's easier, probably smarter, to sell out or at least get out. Besides, clerking isn't all that much fun."

"What would you do?"

"I've been offered a job as an office nurse for one of the new internists who is coming to the clinic. I guess the University is more committed to coming to Burgoyne than we thought. I'll commute to Lexington until the doctor moves his practice down here. I'm lucky to have kept up my license.

I need to move on. I know that you see some sort of conspiracy but even if there is and you figure it all out, it's not going to bring Greg back. I'd tell you to leave it alone, but I know it's not that simple for you," Lynda said.

"I support what you're doing. There are several correct answers to what you ought to do and you've picked one of them. I'll see you tomorrow afternoon, if you're sure that's okay."

"I'll leave the back door unlocked in case Zach isn't home from school. Take care, Vic."

"You guys take care, too," Vic said.

45

THE SHERIFF TOOK VIC ASIDE. "Before I head back to my office, I need to ask something. Do you know if Greg stored any chemicals or fuel in the boat house?"

"There was gas for the mower and boat fuel," Vic said. "As to chemicals, there was nothing flammable ... some Round-Up and a can of wasp spray are the only ones I remember seeing. Usually you have to wait and see if the fire marshal can identify any accelerants."

"I'm not sure whether the fire marshal will be able tell the difference between the gasoline and any other accelerant," Billings said, sounding as if he hoped to pin the fire on owner negligence, not arson. If the fire isn't a crime, only the damage to the boat remains unsolved. Vandalism but not arson.

Vic spent what was left of the morning going over in his mind everything that had been happening. He had no way of knowing whether this latest episode was directed at him or was meant to frighten Lynda and Zach. He couldn't help feeling guilty that he'd been with Julie, enjoying himself and not at the cottage to witness if not prevent the arson. Of only marginal concern was that their tryst took place over a weekend. Vic did have some business he had been hoping to attend to in

Frankfort. The Kentucky Board of Pharmacy Examiners was closed weekends.

Then it came to him. He was being old school. The internet didn't close on weekends and what Vic wanted to find out was public information. Minutes from Board Meetings were part of the public record. After several failed attempts, Vic determined that during the six years since Ali formed her corporation, she and a pharmacist who worked for her were each reprimanded for shoddy record keeping of controlled substances. There were four complaints related to fraudulent Medicare billing. Most notable though, one of her employee pharmacists was arrested for systematic diversion of controlled substances valued at over one hundred thousand dollars. After serving eighteen months in prison and permanently losing his license, he was rehired by Ali as director of corporate affairs. That sounded like a non-position position. She probably wouldn't have taken him back if she hadn't owed him something … like maybe he took a fall for her.

Eventually, hunger disrupted Vic's musings. He ate what remained of leftover tuna casserole he'd made several days before and turned his attention to Greg's materials that he'd accumulated about the Hawkins books. He still wondered if there had been a fourth scrapbook. Everything ended so abruptly and Greg probably would have made entries more recently than seven months ago. Vic thumbed through the books and paid closer attention to Greg's under linings … the cross-references for his notes.

Well into the sixth book Vic found a paragraph that was both highlighted and underlined. The paragraph had nothing to do with the cave. It described Hawkins and another of his club members hearing horses across the river from the cabin. A harvest moon had risen to reveal the silhouettes of empty horses trotting in formation, lead by a lone Ryder wearing a pointed hat. Greg's only margin note was a bold "AHA!!!!" Vic read that chapter. He read the previous chapter and he read the chapter that followed. There was no mention of the cave.

CLAUDIA AND HE HAD A TYPICAL BUSY MONDAY. There was enough traffic that neither one had time to make a second pot of coffee. Lynda obliged but returned to the front before the Mr. Coffee was done sputtering its last few ounces into the carafe. Sheriff Billings had motioned to Lynda from the front of the store.

Vic didn't give much thought to his being there, given the previous days events. Claudia was less charitable.

"He's pretending he's a detective, I think, in case somebody might accept the notion that he has the capacity to deal with anything more complicated than double parking. He wants everybody to believe that it's him who is responsible for Burgoyne remaining this quiet, crime-free community. He swaggers with enough authority that most everybody swallows the myths that there are no drugs in the schools and no domestic violence in the county. Like we're Mayberry North," Claudia unloaded vehemently while sliding prescriptions and vials at Vic to double check.

"I know about the drugs in the high school. What's this about domestic violence?"

"My husband has several parishioners who come to talk to him about their abusive husbands. I sit in sometimes if they need to see him at night. Ministers have to be careful about being alone with female members of their congregations. The clergy is as vulnerable to false accusations of sexual impropriety as is everyone else. And there have been problems. Not with Rex, of course, but within the church ... within all denominations," Claudia explained.

"What kind of violence are we talking about?"

"Oh, slapping, beatings, burns, and lots of threats. The pattern is usually the same. The wife at some point decides that she has had enough. She calls the sheriff. A deputy shows up. It's usually at night. The husband promises to behave. The deputy leaves."

"I don't get it," Vic said.

"Some of the women my husband counsels are married to some prominent citizens, some are even connected to the Department itself."

"The Police Department?"

"I'm afraid so."

"I think I liked Burgoyne better when I only visited on weekends to fish," Vic said.

"You know I wasn't supposed to talk about any of that, don't you?" Claudia cautioned.

"Yes. I understand the confidentiality concerns. I didn't hear anything. Great. I sound like I could be a member of the Department and part of the cover-up."

LYNDA KEPT THE BACKDOOR UNLOCKED AS SHE'D PROMISED. She left a note, instructing him to come on in and to help himself to anything he could find to eat or drink. He grabbed a ginger ale and went downstairs.

Greg's room had no window and was lit by one overhead bulb. His idea of finishing the area into a room was to tack up some inexpensive fake mahogany paneling and to hang some draperies from a rod suspended from the ceiling. The drapes hid the furnace and water heater. There was a doorway but no door. There were three unmatched file cabinets, an old desk, an uncomfortable wooden desk chair, and numerous boxes of papers. A bookshelf was filled with multiple copies of most of the Hawkins books except for the rarest two. Each of the rarities listed for close to $1000 on eBay. Vic had included Greg's extra copies of those two in the materials he brought from the cottage.

As a result of his attempts to make space on the shelf for the books he brought, a tobacco-brown streaked baseball rolled off, hit the desk, and bumped against the ginger ale can. The old ball had Joe Morgan's autograph written with the same green Sharpie he'd used to sign Vic's baseball card. Greg had snagged both autographs at the same time. This had to be Morgan's home run ball. Vic wondered whether Lynda might let him have it.

Vic interrupted his reveries to search through the file cabinets and boxes of papers. While he was intrigued by the story outlines, comic strip versions, and unfinished manuscripts Greg had archived, Vic was disappointed not to find a fourth notebook.

There were several yellow Post-it notes on the side of the bookcase beside the desk. These served to remind him to check certain chapters or to measure precise distances down by the river. One note partially covered two other ones. It simply said, "the other side of the river"

Vic slapped the sides of his forehead with both hands, leaned back in the chair, and closed his eyes. *This jibed with the 'aha' statement. The moon rises in the east. It came up behind the Ryders and Hawkins saw it all from the clubhouse. The shack on the other side of the river must have been Greg's great grandfather's idea of what the boys' clubhouse should be. This means, if there's a cave to be found, it's on the west side of the river.*

45

"Vic. Are you down there?"

Before he could answer he heard the
basement door open, followed by rapid footfalls
coming down the uncarpeted steps. Lynda barged
into Greg's room. "Was Zach home when you got
here?"

"No. I don't think so. I didn't see or hear
him."

"Zach didn't show up at school. He didn't
get on the bus to go to his track meet last night. The
coach thought he'd decided not to go. Zach
canceled out and missed the meet right after Greg
was killed. The staff in Cox's office assumed he'd
gone to the meet. A couple of kids sending text
messages figured it out before the school officials.
I'm going to check his room. I didn't check last
night. I thought he was on his way and was
spending the night in Louisville."

"I'll come with you," Vic said.

Lynda was a half flight of stairs ahead of
him. She'd taken an initial look before Vic stepped
into the ordered chaos that was Zach's room. A
packed duffle bag was sitting on his partially made
bed. His billfold was on the desk. Some papers that
looked like they could be homework, stuck out of
one of the pockets of his backpack.

"There's his I-pad but I don't see his cell phone. Let's check the garage," she said.

"Sure," Vic answered.

Again he had trouble keeping up with her. He knew that Zach seldom drove and he couldn't imagine that Zach would drive without his license. Besides, Lynda had pulled into the garage and would have noticed if their second car was missing.

"His bike's gone," she said.

"His bike?"

"Yes. He claims it helps him to loosen up before a meet if he goes on a long ride. He's good so maybe it does.

We're not going to find him here. I better call somebody."

"I'll contact the sheriff's office," Vic said wanting to do something and letting Lynda know he was taking things seriously too.

"Good. I'll see if I can reach Mr. Cox or somebody at school," Lynda said.

" SHERIFF, GLAD I GOT THROUGH TO YOU."

"What's up now, Fye?"

"What's up is that Zach Ebert is missing. He didn't go to school. He didn't go to the state track meet. His wallet and homework are still in his room. And his bike is gone."

"How long has he been missing?"

"He was supposed to get on the bus at 7:00 last night. Lynda had something to do at church, I seem to remember, so he said he'd get to school by himself."

"Officially, we're supposed to wait 24 hours before we can declare somebody missing but we're better off getting started before dark. He's run away a few times before. Maybe Lynda's told you. We found him down by the river once. We'll patrol around town. Why don't you look around Riverton and I'll be there as quick as I'm able to help look."

"Okay. I'm at Lynda's now," Vic said.

"Sure, get down to the river as soon as you can."

He hung up as Lynda came in to report what she'd learned.

"Stephanie says that he came by her place about 5:30 last night. Her dad wouldn't let him see her. His livelihood depends on the redevelopment and I suppose the river project as well. His attitude seems to be that our family represents the enemy that is holding things up. Steph says when he rode off he was headed away from the school ... toward the river."

Vic said, "I was there last night and I never saw him. I was preoccupied but Zach seems to be comfortable about stopping in. He usually wants to use the bathroom or to get something to drink.

The sheriff asked me to go there now and start looking. I better take off. Will you be okay? Call Julie. I'm sure she'd come over."

"I might do that. First I'll drive by the school. Maybe some of his classmates have seen him," she said.

"Okay, I'll call you as soon as I learn anything."

46

VIC STEPPED OUT OF HIS CAR. Billings pulled in behind him. Ralph followed him into the cottage. Together they walked through the cottage and its garage area.

"Someone has been in here. It had to have been since this morning."

"That means Zach hasn't been missing all that long," Billings concluded.

"I don't think it was Zach. Someone took a few books and a notebook that I left here earlier. I had too many to carry. They weren't materials Zach would have taken. We better look outside."

They talked as they walked toward the river. They no sooner had agreed that the island might be a good place to start looking when they noticed something smoldering in the fire pit. When they looked more closely, Vic identified charred paper and bindings.

"If its the books and notebook. I know for certain that's not Zach's doing. That's several hundred dollars worth of destruction.

But to hell with that. Lets get back to finding Zach."

"While we're on the subject of Zach, tell me about your relationship with him," Billings said.

"We can talk while we're looking around the island."

Knowing that he'd have asked the same thing under the circumstances, Vic tried hard not to show resentment.

"He's my godson. I think he knows that but up until a couple of years ago I was Uncle Vic. I still am, once in a while, when we're kidding around or if he wants something. We've gotten a little closer again these past weeks. He seems able to talk to me about his dad. It's probably hard for him and Lynda to discuss some things. And he tells me stuff about school and about other students, and, you know, things kids can't talk to their parents about."

"I see," Billings said, demonstrating he wasn't trying to be confrontational. "He's a quiet kid. I hear there are rumors at school that he's gay. I guess Ryder's daughter told some of her friends that Zach could never be her boyfriend because he never tries anything. Do you think he's gay?"

"I guess we never talked about sexual preference," Vic said.

"Sometimes you have to," he said. "How about you? Any gay friends?"

"I do. Probably more than I know. Before you ask, I'm not homosexual. Nor am I bisexual," Vic said. He didn't try to hide his annoyance.

"You know I've got to ask these things. I'm looking for a teenage boy who visits a single male in an isolated area. I'm obligated to ask some questions. I don't mean any offense."

"I realize that Sheriff. I'd rather concentrate on finding Zach right now though."

As systematically as they could, given the rocky terrain, they covered the accessible parts of the island. Vic saw scraped places in the forks of two adjacent young cottonwoods.

"Sheriff. Zach keeps his kayak down here. He lifts it up and secures it between these trees. With all the foliage hiding it, it is not visible to anyone who doesn't know where to look. It's gone. His kayak isn't here."

"I better get some people looking on the river, too," he said.

As they got closer to the cabin after their island search, they heard voices. Vic recognized a number of young men from the track team as well as the track coach. The meet was over. Two boys came running up from the dock to report something. The coach looked up and motioned for Billings and Vic to join him.

"Sheriff, a couple of the kids think they see a bike under the dock, down in the water. They want to know if they should pull it out."

"Better let my deputies and I do that," Billings answered, "I think that's Brad pulling in now."

Fifteen kids stood watching as Brad removed his gun, shirt, hat, shoes, and everything from his pockets. He backed into the waist deep water and with some difficulty pulled the bike from the water. It had mud on it but nothing green that would indicate it had been there long enough for algae to start growing. There was a concrete block jammed over the left handle bar. It was held in position by a brake handle that looked sprung.

"Is this Zach's bike?" Billings asked Vic.

"I don't know. It looks like his. His is silver like this," he answered.

One of the kids spoke up, "That's Zach's bike. None of the other kids have a Gary Fisher. Most of the other kids don't ride bikes much anymore."

A couple of the other kids laughed nervously. Several others smiled.

Billings said, "Vic, lets you and I go back up to the cabin. I need to talk to you about a few things."

To the others he said, "Boys I appreciate you coming down here to help. There's still plenty of time before dark so why don't you look for another half hour or so and call it a night. We don't want any of you to miss your dinner or to worry your parents. Thanks."

There was a chorus of agreement from the team members and they started scattering out, walking in groups of twos and threes. Billings and Vic slogged up the incline toward the cabin.

"Fye, is there anything else you can tell me? Anything you're willing to say?"

"I'll do anything I can to help. I'll tell you anything I know," he said.

"I think you better come with me down to the station. We need to talk about this in a more official capacity."

47

"CAN I DRIVE MY OWN CAR IF YOU FOLLOW ME?"
VIC ASKED.

"C'mon. You know better than that. You know the procedure," Billings answered.

He frisked Vic in a manner only TV crime show viewers might consider thorough. When Billings was done Vic said, "You may want to check the ankle holster on my left leg. Let me give it to you."

Billings tossed the holstered gun into the front seat. He offered no apology for having him ride in the back seat but at least didn't cuff him.

As they pulled away Vic said, "My attorney's in Louisville."

"Let's talk before you decide whether you need a lawyer."

"Fine," he said, deciding he didn't want to corner Billings into any legal actions.

The sheriff parked behind the single-story red brick building that, except for the absence of windows on two sides, might have been a physician's or an attorney's office. One deputy looked up from the front desk but other than that no one saw Vic being taken for questioning … well, no one if one discounts the fact that half of the

Burgoyne High School track team saw everything. Billings took him to a small room, undecorated except for a table and two small chairs. Billings offered him coffee and asked him if he needed to use the restroom before they got started.

"I've got to tell you Fye. Every time something happens in Burgoyne, you're somehow connected to it. You're like Father Brown in that British TV program. When there's a crime, you show up. Except Father Brown solves 'em. You don't. I'm saying this so you'll get why I've brought you in."

"I get that Ralph but…"

"Stop. This is my interview. First lets establish where you were," Billings said.

"Starting when?" Vic said. He smiled and tried every way he knew to appear cooperative.

"Lets go back to the weekend. Who can corroborate your being in the Frankfort hotel?"

Johnny had threatened both Julie and him about seeing each other prior to their Franfort tryst. Laine would be angry if not vindictive if he found out they had defied him. Given the tenuous circumstances with the Ebert family and Johnny's influence on county politics, Laine wasn't a person Vic wanted as an enemy.

"The person I was with checked in and checked out of the Frankfort Hilton. I can't say whether she registered as one or two people but I doubt my name was given."

"And no one at the hotel saw you?"

"I walked directly to the room and the next morning I walked directly to my car."

"Is there anyone else who can verify you were in Frankfort?"

"I took my car into Jiffy Lube for an oil change. The receipt is in the glove compartment and it should have my mileage on it. I drove from the Jiffy Lube to the Hotel, back to Burgoyne, then into town and back. Oh, and I've got a receipt for gas at a Frankfort station early Sunday morning."

"Just a second," Billings said taking out his cell phone.

"Are you still down at the river?" he asked.

"Are you the only one down there?

Well try and stop her before she drives away."

Billings turned to him and asked, "Is your vehicle unlocked?"

Vic nodded affirmatively.

Billings asked to speak to Lynda and explained to her that he wanted the receipt and the mileage of the car. She apparently agreed to drop them off on her way home.

Billings told Vic that if the Jiffy Lube receipt and car mileage checked out, he'd probably be free to go but that there were a few more questions. "If necessary I can subpoena the hotel registration records and find out who you stayed with. The person you were with in Frankfort. Male or female?"

"Female. That's why I referred to her as 'she' earlier."

"Yes. I remember," he said.

"Look Sheriff Billings. You've asked me repeatedly about a fire I couldn't start and a boy I would never do anything to hurt. I've given you my full cooperation. I'm the one who called you in on Zach's disappearance. If I'd wanted to hide his bike I certainly wouldn't have done so under a dock where I was living. You haven't charged me with anything and you have no basis to do so. I'm not going anywhere and both of us could make better use of our time looking for Zach ... or we could have, before it got so dark."

"Speaking of looking for Zach, I want you ... no I'm ordering you ... to stay out of it. Assuming you're telling the truth, I don't want anyone accusing you of compromising evidence," Billings said.

"And you don't want anybody accusing *you* of allowing me to hide something. So it's better for both of us. I get it. I'm guessing it's okay for me to keep working unless you order me to do otherwise."

Vic was thinking of other things to say, probably louder and with less self control, when there was a knock on the door. It was the deputy announcing that Lynda was in the waiting area.

"Have her come on back," Billings ordered.

Lynda handed over the receipt and another piece of paper, presumably the mileage. She watched the sheriff as he looked at the materials. He gazed at the ceiling and rubbed his temple as he made mental calculations. Then he nodded and shook his head to affirm that he was satisfied.

"Checks out, Fye. Let me take care of recording this and I'll take you back to the cottage. You're free to go, Lynda."

"Can I speak to Vic first?"

"Sure. I'll wait for both of you in my office."

Once Billings closed the connecting door, Lynda said "Vic, the fact that you're a suspect, or at least the idea that the sheriff hauled you away is being discussed right now around a dozen dinner tables in Burgoyne. Those kids will be twittering and texting their friends if they haven't already done so. My point is, I don't see how I can I keep you at the store. Without a pharmacist, I might as well close up tomorrow. A deputy asked me down at the river if I thought you were gay. That will probably be topic number two among every one in town. Should I call Claudia and tell her not to come in tomorrow?"

"I hear what you're saying, Lynda. Rather than closing the store, we can bring in another pharmacist. One of my associates is filling in at Craft's Drugs in Elwood. Interestingly, my pharmacist colleague's name is Elwood. Anyway, Elwood and I can change places. I'll take his shifts and he can take mine. Call into the local radio station, the one with the inane announcers who think they're so funny. If they report bake sales and students home from college, they'll announce that you've brought a new pharmacist on board. Plus tell every customer who comes in. When I started, most everyone in town knew that I had taken over as pharmacist within 24 hours without the benefit of a media alert."

"Alright. I know I overreacted."

"No I'm glad you brought it up. You've lived in Burgoyne long enough that I've learned to trust your instincts. But my instincts say we shouldn't close.

And is it still okay if I stay at the cottage?"

"Yes. It's okay. We've still got some time before we have to vacate the place."

"Billings ordered me not to get involved in the search. I'll work tomorrow morning so he'll assume I'm complying. If need be, I'll go out to look for Zach once I get back to the cottage."

48

BILLINGS DROVE VIC BACK, THIS TIME IN THE FRONT
SEAT. The lights in the cottage were on and the door
was unlocked. His first thought was that some of the
track team had come in to use the bathroom. That
idea was dispelled when Vic saw that someone had
gone through his things. His checkbook, the pocket-
sized journal, and his Visa receipts, were strewn on
top of his bed. His other gun and the box of
cartridges that he had recently moved to the rafters
above the shower were untouched. He surmised that
warrants were not considered to be requisite for
police searches in Burgoyne. He wasn't altogether
certain, though, that it was a deputy who had
unceremoniously gone through things.

Vic had Billing's consent to work the
following morning in Elwood. That should give him
from 3:30 on and into the evening to hunt for Zach,
albeit without Billing's consent. He knew there'd be
lots of other people searching and maybe one of
them would be successful. If Zach had gone
somewhere of his own accord, Vic knew some of
the best places to look. If Greg took Vic to all of the
Hawkins landmarks, he would have shared those
places with Zach. Vic wrote out a list of places to

check and organized them so that there'd be minimal back tracking.

He was too wound up to sleep, which was fine since he still had several calls to make. The simplest call was to Elwood Barnes.

"Yeah, Vic, I know where the Ebert store is. I've talked to Claudine a couple of times. She seems on top of things," Elwood said.

"Her name's Claudia, so you won't start off on the wrong foot. Thanks for making the switch Elwood."

"Glad to help. Oh yeah, your tech at Craft tomorrow is a guy named Jeremy. I'll let him know you're coming."

Vic was overdue checking in with Patrice Wilkins.

"Patrice, this is Vic. Before we talk about the robberies I need to tell you that Zach Ebert is missing. I'm not sure what Billing's official take on things is but I'm being treated as a person of interest."

"And why do they think you have anything to do with it?"

"They found Zach's bike submerged under the dock behind the Ebert cottage. I'm switching stores with a guy so that Lynda can have pharmacist coverage that doesn't scare away any more of her business."

"And where will you be working or are you taking off to look for Zach?" Patrice asked.

"I'll be at a store down in Elwood. I've got some ideas of places to look when I get off. I'll still have five or six hours before it gets dark.

I can't help but think this has something to do with everything else that's been going on. I need to know. Do you have any news on the robberies?"

"Vic, I'm probably not telling you anything you don't know, but as you suspected everything is consistent with these drug heists being a ruse to cover up Greg's killing. In other words, I'm agreeing with your supposition. Other than the oxycodone and the Parliaments, there's no consistency in what was taken."

"So, are you saying he was an amateur?"

"Far from it. There was nothing clumsy about any aspect of these crimes. There aren't clues other than a vague description of somebody big. No alarms set off. Nobody could identify a vehicle. No. He's good. The other two robberies were close to I-75. He could get away quickly and there were exits a few miles in either direction if he wanted to go onto less traveled roads in a hurry.

Oh. And I might as well share the ballistics report with you. Greg was shot with a 38 ... a 38 with a silencer. Whoever did this intended to use the gun for more than intimidation."

"Thanks, Patrice. I hope I can get back to working on this for you but right now I've got to do what I can to find Zach."

"Of course. Be careful, Vic."

"You, too."

"TRACY, DO YOU HAVE A FEW MINUTES? Things have gotten more complicated down here."

"Sure, Victor, It's not like I've got anything pressing.."

"Thanks. I need to talk. Zach is missing. He has taken off on his own before but never for this long. I was a suspect for a while. I may still be. They found his bike submerged under the dock. I'm going to search along the river tomorrow. Wish the life jackets hadn't all burnt up in the fire."

"Why don't you leave this for the police. I know what Zach means to you but you've always investigated as part of a team with authority or anonymously ... undercover, I mean. You have no back-up, you have no way to conceal what you're doing, and based on the fact that you're calling me to talk this through, you must not have anyone you can confide in down there. And for God's sake, stay off the river if you can't get another life jacket," Tracy said.

"Okay. I'll be careful. I could wear my fishing vest. It's roughly as effective as those inflated things kids wear around their arms. It'll have to do.

I feel like I've done more harm than good down here. I'm not saying all of this is my fault but since I got here, Will was killed; Lynda has sold all of her river front property; the pharmacy's business is skidding down hill, probably will close; and, now Zach is missing."

"Yeah, but you work better when you're under pressure. I can picture your intense scowl," Tracy said.

"Me and Harrison Ford. But it is intense. I'm working in Elwood, probably through the end of the week. Once we know something about ... I mean locate Zach, I think I'll be getting my intense self back up to Louisville," he said.

"Speaking of Louisville, I should tell you that David has reemerged, like nothing happened. He says he was preoccupied with separating from his wife ... moving out permanently."

"Is he staying with you then?"

"Hardly. He says he's getting over being mad at us."

"At us?" I asked.

"Well, mostly with you."

"Why with me?"

"I guess you're not supposed to be a part of my life, not that we're anything more than non-hostile exes. Plus he's still vindictive about your efforts to get the Pharmacy Practice Act expanded. He says you pharmacists act like you're doctors."

"Yeah. We sure wouldn't want to do anything to provide more immediate care or to reduce health care costs. Anyhow it sounds like he's decided to be mad. He could as easily decide not to be mad. So what are you doing about our misguided friend?"

"I'm reconsidering things. There's a man I've had coffee with a couple of times. He's the provost at U.K. Louisville. He has a colleague who has been getting some nasty chemo and so that's how I met him."

"Anyhow, between Dr. Academics and me, we ought to be able to 'beat up' Rothstein the next time he takes your doll or pulls your pigtails."

"My heroes!"

"I got to go, Tracy. Thanks for letting me talk. I needed to vent a little and think about something else."

"I know. Bye, Victor."

"Bye."

49

JEREMY, THE TECHNICIAN, GAVE VIC A BRIEF TOUR. Craft Drugs could best be described as a professional pharmacy emphasized by the sign labeled "apothecary" that hung over the prescription counter. Several antique bottles and other artifacts were displayed throughout the store. Front-end merchandise was limited to popular non-prescription drugs, each in one size only. Jeremy and he would be handling all patients by themselves. The computer system was one with which Vic was familiar and so he didn't expect to have any technology glitches.

Jeremy reiterated what Vic already knew about the owners. From mid-Spring through mid-Fall, the Crafts, both pharmacists, became more preoccupied with managing the Craft Bed and Breakfast on Lake Morgan than in overseeing their pharmacy. The B & B was adjacent to the marina and the campgrounds / RV park that they also owned. The situation meant an extended assignment for Elwood. The Crafts offered Elwood boating and fishing privileges that he rarely used.

Craft Drugs didn't get busy … their definition of busy … until mid morning. Vic had time to familiarize himself with the store and to hear the technician's story. Jeremy had tried repeatedly to get admitted to pharmacy programs but his grade average in science courses disqualified him each time he applied. He seemed resigned, not bitter. Jeremy was no Claudia in his dealings with the patients. Few people could be. But he was technically sound and efficient.

"Why don't I put away the drug order sitting back here? You can enjoy your coffee. Call me if you need me."

"Sure, Vic," Jeremy agreed.

Vic made a habit of restocking the prescription shelves in stores that were new to him. That demonstrated to pharmacy techs that he considered himself to be part of a professional team. It is a small but pointed gesture that lets them know that he will not relegate all of the dirty work to them. Some pharmacists act as if anything not directly involving patients is too menial. Just as important, by putting away stock, he learned the nuances of how merchandise is arranged. Knowing how to find things made him more efficient and helped him behave confidently in front of patients.

Vic moved aside a couple of pint bottles of a codeine containing elixir to put the newest stock to the back. A handgun came into view. It was positioned so that a person could grip it in firing position. Vic pulled it out and broke it down. It was clean and fully loaded. He replaced it the way he found it.

"What's with the gun Jeremy? I mean, I know it's a '32 but keeping it here isn't such a good idea."

"I know. We technicians had a seminar last year about how to cope with store crime ... shoplifting, employee theft, and robberies. They told us that the best thing to do if robbed is to cooperate fully. Never try to be a hero. I tried to explain this to the bosses, the Crafts, but Lester especially has become paranoid about these robberies. He's repositioned it a dozen times. He claims it's now in the 'quick draw' spot."

"I wanted to be sure you wouldn't do something to endanger yourself or me."

"No risk of that. My wife's expecting. She's already given me my orders. By the way it'll be Lester relieving you this afternoon. The Crafts each pull a shift every other day."

A sloppily dressed, younger looking, bulky male came in and attempted to look casual as he walked over to the cough and cold section of the tiny front end. This phenomenon was less common than a few years ago when there had been a change in the law governing the starting chemical for meth production, pseudoephedrine. When stricter controls were initiated a myth circulated among the drugies that rural pharmacists don't learn about new regulations right away, as if electronic messages slow down outside of urban areas or maybe pharmacists in small town settings are slow readers.

Something about this man caught Vic's attention. When he glanced over his shoulder Vic recognized him as Gus Stoner, the guy he had extracted from the hood of his car in Frankfort and a recurring thorn in Vic's side. His response might have been one of puzzled recognition of Vic, or more likely one of general dullness. He looked a second time, showed Vic his smirk, and left twisting his scraggly goatee.

"When do you take your lunch break? We don't seem to be too busy right now, Jeremy."

"Now would be good, Vic. I'll drive over and get a sub. Can I bring you one?"

"Half a meatball on whole-grain. Let me give you some money."

On his way out, Jeremy held the door open for a woman. He turned and watched her as she sashayed back to the prescription counter. The woman was Julie. She was unmistakable even in what for her were baggy jeans, a yellow cap with a broad brim, and oversized sunglasses.

"The Jag or the Ford 150?" Vic greeted her.

"I'm slumming. The Jag. My new truck is worth more than my seven year old Jaguar. I heard from Lynda, you were over here. I thought I'd warn you."

"Warn me? Warn me about what?"

"There's a stalker. Well, I'm the stalker and I'm practicing for when you're in Louisville."

"I've got to have some resolution with Zach first. At least I hope to before going."

"Timmy and a couple of the men have been on the river. I know how this sounds but people are spending a lot of time downstream."

"I've got a few more places to look but I'm running out of ideas, too," he said.

"I've got to go Vic. I only wanted to see how you were holding up."

"Thanks. See you Julie."

Vic was mid meatball sandwich when he looked up to face Ali. She lived in Elwood but he held no illusions. She wouldn't be representing the community welcome wagon.

"I heard you were here," Ali began.

"Bad news travels fast."

Without arguing she said, "I guess we're going face to face with our proposals to John Sennett. I have the contracts in the bag. Why don't you save yourself some embarrassment and drop out?"

"I guess you might want to think about the same. I've been on the Kentucky Pharmacy Board's website. There are some ethical and legal infractions that Mr. Sennett and the board of directors would be interested in if I were to pass on a certain URL."

"Are you blackmailing me?"

"No. I'm doing my best to safeguard the health of the patient base we currently serve and to protect our assisted living facilities from being associated with anything scandalous. A pharmacy board member has agreed to accompany me to the presentations if you insist on not dropping out."

50

"VIC, I USUALLY MAKE A RUN TO THE BANK ABOUT NOW. It's 1:15. We're too small an operation to use Brinks or one of the other armored car services."

"Sure Jeremy. I kind of assumed that you were making out a deposit slip for some reason. I'll be fine until you get back."

Of course, Vic would be able to keep up. This pharmacy made Ebert Drugs look like Wal-Mart on the Friday after Thanksgiving. The owners' other business enterprises had to be showing a good profit. The Crafts had always paid Pharmacists-PRN on time so money was coming in from somewhere. Even if business at the store picked up at night, things seemed very slow.

A large man shouldered his way through the door. He didn't look familiar to Vic. He was dressed in denim including a jacket even though it was 70 degrees and sunny. The jacket collar was turned-up and a hat was pulled over most of his face. He quickly scanned the perimeters of the store, hesitating briefly when he spied each of the two security cameras. Vic didn't peg him as someone there to pick-up a prescription.

He typed a few strokes on the computer and turned purposefully toward the aisle where bulk liquids were stored. He reached behind the elixirs, eased out the gun, and transferred it to his left hand. He unholstered his backup gun with his right hand and took off the safety. He dropped low and moved into a firing position. It crossed his mind that his reaction might be extreme. It was possible he was about to piss off Craft Drugs' number one customer. That number one customer was being patient, or if not patient, he was being quiet.

Vic looked into a mirror that was mounted in a position making it possible to see if anyone might be standing at the register located at the end of the counter. From his low angle, Vic only saw ceiling. He continued looking at the changing image as he slowly moved into a more upright position. He saw the man's hat first. He was wearing Will's fishing hat. It was as if he had taken it like it was a trophy. Like he'd take a scalp. As Vic rose further out of his crouch he made out a left arm and hand. The hand held a gun with a long silver barrel. It wasn't a long barrel, though. It was a silencer.

There was a swinging wooden door at the end of the counter. That door should have blocked Vic's view of anybody from the shoulders on down. The man was tall but not that tall. Vic hadn't heard the door swing. Nor had he heard footfalls on the elevated wooden platform. This guy was good.

The assailant's forward motion, his movement toward Vic, had stopped, evidently to figure out his next move. Vic guessed that it would come quickly. Someone else coming in the store could make things complicated.

Vic's view of the gun dropped from sight as he lowered himself preemptively into a position making him a smaller target. In doing so, the adversaries looked into the reflections of each other's faces. The gunman smiled, knowing that he had Vic trapped in a dead-end aisle. Vic lowered his gun slightly hoping to appear unarmed. But the guy was not easily duped. He was experienced enough to anticipate that any trapped victim will be capable of resisting in some way.

Vic knew that the closer the guy came, the worse his chance of surviving a shootout became. Vic fired first. The mirror exploded. Immediately, bottles began shattering above him and then directly in front of him as the guy shot through the shelving.

Vic tossed out the '32 out in front of the man as he yelled, "I give up. I'm coming out."

The man said, "Listen up, Jerknuts. Step out real slow with your hands where I can see 'em."

Vic moved to where the last shot had exited, stuck only his backup gun and his hand around the corner and fired three times at zones he guessed to be slightly right, slightly left, and dead-center.

Vic heard what he assumed to be a gun falling with a thud onto the elevated platform. As he stepped out of what was now a nearly destroyed hiding place, he slipped on the syrup-covered floor, landing on his back. Vic's hand struck the counter top and his gun skidded toward the gunman.

The man had a red stain growing below his left shoulder but he was pulling himself upright by holding onto the counter. When he saw Vic's gun, he let himself half fall, half crawl toward it.

Although Vic had quickly returned to his feet, he wasn't about to gamble on who would get to the gun first. He picked up the upper half of a shattered gallon bottle and threw it underhand with the same motion and velocity he would if it was a bowling ball lofted half-way down the alley. The man moved to deflect it with his right arm but there wasn't time and he only managed to ricochet the flying object into his own face.

The man was blinded by a combination of glass and grape-flavored syrup. Vic didn't give him an opportunity to recover. He scrambled to pick up his backup Kahr as the guy groped frantically behind himself trying to wipe his eyes with his shoulder. The man grasped his own dropped weapon by the silencer and was in the process of switching it to his other hand.

Vic didn't wait for the transfer. He fired his two remaining rounds ... one for Greg and one for Will ... into the center of the man's chest.

This was Vic's second shooting incident in the past week. It equaled the number of times he'd fired a weapon in the line of duty. Once he had taken part in a shoot out, firing several rounds through a window into what turned out to be an empty bedroom. The other instance was when his partner and he had fired at a fleeing suspect. The ballistics report showed that one of Vic's bullets had stuck the suspect in the leg, the shot that had brought the fleeing man down. Vic knew that when county authorities talked to him about this event, he should act remorseful that the robber was dead.

Vic took a more careful look at the syrup-flecked face. It was not the man who had watched him with interest at the restaurant his first night in Burgoyne. According to his Ohio driver's license, the man was Alexander Zhoban. Vic further compromised the crime scene by picking up Will's hat, leaving the store long enough to stash it in his car. He didn't touch the orange that rolled out of the man's jacket pocket.

JEREMY AND THEN TWO ELWOOD PATROLMEN ARRIVED. Since neither officer knew Vic, Jeremy identified him and verified that he was the good guy at the crime scene. Jeremy further attested to the fact that the unfired weapon had been on the premises and that any pharmacist with a license to carry, Vic in this case, did so because of the string of recent robberies. Vic reluctantly handed over his gun to the officer in charge.

An EMT checked Vic's vital signs and gave him a blanket. Vic hadn't realized until then that he was shivering. By the time the police were ready to let him leave, two hours later, not one but three blankets and several cups of coffee had warmed him but did little to calm him down.

Jeremy insisted on hugging him as he got into his car to leave. Vic complied and then as they shook hands he said, "You ought to retake organic chemistry. You'll be a pharmacist yet."

IN HIS FOGGINESS, VIC TRIED TO DETERMINE WHO KNEW HE WAS IN ELWOOD. Who sent this giant thug, this person he'd identified as Zhoban, to shoot him?

He had told the sheriff he was going to be in
Elwood. This meant that everyone on the town
council, revitalization committee, and river
development team ... many of whom were the same
people ... knew. There was the radio announcement
that there was a new pharmacist in Burgoyne. It's a
small town. Probably everybody knew.

Vic called Patrice Wilkins, explained his
encounter with Zhoban, and asked if she could e-
mail him anything the agency had on the guy that
could be shared. This was Vic's way, too, of giving
her a head start in getting some of the credit for
solving the three pharmacy robberies.

51

IT WAS AFTER FOUR BEFORE VIC GOT BACK TO THE
COTTAGE. He checked his phone for e-mails and
found one from Agent Wilkins. It said simply,
"Thank You Consultant (Agent) Fye. See attached."

The first attachment was lengthy. The
contents seemed extremely detailed but details are
the essence of DEA protocol. The person writing a
background check is typically not the agent who
ends up testifying or otherwise using the
information. As much as possible, the facts are
presented along with any context information that
was unearthed. Anything the person doing the
background didn't personally know or understand
before beginning the process, subsequent users of
the material also might not know. The rule then is,
'When in doubt, include it.' Hence, many of these
reports read more like a narrative than a composite
of facts. As in this report, he'd often found himself
thinking, "Get to the point."

The second attachment was an executive
summary. It gave Zhoban's birthdate and some
family and educational details. It went on to relate
that following a psychiatric discharge from the
military, Zhoban became a professional wrestler
who moved up the ranks to the point that he had

several nationally televised bouts. He "retired" after he went off-script once too often either because of "roid rage" or his natural sociopathic tendencies. Zhoban did not remain unemployed for long. His skills and temperament made it easy for him to transition into thuggery. He had been arrested twice for assault and in both instances the victims, suspected opiate addicts, dropped the charges. A second one-sentence paragraph in a different font followed: "Zhoban always wore orange wrestling tights."

Once Vic absorbed the abbreviated background information on Zhoban, he pulled out his notes about where to look for Zach. There was only one place that he was sure had gone unsearched. The problem was Vic didn't know how to find that one place and if he did locate it, how he would manage to gain entry. All of his investigative instincts told him though that in some way the cave held the key. He had to find the cave.

If Vic's interpretation of Greg's cave discovery was correct, he needed to look on the west side of the river, the side opposite from the Ebert cottage. The bluffs, forming what the DNR called the Palisades, were high and steep with the exception of a lower plain across from Riverton and another one that was the site of the Laine's dock. The Palisades were composed largely of limestone, a substance often associated with caves. The wooded bluff to the north of the dilapidated shack had been searched thoroughly by several of the boys on Zach's team. The bluff to the south was the Laine farm, all pasture and buildings. It was not

unusual for landowners to close off or even to
dynamite-shut cave openings, usually to protect
their own kids as well as to minimize their liability
should other peoples' kids get hurt. Vic's option
that had the greatest potential for bearing fruit was
to look for the water entrance to the cave that Greg
claimed to have found.

The Ebert fishing boat was tied to the dock.
It must have been commandeered by some of the
search crew members. In any case, it still had a half
tank of gas.

Vic tightened the strap on his fishing jacket.
It was designed to provide only a modest degree of
buoyancy. The brochure describing the jacket, as he
recalled, stated that it would help a person in rapids
or fast moving water to think about avoiding rocks
rather than staying afloat. It had a cautionary note
sewn into a seam, stating that it was a swimming
aid not a life jacket. Vic stuffed most of the
zippered pockets with its custom shaped Styrofoam
inserts. He sealed a couple of protein bars, a utility
knife, a small but powerful flashlight, and his Glock
in plastic bags and secured them in the remaining
pockets. He filled a water bottle with ice.

His cell phone rang as he started out the
door. His caller i.d. came up "Lynda".

"I heard about Elwood. I contacted Sheriff
Billings and he said you were okay. Are you really
alright?" Lynda asked.

"Yes, but more importantly, have you, has
anybody found Zach?"

"No. I'm trying to remain hopeful but we're
running out of places to look," Lynda said.

"By the way, one of the victims of the other robbery identified the guy you killed as the person who had robbed her. She said the jacket was definitely his and that the guy had been that big. He's probably the bastard who killed Greg, too."

"Agreed. Let me tell you where I'm looking, Lynda. I think Greg may have found the cave and I think he told Zach. My best chance is if I can locate a water entrance at the base of one of the bluffs on the other side, the west side, of the river. It'll be under the Laine's or the other property right across from the cottage. It's a long shot, I know, but there's no point in me retracing places where other people have looked."

"I know how you are with water. What if you have to swim?" Lynda asked.

"The river is as low as it ever gets. I'm hoping I won't have to do a lot of swimming. I'll call you if I find a way in. I need to go. I don't have too many hours before it gets dark," he said, trying to sound upbeat.

Lynda sniffed. Her voice was breaking up. "I thought I couldn't cry any more.

Oh.

Good.

Rex and Claudia just pulled in the drive.

Call me no matter what."

"I will," Vic said.

VIC WISHED HE WAS MORE COMFORTABLE HANDLING THE FISHING BOAT. He'd watched Greg manipulate the choke and throttle enough that he knew how to start the motor cold and how to start it once it was warmed up. And he had driven it a couple of weeks ago with no problems. Still, he made sure that there were oars on board before he untied the lines from the dock and started toward the opposite shore.

He headed north of the shanty. There were no other boats on the river. The search party had moved their operation well downstream. The vegetation was sparse three feet or so above the water. The silt-covered limestone was typically below the water line this time of the year. The bluffs along this part of the river were steep but not vertical. An occasional root or extension of a vine altered the contour enough to provide demarcations and a sense of movement. Vic cut the engine and let the boat drift with the current close to the shore. He repeatedly thrust the handle of an oar below the water's surface, hoping he'd meet no resistance. With every thrust, he hit something solid, presumably a continuation of the limestone. He went fifty yards or so beyond what he thought was a realistic distance from the shanty based on Greg's notes. Vic didn't want to overlook any possibility.

Vic started the engine and steered the boat to the middle of the river before heading south past the Laine dock. He recognized Timmy's boat among the three tied off there. Timmy preferred to come to work by boat. His commute was three fourths of a mile by water and twelve miles in his truck. The state and federal highway commissioners saw no justification for erecting yet another bridge across the Kentucky River given the sparse Woodford County population.

Vic pulled close to the shore again and repeated his previous procedure, thrusting an oar below the water's surface every two or three feet. But in many areas the bluff face hung far enough over the water that Vic had to stretch further than he was comfortable in order to make contact with rock. The current was slow but the water was too deep for him to see any openings, if indeed a cave mouth existed at all. He maneuvered the boat into a slight recess in the face of the bluff. He tried to make contact below the water surface but couldn't do it. The water felt several degrees colder, colder even than areas shaded from direct sunlight.

Vic's initial thoughts were that this might be a good place to fish. He instinctively looked on the bluff face for an easily identifiable feature ... an unusual shaped outcropping or a natural ledge in the limestone. He saw neither because his eyes were drawn to what looked like a plastic cylinder stuck into a small fissure. He steered closer. He'd seen the orange pen or many others like it. It carried the logo for Ebert Drugs. Greg had marked this spot.

52

VIC TIED THE BOAT TO AN EXPOSED ROOT THAT EXTENDED FROM A SCRAWNY TREE. Somehow, that tree, like randomly scattered other ones, found a way to grow on the sheer rock face. He slipped over the side into the water, holding onto the boat for as long as he could. The jacket provided just enough buoyancy to keep his mouth above the water. Greg was a good swimmer. He would have been undaunted by what Vic was about to try. The water was cool but not cold enough to account for all of Vic's shivering.

Vic took a breath and pulled himself under the overhang, bracing his back against it as he reached forward, seeking an opening. He touched only rock. He pushed himself back out, grabbed the side of the boat, and took in air. He had no choice but to try again. He told himself that he had to make himself stay under the water a lot longer than his last effort. He had tried what seemed to be the closest, the easiest area for a non-swimmer. Greg's pen probably pointed him to exactly where he needed to go, not to the general vicinity. He maneuvered himself into a better position to try again, this time, directly below what Vic hoped was the indicator for the cave.

He took a deeper breath and pulled himself forward again, in toward the wall of the bluff. He could feel a cold current as his fingers curled under a recessed area. He used that grip to pull himself down and further forward. His feet touched bottom and he found himself in a slight crouch. He decided to duck walk ten steps before turning around to get air and to get help. With his seventh step there was nothing solid above him. He stood up and was relieved to find his head was out of the water.

He took a breath and opened his eyes. He was inside the cave. After a minute or so of adjusting to the darker area he made out a glow from high overhead. He pulled the flashlight out of its pocket, took it out of its plastic bag, and turned it on. He walked further forward, looking for a place to pull himself out of the water. He was glad that he had reread the passages in the books that described the cave. He surmised that he must be at the bottom of the gorge that formed the cave's river.

The water became gradually shallower until it barely reached up to his knees. He stepped onto a narrow ledge.

He thought again about Zach. In spite of his body type, Zach was an excellent swimmer. If Greg had told him how to negotiate the opening, it would have been easier for him to get to the point Vic found himself. He would need to systematically search this area but he might require some help to do it. He elected to explore the ledge further before retracing his steps and reversing his underwater excursion. He flashed the light first up and then back down the ledge. It was wide enough for walking, although at times a person would have to move sideways. He didn't expect to see Zach standing someplace, but he wasn't exactly sure where else to start looking at this point. Maybe he would find Zach higher up and nearer to the site of the dim glow. He edged his way up the slight incline, moving the light back and forth from the wall to the ledge to the crevice with its slow, steady flow of water.

He carefully stepped back down into the water and, finding it to be below his knees, walked back toward the under water passage toward the river. He used the light to determine where it would be necessary to lower his head to work his way out. He removed the plastic bag from the side pocket so that he could rewrap the flashlight. He didn't trust the "waterproof" designation. Sometimes the term waterproof for an object meant little more than some degree of functionality if conditions happened to be foggy.

He had turned off the light seconds before he heard a weak moan. He switched the light back on and aimed the beam toward the ledge, the most likely area for the sound to originate. Echoing and the gurgling of flowing water made such a determination more guess work than anything else. Immediately to his right, there was a narrow, teardrop-shaped passage leading from the ledge. Vic raised himself onto his toes and shone in the light. He saw two bare feet and ankles. The big toe of the right foot twitched.

53

VIC HOISTED HIMSELF OUT OF THE WATER. He flashed the beam into the passage. It was Zach. His arms were drawn around his chest and he looked frightened. Vic redirected the light onto his own face and said, "It's me, Zach. It's Vic."

"Hi," Zach answered in a husky whisper.

Vic let him drink most of the water from his bottle, insisting that he sip it slowly. He convinced Zach to save enough to wash down the two energy bars he had packed. Zach revived enough to sit up and to begin to talk.

"There's a bunch of plants, weed I think, up above us. It's not too hard to get up there. I heard somebody coming and tried to come back down. I dropped something and whoever it was must have heard me. He turned on some overhead lights and started shooting at me. I thought I saw a place to hide but it turned out to be a shadow and I fell. I hit the water feet first and hurt my ankle. I think it's broken. I worked my way to the side and crawled in here.

He kept firing shots. I guess he thought he hit me or something. He gave up after a while and turned off the bright lights. I couldn't swim out. My ankle was too painful and I kind of made it worse when I tried to stand up in the water."

"You've been in here almost two days," Vic said.

"I wasn't sure. I was able to crawl over for water but I haven't felt like it for a while," he said.

"I'll get you some more. It must be okay to drink. You haven't had diarrhea or anything have you?"

"No. It probably comes from some underground stream. It tastes kind of metallic but it's okay."

Vic refilled the bottle for him two more times. He examined his ankle and decided there were no broken bones but from the extent of the swelling and bruising it looked like there were some seriously torn ligaments.

Zach said, "Dad told me how to find the opening and about how he wedged the pen into the bank. He said we'd have to swim underwater. The idea was that the three of us would explore it together once you were in Burgoyne.

I was angry with Steph's dad. He wouldn't let me see her. I rode my bike to the cottage as hard as I could but I was still mad. I got my kayak, took off, and before I knew it I was down here looking around. When I saw the pen, I thought what the hell. I'm going in."

"It's going to be okay. I'm going back for help. I'm not sure I trust the sheriff but I'll have a DEA friend of mine call in some state authorities to help get you out of here and to investigate the stuff you found up above us."

"You're going to swim out of here?" Zach asked in wonderment.

"Not exactly swim, but this jacket helps me float and I can walk until I get to the tunnel," Vic said.

"The tunnel was scary for me and I'm not, uh ... I'm comfortable in the water," Zach said.

"And, I'm not. Thanks for reminding me though. I'm telling myself that this'll be the last time I'll have to do it. Here. You keep the light and you may as well take my gun. A little less weight should help my buoyancy."

Vic walked as far as he could until he reached the entrance. He took a deep breath and forced himself through the passage. It seemed a lot longer getting through than he remembered and he didn't want to pull too hard and use too much energy. He popped out on the other side and the fishing vest still held him up. That wouldn't have come as such a big relief to most people. Vic expected to find the boat where he'd secured it. He thought at first that he simply couldn't see it because the sky had darkened so much with an impending storm. But it simply was gone.

He was only 50 yards from the Laine dock, the quickest way to get onto dry land. The slow current would carry him that distance and he could hold onto roots and at times the cliff for security. He hoped that he wouldn't find anyone else hanging around but he heard smashing sounds that indicated he wasn't going to be that lucky.

He edged his way around the cliff until he could see what remained of Greg's boat being unceremoniously broken apart on the dock. One of Johnny's men was straining to pick up the motor. He dropped the engine and stared at where Vic was bobbing in the water. The current swirled a little at the bend and a root he clung to in order to maintain his position snapped. The man pulled a gun from behind his back and yelled to someone else. Vic started pulling himself against the current, hand over hand, back to the cave entrance.

He heard someone pulling on an outboard rope. One man cursed at his companion. After a couple of more pulls, the motor started.

Vic took a breath. He hoped that in his excitement that the breath was deep enough. It had become too dark to see the pen but he was reasonably sure he knew how to find the opening. He pulled himself under and extended his palms to grip the opening. It was a wall of rock. He must have gone too far to the left. Go right. Go right.

Edging right didn't do it. He still felt only shear wall. He'd have opted to face the men except he wasn't sure that Zach would ever be able to get out of the cave on his own. He moved back left to where he thought he'd started. His left hand felt the ridge he must have barely missed the first time. He pulled himself under and forced himself to hold his breath in spite of the fact he was using his head as much as his back to sustain forward motion. He pulled through the water with cupped hands trying to ignore whatever was scraping his neck. He wheezed and coughed several times once he finally stood up.

"Vic? Vic? Couldn't you make it?"

He interrupted his gasping and said, "Yes."

Vic explained the situation to Zach and asked how he should go about climbing to the top of the gorge.

"I don't think they'll expect me up at the top for a while but I better move fast. I'll leave my jacket with you but I think I better take my Glock … the gun I gave you."

Vic edged his way up the gradually sloping ledge. It narrowed the higher it rose above the water. Vic passed a second side passage opening. Zach had told him he had rejected it as a hiding place because it was a major roosting place for bats. Not surprisingly, the smell of their dung was intense. Vic caught a whiff of it as he went past.

He worked his way upward until the ledge almost came to an end. Just like Zach had told him, there was a wide fissure leading up the wall. Vic wedged himself sideways into that crevice in a modified prenatal position. It extended what seemed to be a long way upward, but it was probably less than a dozen feet to the top of the crack. He used his legs to maintain each new position as he squirmed closer and closer to the top. Once he developed a system Vic then understood why it was too challenging for Zach to be able to negotiate it with his badly sprained ankle. Vic had almost reached the second and higher ledge when the plastic bag containing his pistol slipped out of the waistband of his shorts. There was a series of clanks and then a splash. He opted not to take the time to wriggle back down to look for it. Instead, he continued to pull himself up and out of the crevice.

Zach had told him that the light never went out ... that there was always the eerie glow. The glow had gotten brighter and seemed almost like muted daylight from this higher perspective. The aura came from a large number of growing lights that illuminated a thirty-by-thirty foot cavern room ... not a room so much as the widest part of the passage. The lights revealed a sophisticated hydroponics operation. There were several pumps that kept the water and nutrients circulating. There were two other pieces of equipment that Vic thought might function to generate a continuous supply of carbon dioxide. And there was the marijuana itself. There were hundreds of plants in various stages of development. The marijuana looked luxurious, probably derived from Southeast Asian or Latin American varieties. He had seen several such facilities, usually in a basement or in a bedroom but none were on this scale or had attained this level of sophistication.

Vic reasoned that the house and stables above depended on water from several deep wells that probably tapped into the same source that supplied the underground river. The electricity for pumping the water and maintaining the lights for this growing chamber would be a small fraction of that required to run the entire above ground operation. Odors from fertilization or the plants themselves could be vented through the barn to mingle with and be well masked by the aromas of hay and horse excrement. Whoever designed all of this was diabolically brilliant. There would be no utility bills that would seem excessive compared to a working horse farm with several out buildings. There would be nothing to arouse the suspicions of anyone, assuming there was any reason to be looking for a hydroponic farm in the first place.

There was a slightly smaller cavern on the other side of the gorge. Three thick, foot-wide planks formed a bridge that connected the two chambers. That other room had areas Vic's experience told him were used for manicuring. He saw more glass condensers, retorts, and other equipment than Vic had in his entire organic chemistry lab. This was equipment for extracting tetrahydrocannabinol or THC, the psychoactive component of weed. There were empty and filled cartridges that looked to be the right size for vaping pens. On another bench there was a tablet press and several bags of tablets that looked like Percodan. The bottle of powder may or may not have contained oxycodone.

Vic, still dripping from his water excursion, dried himself as best he could on a lab coat. There were cameras with blinking red lights mounted strategically throughout the two chambers. He doubted that they were positioned to detect intruders. It was more likely that they were there to monitor the people who manicured and otherwise processed the plants and made the counterfeit oxycodone tablets.

A heavy metal door with a chicken-wired safety glass window was built into one end of the second chamber. It was unlocked and led to a narrow passage that barely allowed Vic to walk upright.

There was a windowless door at the other
end. Vic regretted that he'd made no attempt to
retrieve the gun he dropped. He could only hope he
wasn't walking into a shooting situation. He slowly
swung open the door. There was a set of steps
leading upward and an elevator door with a single
button with an indicator pointing up. Vic opted for
the stairs. The door at the top took him into an area
he had seen on his abbreviated tour of the stables. It
had two small offices, a conference room with a
table and four chairs, and a space that housed a
coffee maker, an office refrigerator, and a
microwave. He remembered seeing the door that he
had come through. He had assumed at the time that
it lead to an office supply area or maybe to a space
where records and old accounts were maintained

No one should be able to hear him in the
stable area. The weather front that had been moving
into the area all day had arrived with a vengeance.
The rain made machine-gun like rat-a-tats on the
roof. There was a night light level of illumination
that was more than bright enough, given his
familiarity with the building. He had to assume that
Johnny's men would be expecting him but he
doubted that they would have access to the house.

Through the rain he could make out a light
in front of the house's attached four-car garage. His
hair and shirt were soaked again by the time he
reached the garage's side door. He felt foolish that
he had so carefully dried himself off earlier. The
side door was unlocked.

54

JULIE, HER HAND ON THE DRIVER-SIDE DOOR OF HER JAG, TURNED TO FACE HIM. "Vic, what the ...?"

"Julie, I need your help. It's Johnny who killed Greg and Will. Or he had it done."

She put her hand on the front of her head and drew it down as if tightening the skin on her face. Talking through her fingers she said, "I've been trying to tell myself he couldn't have had anything to do with Greg getting killed. I still don't believe it. It's more like what some of his friends would do."

"Julie, a couple of men, men who work here, tore apart my boat, Greg's boat, down at your dock. They came after me but I escaped into the cave."

"The cave? What cave?"

"You don't know?" he asked. "There's this cave system right under where the stables are and right now Zach ... "

An automatic garage door light over an empty space flashed and the door started going up. Julie turned toward it and said, "It's Johnny. He's back early. Hide in my trunk, I'll get you out of here as soon as I can."

She reached down and released the trunk lid. Vic rolled in and curled up in the small compartment. The lid slammed shut behind him. Julie started the car. The garage door stopped its mechanical whine. Then the whirring sound started again until it ended with a thud. The door had closed. The car door slammed shut.

Vic didn't have time to deconstruct what Julie had done. He needed to dedicate his efforts to getting out of the trunk. It was so small he had almost no maneuverability. A blanket was the only thing he could identify. The Jaguar was too well constructed to kick in the seat, even if he could position himself to do it. He found the emergency latch but couldn't release it.

He caught the first whiff of exhaust fumes. He knew that it wasn't the gases he could smell that he needed to worry about. The Jaguar motor was no more efficient than that of any other car. It would generate fatal levels of carbon monoxide within a short time.

Vic got his fingers under the fiberboard spare wheel cover that he was laying on. He curled his wrists forward, elbows to the sides and tucked his knuckles further under the cover. When he rolled his wrists back toward himself he was rewarded with the cracking sound of the splintering fiberboard. He reached down into the well of the trunk, ignoring the painful scrape he got from the broken cover. After a few seconds he located a vinyl bag that rattled. It felt like the standard, minimalist tool kit.

The opening he had created was too small for both a hand and the tools. He rested the tool kit on the spare, positioning it vertically, and drew out his hand. He pinched the bag with his other hand and pulled it out into the trunk. Inside the bag there was some sort of metal rod, maybe the handle of the jack. Vic jammed it into the latch and pulled down hard. There was a snap and the trunk lid popped open.

Vic crawled out headfirst and rolled onto the garage floor. He tried to open the Jaguar door to turn off the ignition but Julie had locked it. The garage was big but he was already feeling the effects of oxygen deprivation on his tissues. He pushed through the side door of the garage out into the storm. The perimeter of the house and the stable area were now brightly lit but that did little to help him see through the rain. He needed to get out of the light, preferably into a dry area if he could, but he also needed to sit down and allow time for the fresh air and its oxygen to replace the carbon monoxide. He remembered that the exchange of the two gases was a slow process ... something about carbon monoxide attaching itself tightly to the red blood cells. He suppressed the impulse to try to breath too rapidly. Hyperventilating wouldn't speed his recovery.

JOHNNY AND JULIE'S MEN GAVE HIM JUST ENOUGH TIME TO RECOVER. There were two of them dressed in rain gear with hoods. One held a handgun. The other had a sawed-off shotgun resting in the crook of his arm. The man with the handgun came close enough that Vic could recognize him as Julie's brother, Timmy. Timmy told the other man to leave. As the man walked briskly into the stable, Timmy stayed where he was, the gun pointing at the center of Vic's chest. Vic's breathing felt like it did on arrival day in Denali National Park but the problem wasn't carbon monoxide. It was fear. Timmy was eight feet away and Vic was in no position to prevent anything Timmy had in mind. Vic wondered if he was any better off than if he'd stayed in the trunk of the Jaguar.

"I've got it now Timmy," said Julie, in a determined tone that up until then Vic wouldn't have identified as her voice. To Vic, she said, "Get up. Don't think for a second I can't or that I won't use this.

Timmy. Have you disposed of Fye's boat?"

"Yeah. Dwayne wanted the motor but I told him to bury it. Everything else is stacked for burning along with the pieces of the kayak," her brother answered.

"Take care of burning it the first thing tomorrow if it's dry enough. Otherwise, bury that too. We were lucky nobody stumbled onto the kayak. Now go ahead of us and unlock the doors leading to the cave. I'm going to see to Mr. Fye."

55

JULIE AND VIC PASSED INTO THE SMALLER CAVERN.
She gestured with her gun toward the plank bridge.
Vic briefly considered jumping but he questioned
whether he'd survive the fall. He obediently crossed
into the hydroponic farm area.

"Lynda's supposedly your best friend but
you killed her husband. I get it that I'm collateral
damage but you went after Zach. How could you
kill Zach for God's sake? He's a kid."

"Timmy gave me all kinds of hell for asking
you to come to Burgoyne. He believed you'd figure
out how to get in the cave. I thought getting rid of
the notebook I found that pinpointed the entrance
and doing my best to distract you would be enough.
Timmy couldn't be persuaded. Then when he saw
you on the island with Zach he decided the two of
you would have to go. And, by the way, Timmy's
not sure if he got Zach. He may still turn up."

"And you, not Timmy, get to take care of
me. Your man Zhoban is out of the picture so it's
your turn to tie up another loose end."

"Seems fitting, doesn't it," Julie said. She
gestured with her gun to indicate Vic should keep
moving.

"You and Johnny put on an act didn't you? Him pretending he's jealous. You promising you'd follow me to Louisville. You had me convinced."

Julie said, "I wouldn't have followed you but I'd have visited you at least until the novelty wore off. I don't give a shit whether you believe me or not but Johnny doesn't know anything about any of this drug business."

"Oh right," he said. "You and Johnny are merely political allies and you've set up this entire system distributing enough THC and Oxy for the entire state of Kentucky. And Johnny knew nothing about it."

"Kentucky and the greater Cincinnati area," she corrected. "No, my first husband put this whole marihuana operation together. Timmy helped set up the expansion and changes after he and I took it over."

"And you explained the drug profits to Johnny how?" he asked.

"Johnny's nothing more than a salesman. He sells himself mostly. He doesn't understand our finances and doesn't want to. As far as he knows all of our money comes from the stud services and the buying and selling of horses.

I tried to convince him not to take on this Riverton Heights project. I was afraid it would draw too much attention to our part of the river. But his partners are his campaign committee boosters; the people who want to make him governor. I had to let him do it.

It turned out that it was Greg I had to worry about. He had everything mapped out in his last notebook. I believed that once I'd gotten rid of him and his notebook, our drug operation would remain a secret. Nobody moving in to the new development would know anything about there ever having been a cave.

Timmy mistook your friend for you when he was fishing near the cave entrance. Timmy took it on himself to contract for our man to take care of you. Will as it turned out.

Unfortunately, I underestimated your resolve and what you'd be able to work out. I guess I assumed that you'd be the same simple guy you always were who I could manipulate with my body."

"You know this is all going away. It won't be long until marijuana will be legal in every state ... even Kentucky."

"Right now we have reliably high potency material and a sophisticated distribution system to back us up. When it's legalized, I'll find a way to tell Johnnie what we've been doing. He'll realize nobody would believe he didn't know what's been going on. He'll use his clout to get us a license and we can move the operation upstairs into the stable. The oxy business is small now but it's getting bigger every month."

"But again what about Zach?" He tried to bring it up less accusingly than before.

"Timmy didn't know it was Zach snooping around until he found the kayak. Timmy told me that he hoped it was you he had shot at. We never did find him. Maybe he got away and made it to shore down stream somewhere."

"From down there?" Vic asked as he casually moved toward the edge of the drop off, as if he was going to be able to see something that would let him evaluate Zach's survival chances.

Vic half-jumped, half-dropped toward the underground river. He'd learned how to do this as a part of his training and he'd unintentionally practiced it on at least an annual basis in his other life as an easily distracted and less than graceful runner. Vic went into a roll as he went over the edge.

It was a drop of eight feet or so onto the wide upper ledge. Vic heard Julie swear and expected her to follow him down the side of the gorge or at least to start shooting. Apparently she wanted to see what she was shooting at because there was a several second delay before the overhead lights illuminated most of the canyon. By that time Vic had reached the opening to the vertical crevice. He sat down on one side of it and eased in, adjusting his legs into a position that could brace him and control his descent.

Vic heard a click when her low healed shoe struck the ledge. Then he heard "Shit!" and the sound of two objects careening off the sides of the gorge. She'd now be pursuing him barefoot and therefore more quietly.

He reconsidered his plan for a slow descent and opted for more of a controlled free-fall down the crevice. He questioned his wisdom in wearing shorts as both legs screamed at him to be gentler. As he slid lower, the rock became more water-worn. But the damage was done.

He maneuvered his feet for the impact with the bottom ... the narrowest part of the ledge. He teetered toward the water but managed to push his forearms against either side of the crack. It was a strong enough hold to let him regain his balance. From above, he heard cloth on rock and a grunt. She couldn't have seen him start down but Julie knew he only had one way to go.

Vic boosted himself into the first and uppermost side passage beside the ledge. He didn't want to lead Julie to Zach. Zach's small cavern might have been submerged if the water level of the river was normal any previous time she was down here. If she didn't find Zach, he might still be able to muster the strength to get out of his cell-like cave on his own.

The overhead lights provided enough indirect illumination into Vic's hiding place that he could see hundreds of bats hanging from the ceiling. He was squatting in their dung but he was more concerned that they seemed restless. He could only surmise that some instinct or some scouting system made them stay out of the electrical storm outside. He assumed that they wouldn't attack him unprovoked but many bats are supposedly rabid. He wondered whether rabid bats were as aggressive as rabid skunks were alleged to be. His legs were scraped and bleeding. Are bats attracted to human blood? The real question was would any of this matter in five minutes. He knew that Julie was done explaining things to him and would have no reason not to kill him at her first opportunity.

Vic heard the slap of bare feet on rock. He heard no splash. Julie was on the lower ledge. He strained to hear her come closer. Even if she hadn't followed this ledge, the lighting would be enough that Julie could see this entrance a few yards before reaching it.

Hearing nothing, he could only continue to stare into the main cave and hope to react appropriately. He had only a vague notion of what that reaction should be. She could crawl past, outside of his range of sight and come from the other side. She could stop below the opening and suddenly stand up and start shooting. She would be unlikely to miss in such a small space and if she happened to be a lousy shot, the ricocheting bullets might finish him anyway. Vic was the proverbial fish in a barrel, waiting to be shot. The squatting was becoming uncomfortable and he would have liked to change positions but he had to assume that she was waiting to hear some sort of sound.

"Uncle Vic. Is that you? I thought I heard you. Are you alright?" Zach called out in a stage whisper.

Damn. He needed to change strategies. He pretended that he didn't know Julie was down there. He tried to make her believe that surprise was still on her side.

"Zach, I'm down here in the other passage. I'll stay in here until the lights go off. Then we'll get out of here," he answered in his own hoarse whisper.

Vic heard a nearby clink of metal on rock and guessed that Julie was moving her gun into position to fire into his passage. He reached up with both hands and scraped several restless rodents toward the opening and yelled, "Bats! Bats!"

The other bats followed their cave-mates and flew in a chaotic swarm into the main cavern. In their frenzy, a few collided in midair and dropped. Vic could see Julie's hand when she instinctively covered her head. He reached out, managed to grab her fingers, and jerked her hand and arm into his hiding place. Her head and gun hand followed. He didn't have enough leverage to push the gun away from his awkward position but he did have a tight hold on the less threatening hand. He pulled it savagely from right to left at the same time bending her fingers back. This twisted Julie sideways and caused her to point the gun up and away from him. Continuing with his only advantage, he bent her little finger back until it cracked.

The unexpected pain did it. She yelped and dropped the gun. It hit the ledge and bounced. He heard a splash. Still holding her left hand, He grabbed her hair from the back with his other hand, holding her until he could reposition his legs to crawl out.

56

VIC PUSHED JULIE IN FRONT OF HIM TOWARD ZACH'S HIDING PLACE. "I'm coming Zach," he said aloud. "Start taking out your shoe laces. We need to tie somebody up. I don't want you to argue. Trust that I know what I'm doing. It's Julie. She's not who she pretends to be."

He had expected her to try to play on Zach's feelings. After he immediately handed Vic the two laces and when he failed to answer the warm greeting she tried to muster, she said nothing further. Vic expertly bound her hands behind her and used the other lace to tie her arms together above her elbows.

Vic said to Julie, "Zach and I are getting out of here. You better hope we make it. I doubt whether anyone will find you otherwise. I didn't tie your feet because the water is rising with all of the rain here and upstream. You may need to move on up the ledge."

"Ever the gentleman," she said.

"No, ever the federal agent. I want to be at your trial," he replied.

He supported Zach to keep as much weight as possible off his sprained and swollen ankle. Vic managed to raise Zach above him in the crevice.

With Zach using one foot and Vic pushing from below they managed to both reach the higher ledge. They hobbled out into the main cavern.

Negotiating the boards across the cavern was no easy task but they eventually made their way into the stable area. They sat down in one of the offices inside the stable. Vic called Patrice Wilkins from the office phone.

"Where are you Vic?" she asked when she heard his voice.

"I'm in the stable at the Laine property. I've got Zach with me. You need to send the sheriff and probably some state troopers. There's at least one guy who is armed and ..."

"We're way ahead of you. Lynda told us where you might be headed. When you didn't call, I called in several troopers myself. A man who the sheriff identified as Timmy Thompson was shot and is being transported by helicopter to Lexington. One of the troopers had a bullet graze his shoulder. The medics put a dressing on him and he's fine."

Patrice walked into the office, still on her phone, and shook Vic's hand. He hung up and told her how to get back to the hydroponics set up and where she'd find Julie. She first called for the EMTs who were still outside. He would have loved to have been there to see her reaction to the pot farm to end all pot farms not to mention the oxycodone. But he had another important call to make.

"Lynda, I've got Zach. Other than a mega-sized ankle he's fine. He's right here. I'll put him on."

After a dozen or more assurances that he was okay and that he "loved her too", Zach was able to explain to Lynda where he was and that, yes, she could come and get him. Vic signaled for the phone.

"Lynda. The EMTs are here to check Zach's ankle. If they have to take him for treatment I'll make them wait until you get here."

"That probably won't be necessary. I'm in the car and I'm only a few minutes away."

"I haven't been outside of the stable yet so I'm not sure what's going on. If Johnny is out there from what I can tell he's not involved in any of this. He's probably more confused than anything right now. I'll fill you in later."

Patrice walked back in and gave Vic a grin. "It's a shame that a mere DEA consultant won't be able to take credit for uncovering a drug enterprise of this magnitude. I'll invite you to my promotion party, though."

"Yeah, and I suppose you'll let me testify too," he said.

"You've still got a few days of consulting left," Patrice said, "and there's nothing that says your days have to be consecutive."

"You know I'll cooperate," Vic said, "But right now I've got a business I'm still trying to rescue and other clients of my company's that I've been ignoring."

He excused himself to make one final call.

"Hi, Tracy. I know it's late but I wanted to tell you. We found Zach and he's okay."

"Oh, Victor. Fantastic. I knew you'd find him somehow," Tracy said.

"What makes you think that I found him?"

"Because anytime you say 'we' did something that means you did it. If you didn't 'take the point', then 'they' did it."

"I guess I'm as predictable as ever. Thanks for reminding me," he said.

"What are best friends for?" she answered.

"Well, best friend, can I take you to dinner next Friday. I'll be in Louisville. I'll be home."

"I'm having dinner with my new friend, the provost. He understands that two mature adults, one mature adult and you at least, can be friends and that friendships shouldn't threaten romantic relationships."

"To test that resolve, I'll expect you to be here for breakfast. There'll be bagels if you bring them."

"And raspberry flavored water?"

"Yes. Please, please, please bring Sheldon. I promise to take care of all the burrs and ticks."

57

"VIC. THIS IS JOHN SENNET. I didn't expect you to be back to work so soon. You deserve more than one day off."

"Coffee and adrenalin work wonders."

"I'll bet. The reason I called is to let you know that Ali Bourne has decided to withdraw her bid for consulting for our nursing homes. The contract is yours assuming Lynda can resolve her pharmacist problem."

"Yours is the second call with great news I've had this morning. Yesterday we hired a full-time pharmacist. Her name is Angela Wray. She's an experienced consultant and in the tradition of Ebert's, a damned fine druggist. She was reluctant to join us until the robber was apprehended. Once she gets moved in to her family's new home in Lexington she'll be taking over here."

"That's great news all around."

"Wait a second John, Claudia is passing me a note. It says 'another town council member had his prescriptions transferred back to us this morning.' We won the trifecta today."

"Wonderful Vic. Print me a copy of Angela's resume and I'll drop by with the paper work."

"Thanks. See you soon," Vic said as he gave a thumbs-up and a grin to Claudia.

"VIC, IT SOUNDS LIKE IT'S SAFE TO SEE YOU AGAIN. What if I drive to Burgoyne for lunch tomorrow?" Pat asked. He wanted to give Vic enough time to decompress.

"Tomorrow is great. I'll see if Rex can join us."

The three of them went to Vic's default restaurant in Burgoyne. Neither Helen nor Gus was on duty so they avoided major distractions.

"It's great to see you guys," Vic said. He hugged and shook hands with both men before they let themselves be shown to a booth.

"So what's new?" Pat asked. He had a grin wide enough for a jack-o-lantern.

Once he stopped laughing Vic said, "Let me think. Oh. I'm going to wear a new pair of socks in the Mini Marathon this coming Friday. Why do you ask?"

A waitress interrupted their horseplay by bringing them waters. She looked at their unopened menus and said, "I'll check with you later."

Rex said, "Claudia says you seem to be okay but how are you doing really. This has been an emotional roller coaster for you."

"I'm still processing. Like you guys I'm sure, I'm struggling with the fact we've lost both Greg and Will. At the same time, it's a huge relief for me that Lynda and Zach are done worrying about the store. Johnny's consortium is going to honor the contract for the cottage. That was a condition of Johnny's when the consortium bought out his share.

But I don't understand how Julie could betray Lynda. She authorized the killing of Greg and then me, Will, as it turned out."

Rex looked directly into Vic's eyes and said, "Greg and you operated under a strong loyalty paradigm. You told me about your Butch and Sundance relationship. In your universe there's no room for betrayal. I think that's why it's hard for you to understand."

"While you're psychoanalyzing me … and I do believe what you're telling me … does this explain my ambiguous feelings toward Tracy?"

"From what you've told me, Tracy tried to rekindle things but now she's drifting further away again," Rex said.

"That's what happened I guess," Vic replied.

Rex said, "If you're given a third chance, the question is can your desire to forgive Tracy, which incidentally is your Christian imperative, overcome your strong aversion to betrayal."

Pat said, "Before you guys end up on Dr. Phil with all this mumbo jumbo, can we please order lunch."

TWO DAYS LATER, VIC FINISHED PACKING TO LEAVE BURGOYNE. His two holstered guns, along with the autographed baseball, were tucked into a separate knapsack. He was sure that Julie and her brother were the parties behind the amateurish pranks at the hotel. It was now a certainty that Todd Ertz, the motel maintenance man who did their dirty work didn't commit suicide. He was probably killed to prevent him from jeopardizing their operation. With Zhoban, the presumed killer, out of the picture, his death would become another Woodford County unsolved crime.

Lynda and Zach were going to be okay, at least financially. Julie and Timmy were arrested and charged. Johnny is being investigated and will probably be cleared if he's charged at all. But it remains to be seen whether his political career will tank. His friends and business associates are already distancing themselves from him.

ON VIC'S WAY OUT OF TOWN, Ralph Billings pulled him over and said, "It's been nice working with you, Vic."

Without replying, Vic shook his head, laughed, manually rolled up the window of his Ford, and continued north. He'd accomplished most of what he'd hoped to in Burgoyne. His self-imposed sexual abstinence was history. Patrice didn't rule out other DEA consultation opportunities. He was behind the wheel of his '57 Ford and he had his sights set on a Frisch's fish sandwich in Frankfort. Maybe a piece of strawberry pie.

Author's Notes to Readers

R.F. Schulkers was an early 20th century forerunner of J.K. Rowling. Schulkers' imaginative writings showed a generation of young people the joys of reading. In his weekly newspaper serials, radio broadcasts, and eleven full length books, Schulkers brought to life the fictional Hawkins, a dozen or so of his boyhood pals, and a host of trouble-making enemies. Hawkins and his friends led idyllic lives with endless free time, a spacious, well-equipped clubhouse, boats and a dock. Hawkins kept minutes of club meetings to chronicle their adventures ... exploits that often ended with penitent villains acknowledging how Hawkins had treated them fairly.

Most of the stories took place along the banks of an amalgamation of sections of the Licking and Kentucky Rivers. The geologic features that Schulkers described are particularly reminiscent of his Kentucky River summer retreat in Clifton near Versailles.

Beginning at age ten, I acquired, read, and often reread all eleven books. I twice traveled to Clifton to visit the setting that most inspired Mr. Schulkers. Views of the river and its palisades were as Schulkers described but unfortunately the entrance to a large cave, a few hundred yards away with its chasm, turns, and side passages had been sealed off during the 1950s.

Acknowledgements

I lovingly acknowledge my wife Sherry and my sons Mike and Dan. They endured and forgave my emotional ups and downs, accompanying the writing and rewriting processes. Dan provided content editing that contributing to the story's plausibility and shielded readers from much that was mundane. I am grateful to my first readers, Margaret Belosky and Nancy Goldhammer, for their careful scrutiny. Voracious readers make excellent editors. Consequently, any inaccuracies and awkward mistakes are my own last-minute concoctions. Merely thanking my long-time friend Don Stratton is inadequate. He provided the impetus for me to undertake and complete this novel and he generously shared his technical, artistic (the cover), and authoring expertise. A special thanks goes to Mike, Jim, Jerry, Joe, Don, John, and Gary for introducing me to the bonding and rituals associated with fishing trips. The Seckatary Hawkins books and characters created by Robert F. Schulkers and the insights provided and archived by his grandson, Randy Schulkers, were inspirational.

About the Author

Rick Morrow was born and grew up in Indianapolis. He graduated with a B.S. in Pharmacy from the University of Cincinnati. He holds advanced degrees from Drake University and Indiana University. Rick was an endowed professor at Drake. He has over twenty-five publications based on his research on the effects of anesthetics on the heart and physiologic and pharmacologic responses of isolated blood vessels. During his academic career, he served as Assistant Dean, Associate Dean, and Acting Dean of the College of Pharmacy and Health Sciences, as well as President of the University Faculty Senate and Marshall of the University. He holds the title Emeritus Professor of Pharmacology. He was married to his late wife, Sherry for 53 years. Together they have two sons and four grandchildren. He resides in Venice, Florida and spends summers in Urbandale, Iowa. A former long distance runner and lifelong Cincinnati Reds fan, his hobbies include golf, reading, and birding.

Made in the USA
Coppell, TX
04 August 2020

32338166R00204